Items should be returned to a library by closing
time on or before the date stamped above,
unless a renewal has been granted.

Swindon
BOROUGH COUNCIL

BY THE SAME AUTHOR

Sister Josephine
Divine

Bitch Money

Joanna Traynor

BLOOMSBURY

My warmest thanks to E.M. for your criticism,
confidence and friendship.

Swindon Borough Council Library Services	
Askews	
	£9.99

First published in Great Britain in 2000

Copyright © 2000 by Joanna Traynor

The moral right of the author has been asserted

Bloomsbury Publishing Plc,
38 Soho Square, London, W1V 5DF

A CIP catalogue record for this book is
available from the British Library

ISBN 0 7475 4792 0

10 9 8 7 6 5 4 3 2 1

Typeset by Hewer Text Ltd, Edinburgh
Printed in Great Britain by Clays Ltd, St Ives plc

For Robbie

Chapter One

'What stuff? And where from?' That's what he wanted to know. Why couldn't he just come straight out with it? But Jonathan chickened out. When Micky had first put the blag to him, he'd been seduced by the mystique. 'You'll be the last to know and the first to find out,' Micky said.

'Micky?'

'Uh?'

'Why me?'

'Coz you're honest, a grafter. I can trust yer. And our Sammy likes yer. Fuckin' 'ell, our Sammy don't like no-one. Not even me.'

'Sammy?'

'Said you were a good driver. The boss likes yer. What's yer problem?'

'He's only seen me drivin' cats. What does he know?'

'An' yer motor. Yer could make it as a racer, he reckons.'

'Micky, I'm a crap driver.'

'That's probbly why he likes yer. Yer not full o' shite.'

If Micky hadn't leant over and flicked the indicator on, Johnno would have driven right past the service station.

'I think you 'andled all that quite well.'

'Yeah, with no box on the back.'

'You'll do.'

'D'yer think? Would I pass me test?'

'Eh, steady on now! Park her over there, next to the Heinz.' Jonathan drove over. And then Micky said, 'There's a damn sight more to it than all this lot, Johnny boy.'

Jonathan hated being 'boy'd but was too tired to pull him for it. And too tired to take in any more new information about lorries.

'Like how to stick a load on, take one off, do yer cables an' all

1

that. An' if yer actually wanted a proper job, you'd need to know about cuttin 'n' shuttin', wheel slicin', doin' a plus, loads o' stuff.' He tapped the cover on the tachograph. 'How to wire up yer wheel o' fortune an' all that.'

Jonathan brought the lorry to a halt. Then wound his window up. In the deafening silence, neither of them moved. Alcohol fumes filled the cab. 'Micky?'

He didn't answer, instead started a raid on the glove compartment. Like he'd had an idea or maybe he'd remembered something. He was quite industrious about it, tossing out oily rags and toll tickets, a Lady Di and Charles mug ringed with tea grime, fingerprint stamps all over it. He shut it all up with a disappointed slam and got his fags off the dash in compensation. Before jumping down from the cab, he pulled the rear-view mirror round, sucked on his nicotine finger and then wet his eyebrows. They only showed up if they were wet. Battle-scarred from acne attacks, on the looks front, Micky Smith needed all the help he could get.

'Micky, are yer still seein' that Chezzy?'

'Me top tart mate. You've got no chance there.'

'She was in my class at school.'

'Comin' in for a brew are yer?' He nodded towards the transport caff.

'No, I'm off home.'

'Why?'

'Why does anyone go home?'

They both jumped down from the cab.

Meeting at the front, Jonathan handed the keys over and did up his donkey jacket. Collar up, then hands in his pockets deep. Micky did loud sucks and blows on his fag. He was wearing T-shirt, jacket wide open. Lovely tits for a barmaid. Nipples like marbles. It was freezing.

'Where's the blag from then, Micky?' Like he was asking for the time.

'Someone'll ring you in the mornin' with the time . . . and the plates.'

'Micky?'

'Stop Mickyin' me for fucksakes.' He was about to flick his cigarette away in anger but went for another drag instead.

'I just . . . well what about the driver then? Whose truck is it? Where's he gonna be?'

'Zat any o' your business?'

'I . . . I just . . .' Well, he'd just about had enough. And he'd had a go in the lorry now anyway. That was all he'd been after really – a go. And besides, Micky's 'need-to-know' bubble wasn't nowhere big enough. If anyone needed to know for chrissakes . . . and if it was all that secret . . . As if Jonathan had voiced his doubts out loud, Micky got a grip.

'Someone's sortin' the driver,' he said.

'He's in on it then?'

'Did I say that?'

'Sounded like . . .'

'I mean . . .' Micky did handcuffs with his wrists.

'So why doesn't this someone sort the whole job, follow through like? Why not get him to drive?'

'Be on his toes, wooden he? Born thief. He'd be off with the lot. Be in Watford Gap before teatime, no problem.'

Micky spun round, the full 360, as if looking for this person. Then, leaning forward, talking quietly, said, 'Now if it was duvets or postal orders . . . but yer don't need a fence for what I've got in mind which is why I chose you.' He tried to poke Johnno in the chest but stubbed his finger on the industrial strength of the council donkey jacket.

'I ain't doin' it till yer tell me right now, what it is, where it's from and who else is in on it.'

'Fuck me! You were off 'ome to yer mum a minute a go. What's up?'

'Micky?'

'Alright, alright. For fucksakes. Yer know where we've just bin, out the back o'town and down the bypass?'

'Yeah.'

'Well, same tomorrer but after the blag, instead o' comin' here, you go straight to ours. And I mean straight. The lads'll be there to unload. They'll weigh you on, alright?' He checked to see it was alright. 'Then yer come right back here, dump the truck, pick up yer motor and go. Got it?'

'Zat the MO is it? Fuckin' road directions?'

Micky grinned. All the green bits in his teeth gone with the daylight. Chinwagging in a dark carpark – they were right on offer. Especially with Micky wearing a fag on his bottom lip, hands in his pockets, doing all he could to look like a villain.

Jonathan walked off. Said fuck to the job. It felt like a wrong'un anyway. Save himself the grief. 'Later, Micky.'

'It's the Astor,' Micky shouted. 'The Astor Hotel. The road goes clean off the bypass. No traffic lights, nothin'. Just a filter. We've just been past it three times. Yer with me?' Jonathan walked back to him then. Got close, girl-close, to be after his every move, every dart of his eye, every twitch.

'Me dad works the Astor. What's goin' on, Micky?'

'Well that's 'andy then.' Micky moved back a bit. He looked unsure. Even through the rank stench of oily tarmac, Jonathan could smell his breath.

'Me dad, Micky?' Loud, that time. He watched again for some reaction, had moved back himself a bit now.

'I 'eard . . .' Taking his last drag. 'What's he do, Johnno?' He aimed his fag at the ground like a dart but then dropped it pathetically. Danced on it and wouldn't look up until he got his answer.

'Security.'

He watched Micky redraw his worry lines into a baffled expression. As if the idea of the hotel having security had never occurred to him. And now that Jonathan could see his own father placed firmly and squarely at the scene of the crime, the daylight of truth dawned on him too. In it, he saw Micky for what he was. Not the skilled operator his public had him down for. Not the mysterious man of few words who'd given him prime responsibility for running top-

4

secret errands into the forbidden territories of Moss Side, to deliver parcels of dubious content to doctors and dentists and a fully lit-up whore house on one occasion. No. Micky was a victim of acne who could get people up before a judge more efficiently than the local CID and it wasn't that wild a leap of the imagination to consider the possiblity that he was paid by them to do so.

With the money from this job and the contents of his bank account, Jonathan had reckoned on enough cash to fund a route to somewhere a lot more interesting than the arse-end of Manchester, well away from the weight of his father's great expectations and beyond a future where he was destined to be juggling the merits and likelihood of more work like this. That was all he was after. The chance to do some decent work. Work that meant something. But once again, it had all gone to cock. And once again, a familiar ripple of relief ran right through him. The job *was* a wrong'un after all. His senses weren't blunt. He was right on the level, sharp.

And this was something his dad hadn't come to terms with yet. His dad. Always fucking it up. His dad who had gone native had to be the biggest disappointment of his life, the cringe of his youth, the lid on his dreams. They were father and son living in the same house but different countries and with very little to say to one another. From Johnno, just words like 'down', 'last', 'base', 'sick', 'never' – grunted local-speak to defend himself from the barrage of Thatcher-speak his dad dished out. Words like 'opportunity', 'interest', 'hard work' and 'perseverance'. Johnno had a dad with a talent for flogging dead horses.

'Not Ole King Cole?' said Micky. He did his 360 again, this time fast.

'What?'

'Speke's bloke? Laughs a lot.'

'I'm sorry?'

'Normally on nights? The black geezer.'

'That's me dad.'

'Funny as fuck that is.' Now looking genuinely pleased with himself.

'I'm crackin' me fuckin' ribs, Micky. What are you on about?'

Micky put his hands in his pockets and swaggered about, playing suited and booted like a businessman now, hands in his jeans pockets, nodding his head like the men in the hotel bar, their deals going down very nicely thank you.

'I'll see yer later on this one.' Jonathan walked off again. Turned and said, 'If me dad's gonna be there, I'm 'avin' nowt to do with it.'

Micky shouted after him, 'He's on the books, the King. Has been for ages.'

Jonathan stopped but didn't turn round. He tried to hear the words again, to make sure he had them all in the right order. Then looked to Micky for confirmation.

'Our Sammy's got the run o' the place, for his brass nails like. Yer dad throws a blind one.'

Jonathan fixed his eyes to the ground, on a crisp packet scrunched up, caught up in a thud of soggy leaves. He squelched it with his foot and breathed in deeply. His dad.

Before asking Micky the ins and outs, Jonathan thought hard for the right face to pull. Puzzled? Not bothered? What he couldn't show was the embarrassment. All men suffered an embarrassing father at some stage in their life, he knew that. But after a while, this embarrassment gives way to respect. There comes a time when the young man realises just how easy it isn't and gives in. Sees that dad's done his best under the circumstances. But these men didn't have a father by the name of Charlie Wilson who was happy to put up Thatcher posters in his bedroom window. A father who'd called the police to have a 'Help the Miners' money collector removed from the hotel premises. A father he couldn't look up to or live down.

Jonathan went for his puddled expression. Crinkled-up nose and head to one side. Looked Micky in the eyes again.

'Me dad does what?'

'Well, I can't see this one blinkin' on us now, can you? All in the family eh?' He did his little boxing dance and followed through with, 'Where's yer motor?'

'On the other side.'

'I'll catch yer later. Wait for the call in the mornin', alright?'

'What exactly is it, Micky? What we in for?'

'Tellies.'

'Tellies?'

'Loadsatellies. Just in time for Chrimbo.'

Johnno watched Micky walk away towards the caff and decided some respect was due, overdue perhaps. The loadsamoney boom hadn't yet reached this arse-end of Manchester but what did Micky Smith care? He was having it off. All around him were holding their breath, waiting for this boom like it was summer – scared to death they'd miss it. But there was a fat ginger bastard with no worries, no eyebrows, full of front and lorry-loads of wedge. To account for the Guzzi 1000cc, the Cosworth and the bat on his houses, Micky Smith could point to the demolition contracts that his brother Sammy never stopped winning, and to top that lot, there was his real business – women. He took women whose men and work had long since gone or women who knew there was none such coming. He took these women and bombed their brains so hard they didn't know boom from bust and never would. He'd taken Francesca and turned her into Chezzy. Took her out of school and, yes it was true and time he faced up to it, put her on the game and for all these years had been working her. He should never have asked Micky anything about her. He should have seen it coming miles off.

He'd seen her just yesterday, waiting outside Sammy's yard. With her mate, parked up in a new white Escort with big spots – just what he was after for his own motor. She looked thin, lithe, healthy. Fur hat and coat. Rosy cheeks. Gleaming white teeth. She was so . . . She had that blue tinge on her lips that always used to be there after netball. Did she work the Astor for Sammy? Was his dad slipping her one for some side salad?

Tarts, tellies, ten-ton trucks and his dad on the firm. Security. Jonathan looked across the motorway to the services on the other side and only then focused his listeners on the noise. Traffic going places. Here he was, on a runway at an airport with no passport.

Not going anywhere except home to get a good night's kip before the job tomorrow.

Cars were playing *Who's gonna drive yer home . . . tonight?* He turned the radio off before the countdown to number one had finished, any youthful curiosity he'd had the week before gone, vanished. He felt old but small. Screwed up. Pinned down. Pressured. After being up high in a six-ton cab all day no doubt. It was high time he put his very small life and very small car into some perspective.

Cars lined his street, both sides. 'Why don't any of these cars ever fuckin' go anywhere?' He felt no better for the yelling and had to calm himself by driving round the block a few times till at last, someone not too far from his house made room by leaving. It was a small space but Johnno was brilliant at reversing. He drove backwards and thought backwards, re-evaluating his last couple of years and some of the advice he'd been given but not taken, such as 'Join the army'. If he had, doubtless he'd be dead now. Another Falkland fool straight from school. He thought back further to his Daley Thompson affair. Fast but not fast enough. Never even made the trials. Right after that, feeling vulnerable, weakened, he'd lost faith in himself. Didn't want to rebel, turn bad. He'd wanted a life to be proud of. In an act of total desperation, he'd even tried the police force. Then the miners kicked off at Orgreave. On the telly, Maggie's barnies with the miners looked a lot scarier than all the Argie-bashing in the Falklands and not half as much fun. So he gave the cops a wide berth after that.

He practised his speech to his father. 'It is impossible to move up and out of the sordid life that is the destiny of any young lad with not too many brains brought up break dancing, breathing in the noxious clout of the dying farts oozing out the arse of what used to be called Majestic Manchester. Do you understand that now, father?' He was looking forward to it. He'd spit it out in one clean gob. Just like that. No grunts. No swearing. He'd say his piece and then slam a door or something.

'There is no escaping this . . . this . . . filth, this . . . this grime . . . This is the disappointment of being ME, father. Do you hear me, dad? This is not the Earls Court of the North.'

He couldn't see out of the car windows. No sky. A torrent of rain closed in on him. Not a steady downpour, drizzle or spit. Hard and concentrated drumming rain. Don't-even-try-and-walk-about-in-it rain. He scanned the decor of his car and pondered the worth of it. It was the only thing he had. It had cost him his two passions in life, smoking and Louise, and then some five hundred quid but . . . He wished now he'd kept up with the smoking. Was gagging for a fag. A touch of Louise wouldn't have gone amiss either.

Lowheeze. Catholic and confident Wheezy. Student at Manchester University. A bird from the south flown north in a bright pink Volkswagen. They'd met at what used to be Henry VIII's, and every weekend he'd spent most of his time in her bed, in a house she shared with a load of southern shites from London. Embarrassed to still be living with his parents, he'd upsticked and moved in two streets away from her. A fire risk of a bedsit with its shower stall out on the landing.

Wheezy was posh learning how to be poor. She was a poor student on all counts, so Jonathan got a job. A proper job. A job he'd told his dad he'd never do. He sacrificed himself to the telesales office of the *Salford Gazette*, his task to sell space to travel agents. When he wasn't ringing out, the world was ringing in but never for him. Wired to the world with a plastic pink nipple stuck in his ear and a Star Trek mouthpiece shackled to his chin, voices were routed directly to his brain, exploding into his thoughts at random and with no warning, all day long. He sold nothing.

At first, it had all been worth it. For legovers with Wheezy, anything was worth it. In the evenings, they ate together, watched a bit of telly and, while he washed up, she'd get her books out. If she had an essay deadline he'd slip her one in early and then go back to his bedsit. If not, she'd re-write her lecture notes and he'd wait on the bed for her, but never for very long. She could do what the others couldn't. Make his stomach go. Every time. She did what he said, what he wanted, every time. She was the right height, weight, the right colour of white, not grey like the Manchester lasses but creamy and where she was pink, pretty, not bloody. She never let him down. And then, half way through her first year, she swapped courses and got in with a new load of London shites that didn't wear high heels or perfume. And so Wheezy moved on and moved her high heels and perfume down to the Oxfam shop. She stopped putting her hair in a bun and went for severe with an Alice band instead. She fought for unmarried mothers, abortions, the right to drink pints and the right to her own body. Saturdays she spent standing outside supermarkets demanding tax-free tampons. Her body, she said, belonged to her, but her life was then in the possession of the great unwashed middle classes intent on curing Manchester of its man problem. These women were rebelling. But unlike fourteen-year-olds who get on with the job of rebelling even while they're sleeping, these women timetabled it to fit in with their exams. And Wheezy timetabled Jonathan to fit into the minutes and moments left over. Her reasoning? He was just like her father, she said, which was some indication of how far the psycho rot had set in. Clearly she was hallucinating. She said that he didn't . . . and couldn't . . . ever own her.

It ended as so many relationships do, on Valentine's Day. He was sacked. Simple as that. She said she had to concentrate on her work but what a coincidence. And so, unemployed again, he moved back home, gave up smoking fags and saw his own Thatcher-loving union-hating father for the first time, in the fresh. His father who saw nothing wrong in asking complete strangers to buy local bog paper space at fifty quid a centimetre. It was a good job, his father said. Warm, clean, safe and, if he worked hard, not too badly paid. A good job Johnno had found out sooner rather than later, that was all. And that's what his mother had said about Wheezy.

Alone in the world of his car, Jonathan worried. He'd reached yet another turning point in his life, but knew he wasn't going anywhere. Round the block and back again. He felt manipulated, as though someone, somewhere had mapped this small life out for him, the streets, the ambition, the limitations. Someone, somewhere had decided that for people like him, this would be enough.

He predicted the Cult playing their 'Rain' song and turned the radio on to see. They weren't. Then the rain stopped almost as suddenly as it started. Slowly a steamy view of the street dissolved through the windscreen. He got out of the car, slammed the door and wished he'd never bought into the idea of being the handsome young man with a racy motor. Wished instead he'd gone to Spain with Jack. And fuck to this rain. Jack's last postcard had read 'Plenty of work. Plenty of birds. Plenty of sun. What more could a man ask for?' Johnno only asked that all the babble in his brain would stop. He didn't believe in Spain.

Up the entry and round the back and just a quick peek in the kitchen window, under the nets, see if there was anything going on not to walk in on. He opened the back door. Washing everywhere. The washing machine still on, as always. He felt the weight of the kettle, flicked it on and walked through to the front room. Shirl was huddled in the corner, feeding Malcy. She did her eyes to heaven. Mum was upstairs.

He sat on the end of her bed. Vying for her attention. The TV was turned off but she was reading or pretending to read a magazine, holding its bottom corner between thumb and finger, her hand rigid, dug into the covers so he couldn't see it shaking. 'Me dad'll be home in a minute, mum. Are yer gonna get up?' She moved to get more light on her page. Wouldn't look at him. He leant over to see what could be so interesting. Upside down he read 'Jesus and the Mary Chain'. No way was she reading that.

'Don't start, Jonathan.'

'Well get up then.'

'Yer beginnin' to sound like yer father.'

'That's a laugh.' He stood up and went to the window. Picked up the photo of grandma, his mum's mum, and scoffed at it. Flung it back down. It didn't land right. Face down flat. He picked it up more gently then, feeling apologetic. 'What's wrong, mum?'

'Who said there was owt wrong?'

'Mum?'

She wouldn't look up. He sat down and stared hard at her. She couldn't stand it, the staring, so she reached for her watch off the bedside table which wasn't a bedside table but a mini-fridge. And on top of the mini-fridge, a little tray with a miniature kettle and teapot. A dirty cup and saucer. On the wall either side of the bed, matching lamps in need of new bulbs. 'Is that the time? I nearly missed *Corry*. 'As she not put Malcy down yet?' She rolled to the other side of the bed and reached for the back of her teasmaid clock, always slow these days, so old it couldn't keep up with the time even. 'Turn telly on, love.'

'I'm leavin', mum. Leavin' 'ome.'

'Again?'

'I mean it.'

'Oh aye. Turn telly on, son. Let's see how Hilda's copin' without Stan.'

'Me passport's valid for a year yet, mum. I'm gonna get some use out of it. Go to London I think.'

'Yer don't need a passport to get into London. D'yer think I'm stupid or somat?'

'I'm gonna start off there.'

'Well if it's trouble yer after, you'll not go far wrong, down London. What's brought this on? Robbed a bank 'ave yer?'

'I'm sellin' me car.'

'That'll keep the noise down.'

'About sums me up that, doesn't it?'

'Zis about yer father I suppose.'

'This is me, mum. It's about me. I wanna make sure . . . I wanna make sure there's more than this goin' on. I want somat different to all this.'

'Aye, well there's plenty different goin' on in London no doubt.'

He got off the bed again and walked away, hands in his pockets, face to the floor. Then a look up to the walls which were a grid of pictures, some colour, some photos, black and white. Manchester in the twenties, a lady with a bare neck and a string of pearls, a street party scene outside the big Post Office where his dad used to work, some bad Lowry reproductions, as if the originals weren't bad enough. All out of the Astor. Except the Jesus Loves You poster pinned to the picture rail and a palm leaf bent to a cross. A framed Lady Di wedding photo she won on the bingo, limited edition. There were millions of them. And, of course, the Thatcher.

'Where d'yer keep yer weddin' photos, mum?'

No answer. Mum looking up at the ceiling.

'In the attic?'

On the ceiling, a lampshade, antique, dad said. A green and white marble effect. The light from it made everything look antique. The wallpaper, pale flowers, bleak. Behind the door there was a fire extinguisher. There was one for every room in the house, all the ones downstairs empty, funned out. Next to the wardrobe, a trouser press that dad used all the time. There was a pair in there now. Jonathan had never used his. And on the back of the door, a barometer stuck on sunny which mum thought was funny because the sun never got near that bedroom. Two ottomans, one each side of the room, against the wall. Mum's legacy. Full of stuff she didn't want and couldn't chuck.

The curtains pulled only slightly apart didn't match anything in the room. They were for downstairs really, the front room. Red, to go with the carpet. There *were* curtains that matched the bedroom spot-on. Thick green velvet ones with lining, frills, hanging pelmets and tie-backs. The laundry woman at the Astor Hotel wouldn't do them. And now no-one had the nerve to go and collect them from the dry cleaner's. There was a continental quilt and a suede coat in there too. All taken in on the same day by an optimistic mum who'd just won a ton on the bingo. He pulled the curtains back wider. Picked up granny's picture again and looked at it for the millionth time, the woman in dark clothes with the curious nasty smile, wanting people to believe that she didn't think much of having her photo taken but in fact, plain to see, loving every minute of it.

'Don't you ever wonder about Aunty Margy. What she's doin'? She might be dead rich yer know.'

'*She* was always after runnin' away.'

He looked her dead on in the eye. 'I ain't runnin', mum.'

'Well, it had to come I suppose.'

'Yer should've gone with her . . . Aunty Margy.'

'Was only a fiver 'n' all, that boat.' Saying it now like she wished she'd gone on it.

'Australia for a fiver. Jesus. I wish . . .'

'You'll need more than a fiver for a bag o' chips in London.'

'Are yer gettin' up, mum?' He looked out the window. The top part. The bottom part was netted. He could just make out Mrs Geno under the glare of a street lamp, next road over. She was taking wet washing off her line, the rain still drizzling. She looked sad, doing all that, on her own, in the dark. 'Was you in love with me dad, mum? Is that why yer never went with her?'

'I needed the wage. You were on the way and I needed the wage.'

'I want to be wanted for me, not for me money.'

'Well that's 'andy isn't it, son? Seein' as 'ow you've got none.'

'Mum, why don't you ever get the photos out.' He looked up to the attic. 'The weddin' photos.'

'What for?'

'Coz I've never seen 'em.'

'There's nowt to see.'

'Yer weddin' day? And when I was a nipper, a babby.'

'Most of 'em got fired. Burnt. How many times 'ave I told yer that?'

'I don't believe it.'

Still staring out the window, he heard the mattress springs zing into action behind him.

Chapter Two

'You are comin' in tomorow I take it?'

Charlie had been hoping he wouldn't ask. But now he had, 'I don't think so.'

'It'll look dead obvious if yer don't. They won't suspect a thing if yer there.'

'Inside job? Rare as ratscakes they are, aren't they?'

Speke was losing his nerve now that Charlie had other options. Charlie felt flushed.

They were in the Queen's Arms just down from the hotel, a spit away from the clink and full of off-duty screws most of the time. They'd modernised it, put tellies in, both ends, taken most of the seats out and put shiny silver firemen's poles all over the place with tiny little shelves all round for drinks to go on and the odd bar stool if you were quick. Make more space for standing, said Macky, the landlord. An American idea. Charlie liked American ideas usually, part of his heritage coming home to him was how he saw it. But not in the pub. He didn't want America in his pub.

The seats around the sides were covered in orange and blue zigzaggy stripes and hard as nails. The music, when they had it on, was disco loud but early evening Macky did them all a favour and kept it down. That left them battling with electronic noises from the games tables and car-crash crunch sounds from the one-armed bandits that didn't even have arms on any more. The Queen had 'em no doubt, Charlie chuckled to himself. He was well on the way. Burping.

Speke got up for the bar. Charlie nodded. His fifth pint. He didn't want to go home. Home was eggshell city these days.

'I promise yer, it'll look worse if yer don't turn in.' Speke put the pints on the glass table really gently, rubbed his hands and sat down as if his first that night. Took a testing sip, sat back and sighed, like Clint Eastwood in a saloon. Without the tan of course. And the frame. But he had the right sideboards and shock of hair.

'For who exactly?'

'You, yer daft bastard. They'll all be on yer case, won't they?'

'All?'

'Charlie, why d'yer think Sammy Smith's botherin' with a wagon load o' tellies? Not exactly 'is game now, is it?'

'He's fuckin' greedy, that's why. Pardon my French.'

'He's a loser, Charlie, that's why.'

'Yeah well, that goes without sayin'.'

'No. You don't get me. He loses money. Lots of it. All the time. He thinks he's so shit hot on them neddies but he's not. He's got a system see. He's got shares in 'alf a dead horse and a system that don't work.'

'So yer tellin' me he's skint? Drivin' about in that car of his? Half the fuckin' neighbourhood on his payroll? Do me a favour.'

'When he runs out o' money, he can't stop them horses runnin' round his head, can he? He can't help himself. So he helped himself to someone else's hard-earned and they're not happy. Whoever he owes money to, they mean business, I'm tellin' yer.'

'Serves him right.' Charlie swigged.

'That's why he's doin' the blag and that's why I'd get me arse down there if I was you. You don't wanna make this team jumpy.' He took a drink and pulled out his cigarettes, a pack of ten Embassy, crushed. He was trying to give up. 'I ain't ever seen Sammy look as scared as this and he's been in some shite over the years, let me tell yer.'

'You after someone to hold yer hand? Not losin' yer nerve now are yer, Speke? Sammy this. Sammy that. That's all I've ever 'eard off you and now look at yer. I'm stayin' out of it.' Speke straightened his cigarette, stuck it in his mouth and felt about for a box of matches. Charlie sat calm, relaxed, like he had everything he needed.

'You 'avin' a new job lined up at that supermarket . . . well, the coppers'll think yer in on it for defo. They're bound to tip 'em off about yer. If yer came into work though, and faced the music, you'd be totally innocent. That's how I see it and that's how they'll see it.'

Charlie didn't answer. Three screws had come over and sat down at the next table. All five men nodded at each other. Speke stood up and walked over to them. One of the screws pushed his fags and lighter forwards before Speke had a chance to ask. He lit his fag, returned to his pint and changed the subject.

'Wife still sick is she?'

'She's gettin' there.' He took a sip, just like Speke's. They were both dying to get a glug going but they'd be on the sixth before eight bells if they went any faster. And now the screws were there, it was hard to think up something good to talk about.

'I expect she'll come full circle when you get back on nights. They get stuck into a routine don't they, the women?'

Charlie didn't want to talk about Hilda. She wasn't a topic of conversation. More the end of one. He wanted to talk about the job tomorrow. To ignore Speke's question, he turned away and threw a scowl across to the screws.

'What about the lad then? Is he workin'?'

'In a fashion.'

'What's he up to?'

'Cash in 'and. Though we don't see nowt of it. I wish he'd get off his backside and leave 'ome. It's the Mrs tho' innit. Mollycoddler. Always 'as been. Every time he mithers her, she forks out. He ain't goin' nowhere is he? Why would he?'

'What work's he at?'

'Fannies about on tractors an' you'll never guess where.'

'The Smiths' Yard?'

Charlie scrunched his face, chucked his beer mat bits in the ashtray, took another swig on his pint and wiped his mouth.

'I guessed right then I take it?'

'Guessed my arse. Too bloody close to home, all this lot is.' He took another look at the screws to see if they were listening. They were sitting in a row, leaning back, eyes straight ahead like con-

17

demned men. Cheered Charlie up a little, enough to stop him ripping another beer mat up.

'I wish you'd calm down, Charlie. Yer makin' me nervous.'

'You? Nervous? Can't think why. 'Snot as if you'll be there, is it? I mean . . . right there. Gettin' the load in.'

Speke glugged on his pint and changed the subject again. 'I wish yer weren't leavin' us. Specially now we've got this new manager in.'

'You'll 'ave to watch him.'

'Sammy'll sort him,' in a whisper.

'Sammy can't go round sortin' everyone,' Charlie said, loud.

'Every man's got a figure in his head, Charlie. Pound signs flashin'.'

'Every man's got a *price* on his head yer mean.' He put his empty pint down.

'You'd better come in tomorrer then, 'adn't yer.'

'What?'

'I'm just passin' on a message, Charlie. Gentle like.'

'Doin' me a favour like?'

'Somat like that.'

'Cheers, Speke, I needed that. You tell 'em I'll be there on the dot, nine o'clock.'

'I'll get another round in then.'

A car-crash crunch sound then, from an armless one-armed bandit.

He left his van in the pub carpark and was glad to walk home. The think. The big think, plink, plank, plong gonk. Drunk. Dread for the day ahead. Knew in his bones it was all wrong, gone, son of a bitch this business, he said to himself out loud. And then the rain. Into the Dog and Dart for a swift one, wait, think, drink. Stand at the bar. Safer at the bar where the landlord can see who's startin', fartin', takin' the piss and yes, that's an idea. Have a whazzer and wash his face. Get the stain of the rain off him. Acid in it now, they say.

He went into the loo and sat down without undoing his trousers. Safe there. Foot against the door. Holding his breath through his nose, breathing out slow. Shit and toilet drains and stains and finger poo all down the walls and god he could cry now. He never asked for this. Shit smell. Life in hell as a proper person would see it. A proper person would look at him now and mark him down, steer clear, get rid, make sure not to mix with the likes of. But Charlie never asked for it to be like this. He wanted the best for all of them, himself, Hilda even though she's done her damndest to bring him down and here he is now, fraid o' going home for stares and silence and that horrible feeling of guilt for all the things gone wrong. Pants down. Bear the idea of his arse on a toilet with the bums from that shite hole.

He was an empty man with all the makings for a good life, wife, kids, grandkid, house, job, van, a future not worth contemplating though. What happened? Where did it all go wrong? He worked, came home, fed and went to bed and at the end of the week brought the money in. But he was still to blame. No prospects the lad said. No brain for colleges and exams he said. No drive to be top man at the supermarket. No money to be top man of a builder's yard. And it was all Charlie's fault for not giving him more leeway, rope, direction, money. Thousand pound he was after for some enterprise allowance he called it. Fuckin' enterprise gettin' 'old of a grand for the likes of him. Fuckin' enterprise my arse, said Charlie, wiping it and making a mess. And no toilet paper left. He wants money. He wants to believe in something. He wants to bleed me dry. Self-pitying ungrateful swine with no guts and no idea.

Just the thought of the job tomorrow had him with his pants down again, opening bowels, the pile inside falling through his stomach like soil heading for the coffin, stinking to high heaven. Earth moving, the full load of it coming away from him in a hurry. And then his neck started. He'd be in full rash by morning, he knew it. He cleaned up as best he could and got out the Dog and Dart the back way, into the carpark. The rain had cleared off and once more, he set off for home, biting his lip and smelling the shit on his fingers every time he rubbed the rash on his neck and tucked his scarf back in. They'd turned the taps off at the Dog and Dart to stop the gypos coming in and out, filling kettles and the like.

19

Charlie hated the smell of shit. Even baby shit. Even Malcy shit. He hated it.

He'd raised a family that did nowt but scrape barrels. They weren't starved but weren't going anywhere either. Getting Hilda off her arse to go for anything less than a fifty quid jackpot down the bingo was a full-time job in itself. When did he stop loving her? He hadn't. Not really. It was Johnno who'd burst the bubble. Johnno coming along, that was all. A tiny baby that could cast a shadow dark enough to dim the light of the brightest lovebeams. A tiny baby that snatched all the moments for himself. Turned his woman once a dreamer into a scheming screaming hag.

Got into the house and saw the old washing machine connected up. The last new one already down the scrap yard. Another new one on the way. This one had pipes for the kitchen sink taps. A museum piece and thank the lord he'd not shifted it out the shed. How long does it take to deliver a bleeding washing machine for chrissakes? The bathroom door was locked. He could hear Shirl and the babby in there. The kettle was empty. He wanted clean hands. He shook the pipe hanging over the sink. Good. There was still spare spin water in it. He shook enough out to wet his hands but not enough to do a good job. He wiped off as best he could no the babby's dirty bib from the pile of dirty washing still to do, all over the kitchen floor. God knows there was enough kiddy cack round the house to start a plague.

Jonathan stayed staring out the window, till he felt sure his mum was decent. Put his head on the glass and blew for some steam. He knew the fire story was a lie but had no idea why they'd want to lie. It was true, there were no pictures. Not of him or Shirl or the wedding. It was like they all started out in 1968. His earliest picture was in black and white, in the back yard on a three-wheeler. Must have been eight then. His face miserable, half hiding behind the washing. Disappointed, he looked like. That was the beginning of the end of his childhood calm. The man not yet born and the scream of his future disappointments barely audible. Pitched on the scale of a dog whistle then. Horribly loud now.

Wheezy and her like – they were born too high for dog whistles and disappointments. They were born into rooms with high ceilings and heat and carpet, all wall-to-wall with underlay. Wheezy had told him that back home, she had huge trees in her garden. Her great grandad had planted them. She used to sit in her bedroom window and imagine the branches the arms of her ancestors reaching out to her. Always there and rooted to the ground. Then she ruined it all by saying she felt closer to the trees than her parents. Would the trees be leaving a will? he asked her. Would they buy her a car, feed and house her? She had a future she could bank on, he told her. Johnno's future could only be read in tea leaves and his past hadn't managed to survive the Kodak Instamatic.

Wheezy and her like didn't know the meaning of the word disappointment. He could see that now. A death in the family. A marriage gone sour. That would be their measure. He had danger, dad and the dole to contend with and no reason to raise kids or plant trees or even dream of a future. None that he could see anyway. And that was the trouble. He couldn't see. The walls were too closed in, the light too grim, the house too small and full of things. He needed space, air, a view.

She was at the tallboy pulling out drawers. Wearing her Astor Hotel dressing gown that didn't fit any more, didn't reach all the way round. And her Astor Hotel slippers. He went over to her. Wondered if she felt shamed for having gone along with it all. He couldn't even hug her any more. When he tried to get close, she told him to stop mithering. Scared dad would see, find out, go on at her with his eyes, his silences. All physical connections from childhood gone now. Like everything else. To hug her was a lean towards some taboo. A touch too close. But how come it was OK for Shirl to touch? Why didn't dad kick off then? How come Shirl had managed to stay in with both of them? What did she have that he didn't, besides a baby? And a job. And a tidy room.

He thought he saw her shudder, about to yarl maybe, or maybe she was cold. It was cold. Even with his coat on. He could feel heat coming off her. She smelt of mints. The elastic in her face all gone now. Like knickers fallen down, her cheeks sagged heavy with fat. So much sagging fat, her eyes had dropped like the penny slot-holes of a one-armed bandit. Her hair was perfect though. Like she'd just come back from the hair dressers. She hadn't. It grew like that naturally, curly. Grey now. He could remember her being little, blonde. She'd blown up a lot. Small eyes. Middle age. Big arms. Big arms that did nowt but eat and worry and hold Malcy in check. She was all closed up now.

She used to be open, laugh wide, like people, meet people, follow strangers home sometimes. His dad went mad for her getting carried away with the strangers. In and out of their houses whenever the fancy took her, posh houses where all the furniture had skinny legs, the cups skinny handles. Where the women wore rings, all diamond clusters, rows of them tight, right up to the knuckles. Where the kids scoffed chocolate biscuits with a towel on their laps and hankies down their front so they were tired out before they even started.

'Shall I get the tea on, mum?' Now he'd got her out of bed, he could move on.

'There's nowt I fancy.' She didn't want to go that fast. First she had to get dressed. She kept taking clobber out of the drawers and then putting it back in, like they weren't her clothes. She used the same face for sorting dirty clothes as clean. No pleasure in it at all.

'I'll go and get somat.'

'If yer like. We've ran out o' butters and strawberry jams yer know. S'all lemon curds now.'

'There's a great big bag o' . . .'

'There's coq au vin bags need defrosting. Yer could stick 'em in microwave.'

'Me dad doesn't like . . . where is he anyway?'

'Pub I expect.'

'How about . . . how about I do me spaghetti thing eh?' As if this would cheer her up.

'There's a ton o' mince in the freezer.' She sounded happier. She'd found something. A big blue cowl-necked jumper. He didn't like her wearing that. Reminded him of a baby being born, head coming out the neckhole having done as much damage as possible.

'I'll do somat with that then eh?'

'The mince?'

'Yeah.'

'No onions.'

Then they heard him. He wasn't exactly quiet. He banged the back door and came banging straight up the stairs. He usually stayed in the front room, demanding cups of tea and telly pages. He'd sit there demanding all night till bed. That's how it'd been, since he'd been on days, for the past two months.

Jonathan didn't feel good. Being in the bedroom with his mum. His dad walking in on them. And then he remembered. And then the door swung open. And there was his dad, shocked just for a second, loosening his collar.

'What yer doin' in 'ere?'

'Nowt.'

Jonathan moved so his dad could see her. He felt guilty then, like he'd left her to be mauled. 'What yer doin'? Still in yer dressin' gown?'

'She was gonna get a bath.'

'Who asked you?'

She hugged the clothes to her chest and pushed her feet further into her slippers. Dad came further into the room then. Walked over to the unmade bed. He'd shrunk, no doubt about it, he'd shrunk.

'Bin in bed all day 'ave yer?' He pulled the blankets straight, like he was covering up. Not wanting Jonathan to see something. He fiddled with the fringe of the counterpane as he pulled it over the pillows. 'You need help you do. For up 'ere,' he said, pointing to his head.

'She's comin' down now,' said Jonathan, not sure who his dad meant. 'We was talking. She'd have been dressed by now else.'

'Bin in it all day 'ave yer?'

'No.'

'We're all workin' our arses off and you take to yer bed all day.'

'How can she, dad, lookin' after Malcy?'

'Who asked you I said?' Shouting now. He lunged, grabbed Jonathan's arm and pushed him. Bang, out the room. 'And stay out.' So certain of his power still.

The door didn't click closed after, just closed to. Jonathan stood and read the gold plate on it, The Pankhurst Suite but changed to SPankurs, with the scratch of a screwdriver and a felt-tip pen. He tried to drum up the courage to hurl himself back in but, tooled up with enough information to floor him, he still couldn't stand up to his father.

Shirl stood at the bottom of the stairs with Malcy on her hip. She was wearing her Astor dressing gown and he was wrapped in a matching yellow towel. His cheeks were red raw, like he'd just had a good slapping.

'What's goin' on?' she was after.

Jonathan waved her away and, wrestling with Malcy, she went.

'I'm not 'avin' this, Hilda. Where's them pills? You'll be welded to that bed if yer don't get off it. Where's yer smarties eh?'

'I've stopped 'em.'

'An' this is 'ow it's gonna be is it? Look at the state of yer. Just look at yer. Come over 'ere and look at yerself.'

Jonathan heard the wardrobe door yanked open.

'And look at all the crap in 'ere. Everywhere I look it's crap, crap, crap.' And then the sound of flesh on flesh. At last, Jonathan's cue.

'If you lay one finger on her . . .' He stood taller than both of them now. 'Mum . . .'

'She hit me as it 'appens.'

'Good,' said Jonathan.

He looked at his mum sinking down to her knees. Head down. Quietly blubbering, once again trying to get the two men in her life to feel sorry for her. She'd been working up to this. She should have been out of bed and down there, making the tea. There wouldn't have been any need for all this. But she wanted the attention. There were never tears, real tears. And his dad never paid her snivelling any mind. Never had. One reason why they'd fought so much, Johnno always falling for it and then piling into his father for not doing. Over the years, the form of this fight had changed. When he was a kid, he'd mark his distance by throwing a silent one. This was the best way to punish a father who constantly complained about noise and too much laughing in the house. But as Jonathan had got older and naturally quieter, these silences were just a preliminary to lots of shouting and door-banging, the distance then both psychological and territorial. And when the door-banging stopped, when the hammering-in of that wedge was over, when their connection, their join, was all but hanging by a thread, then came the jolt. Then his mother really would cry. And father and son would do what they could, as fast as they could, to make it up to her, to make her smile. Then it was a race for forgiveness. Whoever won the race, won the argument. Whoever won, won her. He could see right through it all now of course. She wasn't the victim in the middle, she was what kept them apart. Another disappointment. They don't stop coming once you start looking for them.

'Were you threatenin' me, son? In me own house? This is my house and I say what goes . . .' His father was jabbing at his chest now. Jonathan grabbed him by the neck and flung him on to the bed. Then put his arm across the throttle of his throat to hold him there. He lay still, half on, half off his dad who was staring back at him, trying to stare him out. 'Gangin' up on me now are yer, son?' Jonathan felt her pulling at his coat from behind, trying to get him on her side. He felt OK until the fumes of alcohol reached him. Then he got jittery. Fumes were the signal to retreat usually. The calm before the fit.

'Leave us, mum, would yer?'

'Son don't start . . .'

'Leave us, I said. I've got a bone to pick with me dad.'

The bedroom door closed with a click this time. A finale. He felt sealed-in. It was his show now. Time for his speech. At long last. He was in charge. His dad under him. The turning point. No manhood pint down the pub with him. This. It was an end that couldn't end like this, his dad just lying there. He got off and let him sit up, watched him stroking his throat.

'Musta bin hard this last couple o' months eh? What with the hotel being closed and no tarts comin' an' goin'.'

'I don't know what yer on about.'

'No wonder *she's* at her wits' end eh?' He looked to the door to make sure it was closed.

All of a sudden, he smelt such a waft of shit . . . Jonathan clocked him one then, fist on face. Hard. Watched him fall back. Holding his chin.

'I'm sorry, dad.'

'So then. Yer can take a swipe but yer can't stand yer ground.'

'Dad.'

'Who's it gonna be? Either you go or I go.'

'Me, dad.'

'Right then. Pack yer bags and get on with it.'

'Dad.'

'You heard.'

'About tomorrow.'

'What about tomorrow?'

'The job.'

'What job?'

'Micky's job. The fuckin' job, dad!'

'If I hear language like that in this house again . . .' And he came at him then. Swung for him. Jonathan pushed him back, with one arm. He watched his old dad fly backwards, fall into the telly trolley, trip on the rug and topple to the floor. Then hold on to the bed leg to steady himself. A right old tumble that left him so startled, his teeth were showing. When his dad wasn't smiling, teeth showing was bad news. Jonathan held firm though. That tumble was what he'd been looking for. Some proof at last.

'Yer not listening to me are yer? . . . The job, dad. Yer doin' a job tomorrow I hear. Well?' He had him. 'And what about all them tarts, dad? What about 'em eh?'

Then they heard the music. Hark! A family ritual. They gave it time to settle in, time to get to the melody. God songs. Hark an angel sings by the name of Aled Jones flying high on his Wings of a Dove.

26

Mum's calming music sometimes worked and sometimes didn't. When it didn't, when the shouting and swearing won the day, the added din of young Aled in the background was more like a cat being gutted alive. The eerie chorus coming up the stairs right now, though, was OK. Made the situation in the bedroom more holy than angry. Father and son had landed.

'It ain't Micky's job, it's Sammy's. Sammy Smith's the brains behind it. He's got debts to pay.'

He sounded weepy. Weak. Looked terrible sitting on the floor, head down, knees apart.

'Sammy's, Micky's. What difference does it make. For cryin' out loud, dad, get up will yer.' Jonathan turned away to the wall. To give him some dignity. Not much but something. When he turned back round, the old man stood one hand on hip, the other stroking his head, front to back, front to back. He was bald at the front and the rest of his hair cloudy patches of grey that were nearly all over. He was growing a beard to compensate. 'I'm the driver, dad.'

'Oh Jesus. We've been set up, yer know that, don't yer, son?' Jonathan moved in then, chest and shoulders forward, his head so on fire his mouth was twisted. He could throw a punch at him, any time now. His dad stood his ground, put his hands in his pocket. Said, 'You can't drive no truck anyway.'

'I can now, dad.'

'Yer can't,' he shouted, moving in closer, less than six inches nose-to-nose, thinking he was still in with a chance.

'I was out practising today.'

'But . . .'

'But what, dad?' One of them had to back off. Jonathan turned back to the wall again. He carried on talking but to the wall. '*Get a good job, my son, and you'll not go far wrong.*' Then turned back round and pointed. 'Like you eh? My Dad. If it wasn't so fuckin' tragic, I'd laugh.'

He had no idea, the lad, thought Charlie. He'd come all this way and . . . well he wasn't too bright, that was clear now. None too bright at all. What did General Patton say? 'Show your son where to head for, but don't tell him the way.' Well General Patton was talking through his backside.

'I 'ad no choice, son. Who d'yer think was doin' *my* job before I got it?'

'Oh, I see. Yer just carryin' on a tradition like.'

'It was Smithy. Micky and Sammy's old man. Can't yer see it son? I 'ad no choice. He used to be a copper. Still knows 'em all doesn't he? He's got the whole place sewn up. If I'd said owt, I'd have lost me job and what good woulda come o' that eh?'

Charlie couldn't help but feel sorry for the lad, looked just a touch like he'd had his heart broken. Well perhaps some good would come of it. Perhaps the lad'd try that bit harder – would hate his old man enough to not turn out like him.

'An' you 'ave the nerve to 'ave a go at me?'

'I've got a job at the supermarket just opened. Back door man, nights. Start new year. Got the letter today. I'll be out of it for good then.'

'All this time you've been Sammy's dummy and . . .'

'Don't be comin' it all 'igh an' mighty now. You wouldn't be shellin' out on new pumps and gear boxes if it wasn't for Sammy's tarts and the rest of it . . . Every penny you make off him . . . Where d'yer think he gets it from eh? Dumper trucks and demolition? Grow up, lad.' He stared at him hard now. He wanted his son to see how powerless they both were. Arm outstretched, he pointed. 'So you think on before you 'ave a go at me. You think on, my son.'

'An' me mam's been goin' short coz the hotel's been closed, is that it? She's been livin' off his bitch money 'n' all 'as she?'

'Blowin' it down the bingo yer mean.'

'Oh, well that's alright then.'

The lad was squeezing it for every last crumb of victory he could muster. Did he really think he could win on morals after the shite he'd been into for the last god knows how long? Charlie weighed up the odds carefully and decided to give him one last chance. He could give in or bugger off. Find some other mug to scrounge off.

'Well we're all square now aren't we, son. You've 'ad yer fun. Now get out me road.' He shoved to get past but Jonathan followed him, over to the tallboy.

'Why yer doin' it, dad? The blag. Why yer gettin' involved? Why not . . . why not take the day off?'

Charlie opened his shirt drawer. He turned and saw the lad sneering at Mrs Thatcher looking down on the pair of them. He pulled out a pale blue nylon one.

'How d'yer square all this with her then?' said Jonathan pointing up at her.

'That's right, son. You go for the easy targets.'

'Well you said it.'

And from another drawer, a pair of blue trousers, still with the belt drawn through. He laid these on the bed and began to undress, blue shirt and black tie and thick black trousers. His security uniform. He put the nylon shirt on before taking his trousers off. Jonathan sat on the other side of the bed, watching him as he used to, the last time he couldn't have been more than ten years old. Charlie bit his lip hard, the full size of his son a real problem now. A son with some power and no idea what to do with it. If it was power he was after, he ought to think about the consequences. He walked over to the trouser press, unclipped it and took yesterday's trousers out. Then put today's trousers in. Then reached for the hanger up on the picture rail, gold writing all along it.

Jonathan felt he'd earned the right to be here. To be on the bed, watching his father. His eyes resting on the old spindly legs, the tail of his dad's shirt like a skirt now, a sick joke. How old was he? Forty-three and fucked. Now on his tiptoes, reaching up to hang his trousers. Legs, brown but veined. They used to be dark, dark and hairy but the hairs had gone grey or gone completely so now they just looked like old women's legs. It was like it was all over for him.

'Dad?'

'What?'

'How much they payin' yer?'

'They'll give me a scratch and, if I don't play the game, somat else I don't wanna think about.'

'Yer leavin' anyway yer said?'

'So?'

'So what can they do?'

'They've a dozen young lads who wouldn't mind the kickin' practice. Grow up, Jonathan.'

'How much yer gettin' then?'

'I told yer, a scratch. A fifty-pound note.'

'And what yer gonna be doin' exactly?'

'I stay outside with the delivery van. Eyes, ears and gob shut. What I usually do.'

'Who else is on?'

'Speke's got a sparky gonna keep the manager busy with his new uplighters as he calls 'em. In the conference rooms. No windows in there see. And there's a trainee villain on porter duty downstairs. Started last week.'

'Fifty quid for fuck all then.'

'I'll be glad to be out o' there. They've tripled the number o' rooms now yer know. Made 'em all smaller. The place'll be heavin' with tarts new year.'

Earlier, when Johnno had told his mum he was leaving, he'd been trying the plot out, seeing how it sounded, how real he could make it happen in his head, but now his heart had caught up with the idea. Limits and boundaries hurt, press down, but once gone . . . the uncharted territory of responsibility. Might as well get off, he thought.

His dad was brushing hairs off his jacket now, hairs that weren't there. 'They didn't 'ave to twist *your* arm though, did they? I can see that alright. It's a set-up, yer know that, son, don't yer? If yer don't go along with it, we'll all be in the clear.'

'Zat you tellin' me what I can and can't do? I'm gettin' the money off this job, sellin' me motor and goin'. Leaving. It's just scum round here, far as the eye can see.'

They clocked each other then. Jonathan looked down. Then his dad piped up, 'What else 'ave yer been up to then? Up to yer neck in it I suppose.'

His dad looked so stupid and dumb, all the glory had gone from Jonathan's victory now. In his father's eyes, he saw just a glimmer of pride left standing, a thin disguise over his lack of control. It was horrible to see it.

'They roped you in on it coz o' me, Johnno.' In a soft voice. Pathetic.

'That's it, dad. You blame yerself.'

'I didn't . . .'

'Not coz o' you, no, dad. They asked me did I want an earner and I said yes. They're short o' drivers. They think I'm good. That's why me. It's one job dad. Just one job and I'm away.'

'You've been eatin' too many Yorkie bars, my son.'

'Now yerv lost it, yer up to crackin' jokes about it are yer?'

'Lost it? Lost what, son?' It was no great loss. He'd never had the boy in the first place. For years, Johnno had been working up to this, angling to take control. And that was about the strength of it. The lad was too big for his boots and would keep falling over until he wore a pair that fit. Now he wore the exact same look on his face as when . . . well he could make a list but the most chilling time . . . the time when Charlie had seen ahead of the boy, had to be on that famous fishing comp. Johnno had gone off to have a whazzer so Charlie baited. Then he cast in and, in just under a minute, caught the biggest carp to come out of the Shropshire. The look on Johnno's face was of a man, not a kid but of a *man* who'd been robbed. And now here it was again, the full disgust of him from the inside out. Spark and spirit gone. No fun in there any more.

The lad had no more chance of pulling cash from that job tomorrow than Charlie had of pulling out of it. And there was no point telling him. None whatsoever. He'd do it just to spite him now.

Charlie rubbed his leg and then his throat, his Adam's apple quite sore after the throttling and then he smelt the shit again. Everything he touched turned to shite anyway. What he needed was a drink.

31

'You know,' said Jonathan. Charlie could tell the boy wasn't altogether comfortable now and had no idea what came next. Charlie crinkled his nose and squinted his eyes and shook his head. If it came across as disappointment, it wasn't meant like that. It was more disbelief the lad was so slow. Christ, he needed a drink. Then Hilda shouted up,

'Coq au vin alright for yer?'

'She's still not very well is she?' said Charlie, to get the lad to see the big picture.

'Well steamin' into her don't help, does it?'

'What d'yer want me to do? What am I supposed to do?' Charlie moved fast towards the door and shouted down, 'Nowt for me love, ta,' and then closed the door again, trying to think of something useful to say to the boy, something the lad could accept at face value without turning it into a weapon, a way of getting back at him.

He walked over to the wardrobe mirror and did up his shirt, kicking at a pile of papers and magazines on the floor, all fallen out of the wardrobe. He did another worry rub across his forehead. He saw Jonathan look away. Saw that Johnno's face was all finished now. Worn-in like a man's. It wouldn't change again. Not till he'd had some kids himself. Perhaps the lad *would* be better off going away. Perhaps this was a god-given, a chance not to be chucked.

'Where d'yer think you'll make a start then? London I suppose.' Charlie, still at the mirror, watched Jonathan's face for a reaction. There was none. Just a short sharp answer.

'That's the plan.'

He couldn't give it a rest could he? Caught his dad with his pants down and couldn't give it a rest. *'That's the plan.'* Like Charlie was too old to make plans now. 'Oh, yer planned it like this then did yer?'

'No, dad, not exactly.'

Aled was on to 'Hark the Herald Angels Sing'. Charlie was dreading Christmas. 'Shirl's got her name down for a flat yer know?'

'I know.'

'Her gone. You gone. Yer mam'll be on her tod.'

'If I go, Shirl won't have to. Malcy can 'ave my room.'

'She can't wait to get away, sounds like. I'm worried about yer mam I am.'

'I'll talk to her.'

'Who?'

'Shirl o' course'

'Oh . . . Right.' A long silence. Then, 'Whose truck yer gonna be drivin'? One o' Sammy's?'

'An empty one from the services.'

'You'll be goin' away sooner than yer think, sounds like. Yer turnin' out to be a bigger disappointment than I thought.'

'Thanks, dad.'

Jonathan liked it. Liked talking with his dad as an equal for a change. Up there, with him. Wanted to savour it – and so much so, he looked for something profound to say, to make a mark on the day, the moment. But no words came. So he sat on the bed and watched his dad doing what he himself had been doing not five minutes since, standing at the window, hands doing tripods on the sill, looking out, nothing but reflection and rain staring back.

'Me nerves are all over the place, son.'

'Yer just drunk, dad.'

'Not drunk enough. Don't say nowt to our Shirl . . . about . . . about any of it will yer?'

'Scared she might think even less of yer?'

'She's a good girl, our Shirl.'

'Listen to yer! Dad! Yer just make it up as yer go along, don't yer?'

'There's no book, son.' He turned round. His eyes huge. Great black nuts, shining. The rest of his face dissolving away, sad. Lips small and tight in on themselves. Holding in his words. Was this man to man now? It felt like.

'D'yer remember what yer put our Shirl through, dad?'

'Preggers yer mean?'

'You know what I mean.'

'Yeah, well she was too young to be runnin' round for my likin'.'

'It wasn't because she was yer favourite then?'

'No, son.'

'Don't lie, dad. I don't care any more. I don't even mind any more.'

'I didn't want her ruined that was all.' Then quiet. A look away. 'And we've got our Malcy now 'aven't we?' Then quiet for Malcy. 'And look at our Shirl . . . she'll be a *proper* nurse one day, you mark my words . . . I know what . . .' His dad sized him up and down. Then said, 'How's about we go an' 'ave a drink, son? Down the Spike. What d'yer say?'

'Where's that shit smell comin' from, dad?'

Chapter Three

The call came. Jonathan wrote the plate number on the back of his hand. Then went back to bed. When he woke up, his gut told him straight off, 'Don't do it.' The first law of villainy is to listen to your instinct. Jonathan wasn't villain. Lying in bed, seeing the scam in broad daylight with a giggling toddler bouncing on his stomach, rammed this home to him. He could hear the rain, could tell it was the lashy stuff, could have done with the morning in bed. Pretend it was all a dream. The kid was wide-eyed, laughing at him. And then the alarm went off. And mum was suspicious. Saturday. Alarms on a Saturday? Overtime, he told her. It happened. From time to time.

Even little Malcy knew things had gone too far. Jonathan was on the loo and copy-catting; Malcy was sat on his potty. Looking like he had no idea what he was supposed to be doing on it. Then, all of a sudden, he picked it up and ran out, his nose all crinkled up. The stench too strong for him. It was too late now. The show must . . . On the bright side . . . if all went to plan . . . if all went to plan he'd be away after Christmas. Buy Shirl a new buggy so she could hold her head up straight. The one she had was plastered with gaffer tape. A disgrace really, considering.

Jonathan had good reason to feel jumpy. But not the sort of good reason a villain would come up with. He was jumpy because of his record, his form. Probation for twocking. Fined twice for hoisting. His only crimes and every one a balls up. No wonder he was bottling. There were loads of faces with better records than him. Why the fuck did Micky trust him on this one? A forty-foot lorry full of thievery? He pulled the chain and turned the shower on. The brain work hard. Very hard. Standing in the wet with nowhere to go but against his better judgment.

He gave it a stroke to bring himself on and then took a quick peek.

Masquerading as an add-on – the very crux of him. And he wished he'd not woken it up now. He was *too* jumpy. Vulnerable. Worried that even this, the very man of him wasn't up to it, wouldn't last the course, would in the end turn out to be just a very efficient wanking tool. The great hope of it being central to his main event was fast fading. The main event? The blood and passion of his future, the very him. Looking at himself, at his situation, his scope, and then at the great glory between his legs – well it didn't pack much of a punch in reality. It was nowhere near man enough for the job in question. The jail of choices his life had thrown up was inescapable. A bald fact. *Nothing good comes to him who waits in Manchester.* Not even a decent woman.

Someone for everyone. His only inalienable right, as his dad liked to call them, was his right to a woman who could do something for him. Something other and more than what they usually did for him. This hope, this great unknown, used to be and should really be enough of an ambition. This great hope had got him through great long stretches of the all too predictable. On the hunt for Wheezy Mark II, his seed, like Cinderella's slipper, had been deposited in addresses all over Manchester. No girl could wear him. Manchester girls were too big and mouthy and mad for the beer. Too cocksure of themselves. Either that or too tarty, tight and too much like hard work.

For all he knew, he could have had kids out there already. He'd not been accused but that meant nothing. Orphans. Abortions. Look on the bright side, Johnno. He looked down at his dunker and, even now, at this low ebb, the pride rose up inside him. It was a pride he'd been born with. Had to be. No matter how mad or sad or disappointed he was, this pride never left him. When he looked at himself, felt himself, compared himself, he was proud. As if he'd fashioned himself with his very own hands. Stood in a hot shower, thinking cold shower shite such as this, had the desired effect. He got out, went to the mirror and thanked god. Even though he said it himself, he was fucking gorgeous. And then he thought about Micky's eyebrows. And then the job. And then he was back on the loo. His mum was banging on the door.

'I've got a bone to pick with you,' she said.

He'd been in there too long. For some reason, it wasn't done to stay in the bathroom too long. It suggested a 'problem'. It worried everyone. The house became restless.

He found her in the kitchen filling the washing machine. 'What's the problem?'

'Problem?' she said, turning for just a glance, a slap of a glance that stung him into an examination of his conscience. What had he done to deserve that?

'A bone to pick, yer said.'

'Oh aye. The bone.'

'Well?' He was already angry at himself. Whatever he'd done, he was sorry. That's that. All over. Done and dusted. There was no point in dragging it out. 'What is it? What've I done?'

She jammed down the door on the tub, made sure the pipes were tight on the taps and turned the washer on. Turned round and looked at him. 'The new washin' machine's comin' this affy. We'll 'ave room to bring the table back in.'

'Don't harp on, mother. What've I done?'

She wiped her hands on a teatowel and then hooked it on the side of the cupboard. He stood in the doorway, taking up the whole frame, leaning, arms folded. She walked towards him as if to get past but he didn't move. He wanted his answer. It felt like he'd got her. Talking washing machines because she didn't have the power any more. There was no door to protect her, no husband. She had a bone to pick but she couldn't tear the meat off it now. He was too alive for her – man alive. The only dead meat in the house was hanging off her bones. Frozen to a chill. Dad had been picking on her for years, trying to liven her up. Picking on her with good reason and no appetite. Now Johnno was up there. He'd taken his seat at the table with the men. Reached the world where women can't go and she knew it. He was old, strong and able enough to keep his dad in his place and her out of his face. He was the man of the house now.

And before the burn of this blasphemy had passed through his mind, she was there, as if she'd heard every word of his mutinous wishful thinking. She stood in front of him and stared hard. Almost a sneer on her face. Gone the metal jaw of her industry. Gone the housework grey of her drudgery. For a minute *she* was man alive. And not friendly. Not reassuring and it was not really like him to forget his manners like that. He now wished he hadn't cut her off quite so confidently. It was his nerves, that was all. She was playing on his nerves. He felt so uncomfortable he made to move out of her way. She grabbed him by the arm then.

'Remember what I said to yer father the last time he took a swing for yer? Do yer?'

'Sort of.'

'Well you listen 'ard, my son. Don't you ever do to him what yer did to him last night or else you'll not see the inside of this house again. Do you hear me?'

It was a cheeky job. The hotel had been closed down for a complete makeover. Due to re-open in the New Year. At the front of the hotel, two huge glass revolving doors, and round the back, where the carpark was, two more. It was the revolving door system that had given Sammy the idea, apparently. Micky's contribution was the intelligence, something he wasn't well known for. Bottle, brawn and bullshit yes. Intelligence no. This intelligence amounted to finding out what day the new tellies were arriving and who'd be parking up an empty truck, over at the services.

Jonathan got out of his car, locked it and tapped a goodbye on the bonnet as he walked away. This time, because it was raining so hard, he decided to walk through the service station main entrance and then on to the transport caff to get over to the lorry park. He looked at his hand for the plate number. The long shower had done a pretty good job of cleaning it right off but he could see enough to match the letters with the type of lorry he was supposed to be driving. He looked around before trying the door. He climbed up, jumped in and checked the keys were in the ignition. Three red barrels of rum on the keyring. He started her up and then leant forward on the steering wheel. The TVs weren't due to be delivered for another half hour yet. No rush.

He made himself familiar with the controls, lights, gears, air, sounds. He kept the CB turned off. That was a worry. Maybe the driver signed on with someone at regular times, on regular days. Maybe he'd be missed. He was a tidy bugger, whoever he was. No fags or sweet wrappers in the ashtray. Glove compartment tidy with manuals and time sheets. The windscreen wipers were sound. He turned everything off. And then he heard what sounded like a mouse squeaking. Then a rustling sound. He listened again. It was definitely coming from inside the cab. He turned around to check and saw immediately how much trouble he was in. He saw just the crotch of the guy first. He leant back further, got a bigger better look and saw the whole man lying there, hands tied behind his back, a balaclava on backwards, cheeks blown up full of something, squeaking away and wriggling about for all his dear life. Jonathan sat forward again. How much had the man seen through that balaclava? Was there any tape on his eyes underneath it?

He turned the engine over. There was worry enough in the back of his mind but now he had the driver in the back of his cab. Everything was crunching out of synch, the wheels of the gear change, the mind change, that noise that comes with a wrong'un. This was a true amateur at work.

Micky should have put a genuine Class 1 on the job. Someone experienced with weight. With some idea. He said all Sammy's drivers had gone to work for the big boys on contract. And these big boys had driven the pallet prices so low down, the little Sammies of this world had been forced to diversify. So Sammy had sold off most of his lorries and gone into earth, digging, dumping, moving. Did a bit of Thatcher's scab work when it came up, the first time shifting scabby coal out of Yorkshire, and the last time, when the bin men were out. That was his other line, tipping. He'd move anything except shit and drugs. He didn't want his men coming down with diseases, he said. Or criminal records. Now that would be bad for business.

Yesterday Jonathan had thought Sammy clean, straight, a businessman, the one to watch, the good half of the Smith family.

Sammy was his boss and as such owned his future, his daylight. That he was a ponce using men like his dad to fund his gambling habit put him in a different light altogether. Jonathan didn't object on moral grounds – there were very few muckers mad for morals round that neck of the woods – no. It was the blatant usage that got him, that had got Jonathan driving a stolen artic all the way up the M62 and would get Jonathan locked up if he didn't look out as he did now, through rear and side mirrors, one two three, all the way over to the hotel. Sammy said he was a good driver. Yet again, Jonathan had got it all so wrong.

Sammy the suave, Micky the mover, that's how it'd been. Sammy up the casino giving it large, Micky down the motorway, counting tricks and shagging chicks, whores or not. How did he manage that? Money. Scag money lately, so he'd heard. To keep the bitches on their back, Jack had said. But Sammy was above all that, or so he'd thought. And now Wilson and Son were grafting for the pair of them. About as low as Jonathan wanted his family to go.

When the telly lorry turned up, security – '*our Charlie*' – would tell the driver and the porters to unload round the front, for easier access to the service lift. The lift was sent down to the basement. The trainee villain and Barny, another mate of Micky's, emptied it. They threw those tellies about like chuck-ins, at footer. Jonathan stood in the back of the lorry and caught them like blows to the stomach. They had an hour. What they couldn't clear in an hour they had to leave. Between lifts, they caught their breath while Johnno stacked the tellies straight, in the lorry. Some boxes had 'Conference Rms' scrawled across them in black felt-tip. These he guessed were the best and he put them to one side, by the door. They were his side salad, just in case he didn't get weighed on, after all. Two tellies and two video recorders.

He wasn't supposed to have done any lifting really. Driving, that was his job. Barny had dragged him out of his cab though. Asked him if he wanted to discuss his new job description with a fist. So he figured, on account, he deserved a skim.

'Hour's up. Loading done, Barny!' Jonathan jumped out of the lorry and looked down the length of it, both sides. Barny was in the cab, checking the driver was still tied up. He jumped down and handed Jonathan some keys.

'I'll go and get some bodies and meet you over Micky's lock-up. OK?'

Up in a lorry, after a scam, is a high feeling, everyone else so small. That Cavalier was so small Johnno almost never saw it. The rain, the steam on the window. The adrenalin. That's what did it. A lorryload of tellies. It was a buzz. He'd been too happy, too relieved. Forgot about his passenger. The sweat of the fear was gone. The heat off now. He felt cold. Sliding off the roundabout to the slip road, he got busy. It was always the same, just before the open road. He whacked up the speed and the sounds and the window-winder to keep the tunes in and the rain out and to make the mouse in the back go quiet. Got his fags out. Hunted around for a lighter. He might have been settling down for a night's telly. So it took some time to register that the diddy Cavalier wasn't moving very fast, in fact not at all. The idea of swerving quick and wide didn't appeal to him. Instead he gently wheeled the load over to the right. He figured his back end might just tap it. Clip it. Might even miss it altogether.

The Cav was shunted off the slip road. It rolled forwards fast, the body in the driving seat not even attempting to control it. It veered off the road, on to the verge and then into a ditch, landing there, arse-end upwards, smoking.

Maybe the guy put his foot on the gas, just as the lorry made contact. No way could it have shifted that far, just from a tap. Unlucky. There was quite a lot of smoke coming off it now. Looked like it was getting worse, maybe getting ready to burst into flames. Hopefully it was just some salesman. A fit able-bodied soul with the nous to climb out and get the fuck away.

He was taking such good care of his driving now he only went and missed his exit. Instead of taking the turn off to Micky's yard, he carried on, over to the motorway, and then on to it, and then he found himself on his way back to the service station. There were too many bodies on this job. One behind him. One probably charcoal by now, dead in the ditch. He'd seen all this coming. When he woke up, he got the call, not to do this job, and here he was, bottle well and truly gone.

Maybe now, though, his instinct was working for him. The crash was all heat, smoke, noise. The sort of heat that leaves a trail. The image of a smoking car and dead body kept coming at him. If he changed his mind, if he ignored gut instinct one more time . . . he'd have to drive back to Micky's place and down the bypass with the greater part of Greater Manchester police force on it. He'd read somewhere that a large percentage of criminals were caught because they lost the plot and returned to the scene of the crime to find it again. He wasn't falling for that one. He came off the motorway like a real professional. Concentrating, he got on with a new plan all of his own making. And then another plan and another . . . he could drive straight to Watford Gap, sell the tellies and lose himself in London. But then he'd have to dispose of the driver. Corpse was the word that came to mind. Or . . . he could go back to the service station, ring up Jack's brother Doc and ask him what to do. Doc had his own lorry and had driven half way round the world in it. He could get on his CB and find a fence for him quite quickly. And if Doc wasn't home, and there was every chance he wouldn't be, he'd park up in the service station and just walk away.

He drove round the service station scanning for lorries that looked just like his. There wasn't one. He slid in between two Tesco juggernauts. No sooner had he done so than a car drove across his front, its headlights flashing. He hardly dared look at it, expecting it to be cops unmarked. Matey in the back was doing his head in, banging with his feet now, still whining, after all that time. Really irritating. Really stupid. More headlights flashing. He looked down. It was a Rover. A girl was sat in the passenger seat shoving her tits out the window. Big white tits in black lace, just hanging there, in the rain, seemingly unattached to any face. Jonathan stared at them for a while wondering what she thought she was up to and then thanked god. But something about the girl stuck in his head, something he recognised.

Until jumping down from his cab, he'd felt reasonably in control considering what he'd just been through. When his feet hit the tarmac, though, he just collapsed in a heap. Thought he'd broken his legs for a minute. The car was still there, the window up now. He felt a prat. If he'd seen *them* then they'd definitely clocked him. He brushed himself down. Then, his mind made up, he knocked at the drizzle on the car window. He could see she was covered up, no white flesh glaring. The window hummed and as it went down her top was yanked open by the driver. In the back of the car, there were two girls both with frizzy hair, squashed up together, handbags on their knees, one of them smoking, their lips caked black in the dark.

'Are you in for some o' this or what, mate? If so, stay in yer cab and be a good boy.'

'Val?' He could hardly see her face. She'd closed her shirt up and was looking down, away from him. On the dashboard he recognised the keys to her house. The plastic willy she'd won for a line on the prize bingo in Blackpool.

'Know him do yer?' said the man, more a young lad really.

'Old school friend,' she said.

'Are you in for some or what then, mate?'

He actually thought about it. He was that keyed-up, he thought about it. Sitting room only in his cab, though.

He'd have liked her lying down. On her back. And for free.

'I thought you were working with our . . .?'

'No,' she said.

The car reversed away in a skid.

He snook his way round and between the lorries and over to the transport caff. Hating himself. Hating her. Hating Micky. Then it all came back to him. Like a blood transfusion. The job, the car, Barny. Jelly legs. He'd go straight to his motor, straight home and, after that, straight to the train station. Get out. Bottle gone. This was the kick up the arse he'd been waiting for.

By the time he got into the caff, the accident *and* the robbery were all over the place. They were all on about it. Definitely a lorry involved. They all looked at him, like they knew exactly what he'd been up to. The sight of the swirling Coke in the drinks machine made him gasp. He hadn't realised how thirsty he was. Drenched through with rain, but his throat as dry as a chip.

'I'm off. Harry's just got it on the radio, they're all over the fuckin' place. After a Stobart, aren't they? And they're not lookin' in mine, not today they're not.'

From the caff windows looking out on to the motorway, there were blue lights all over the show. In all the rain and mist, it was hard to make out where they were going, coming from, headed for. Fire, police or ambulance? It was definitely an emergency.

Jonathan rang Doc. Doc's lorry was off the road but he could use his mate's. His mate was off the road with backache. Hang on two ticks, he said. He'd ring back.

He rang back in less than a minute. There'd be no mileage in driving red-hot tellies down to London today, none whatsoever. He had a lorry and the Grove Corner Under-15 football squad at his disposal. It would be late kick-off but with the wagons back-to-back, they could clear the load in less than fifteen minutes. Did he want to chance it?

The lorry only just fitted between the two rows of parked cars on Jonathan's street. There were only two tellies left in it. Too paranoid to go back for his motor and intent on claiming at least some wages for his trouble, Johnno had stayed with Doc and watched with awe how fast a consignment of cheap tellies can disappear. They did three drops, all on Ridley Avenue, which, before Thatcher, had been known as depressed, a label that afforded it some mystery and sympathy. Now it was simply and obviously deprived.

He shared the takings with Doc fifty-fifty and, still flushed with adrenalin, agreed to accompany Doc all the way to Spain to see Jack, the man missing from both their lives. First of all, though, to London, to pick up a load.

'What load?'

'Any load,' said Doc. 'Any load goin' Spain.' He was past forty easy. Hairy and heavy from the waist down. His arms got all the exercise. He wore a woolly hat, a beard and eyes that never left the road, not for a second. Even at the traffic lights. He was wearing gloves too, grey suede ones.

'And then what?'

'Down to Portsmouth and on to the ferry. I'm lookin' forward to drivin' this thing for a distance. It's better than mine.' He hummed his way through the gears and gobbed out the window. He gobbed out the window a lot.

'Shouldn't yet be askin' yer mate first?'

'Eh?'

'If yer can take 'is lorry to Spain?' It crossed Jonathan's mind that Doc wasn't fully engaged with what was going on. Was perhaps a little too high on the excitement. There were more traffic lights. Doc rolled a cigarette and, for the very first time, looked Jonathan in the eye.

'Listen. I ain't stickin' round 'ere. Not now you've told me the whole story. I ain't feared o' Sammy Smith, so let's get that straight. But I do get scared when I 'ear that he's scared. If he's jumpy, I figure all this lot's a damn sight more serious than a wagon load o' tellies. You're miles out o' your depth, d'yer know that? Spain's as a good a place as any.'

Johnno would have to pay half towards the diesel. Johnno would have to go home and pick up his passport.

'Are we goin' yours after I get me passport?'

'Look behind yer. What d'yer see? Bed, blankets, wanking material. A crate o' Stella.'

'Yer passport?'

'Always close to me 'eart.' He patted his coat hanging off the back of his seat, a black three-quarter-length, the really heavy sort. 'Habit. I'm long haul, remember.'

'An' yer wife?'

'Shaggin' Dylan from the garage. She's 'appy enough. I know I'm not. And by the way, you'll have to kip where yer sat I'm afraid.' And he gobbed out of the window again, just as they turned into Jonathan's estate.

Even before they reached the house, Jonathan knew there was a major flaw with this Spain plan. He'd need to know what it was before it was too late to change his mind.

First off, it was more than risky driving down Lincoln Street in an artic. Overweight. Over noisy. Over the top. Too risky for a two-telly drop, one for Doc and one for Jonathan's mum.

Doc helped him lug the boxes up the stairs and Jonathan stood on a chair and put them in the attic. He was nearly crying by the time he'd got them in safe and pulled the board over. It was the come-down. Doc had already gone downstairs. Said he'd wait for him outside. Hurry. Jonathan was leaving home. He didn't have enough adrenalin to get excited about it. Not under these circumstances. He was drained. The blood gone from his head. He felt pale. Fainty. The top of the stairs was a long way up and, with him stood on a chair, it looked double the distance. He wavered a bit but caught himself. He got off the chair really carefully. Then saw his mum's face looking up at him. She seemed miles away. Malcy sat on her hip. He was too big to be carried now. She had her quiet look on, the one she used for Dad's bad moods. The one that said she was ready for anything and used to it.

'Where's me dad, mum?'

'Work o' course. Where d'yer think he is? I thought you was me washing machine come. What's goin' on?'

'And Shirl? Where's our Shirl?'

'In bed o' course. What's goin' on, Jonathan?'

'I've gotta go, mum.'

Then Doc pushed the front door open. 'Come on, lad. I'll be gettin' that pull I don't want in a minute.'

'Mum, this is Doc. There's a telly up there for him. He'll be back in a couple o' weeks for it. There's one there for you 'n' all. For Christmas.'

'Where yer going? Where d'yer get the tellies from?'

Doc went back out again.

'Off the back of a lorry, mum.'

'They don't normally deliver.'

'There's nowt to fret about, OK?'

'You've not been out burgling 'ouses 'ave yer?'

'Mum!'

He rifled all his drawers for funds, a few clothes, his cheque book, the last postcard he'd got from Jack and his passport. Then his beads off the bedstead. He tapped his pillow, then smelt it, smothered his head in it and threw it down, told himself to grow up. Then he pulled a squeeze on the curtain and looked out into the street, a street well worth leaving. Pulled out his box of tapes. Gregory. Uhuru. Toots. Sly and Robbie. Ranking Trevor – roots all over the world, he said. Well, time to find out. He took a deep deep breath and was out of there.

'I've gotta go, mum.'

'Where?'

'London, I told yer. I've got a lift sorted.'

'Trouble isn't it?' She was having trouble keeping Malcy still, he was doing that rigid stretching stuff, to get down. But she held on to him, tight, struggling with him. And then, as if the kid had been given the nod, he went all quiet and relaxed. Like he knew something different was happening. Something important. Like he wanted to listen in.

'Mum?'

'What?'

'I need money, mum. And I'm in a rush.'

He didn't need money right then but knew he soon would and, when he did, she wouldn't be there to give it to him. He didn't like asking for it either. Never had but always had to. 'Have you got a few quid', his usual, meant just that, a few quid. The only word guaranteed to hit the spot was 'money', a word strenuously avoided most of the time, unless of course it went missing. In his pocket or down the bingo. She'd been trying to get off it. Not doing too badly either. And he'd been working lately so the chances were she had quite a stash somewhere. Doc was making a right racket outside. He had to go and quickly. He was on the run now. He liked the sound of that. On the run. No fannying about. No mind to make up.

She laid Malcy down on the couch and went upstairs. Malcy's eyes followed the flash of the television. He was sucking his thumb. Thinking. About what? Jonathan picked him up, hugged him and kissed his face with big sucks. Then laid him back down. The kid's eyes went straight back to the television.

When she came back, he noticed her eyes were full. It usually took time to get to tears but she was at it already. She had in her hand some notes bound in elastic.

''Snot yer catalogue money is it?'

She shook her head. 'Christmas money.'

He hugged her, took the money and went, banging the front door hard behind him.

His mum opened it up again, still with eyes full. Real tears they were. He was pleased.

'Don't get that telly down till after Christmas OK? And tell our Shirl to keep our Malcy sweet.' He ran back and pecked her a goodbye then.

It was a Stobart spotter that had nailed him, got the plates, fucked the whole job up. The hotel manager's son had been taking advantage of his dad's new job, living it up in one of the newly done-out suites. He'd been hanging out of his window, bored, waiting for his new telly to turn up.

The word had gone out on the CB channel that the police were checking all Stobart lorries. These lorries apparently held some significance within the motorway community.

'Doc, what's so special about a Stobart?'

'Keep yer eyes peeled an' you'll see.'

Jonathan was spotting Stobarts all over the place after that. When you really look, there are millions of them. He felt so much better.

They weren't out of Manchester before it was all too apparent that Jonathan wouldn't be able to stomach too many more of Doc's tales of the unexpected and mostly the uncalled-for. And his humming and snotting and gobbing. Back in the city, he'd given

48

him the benefit of traffic fumes, asthma, nerves. But now Doc explained that he needed constant noise because he had tinnitus. He'd be humming all the way to Europe in fact. Doc was the major flaw.

'I want out, Doc.'

'Not recommended, I'm tellin' yer. I wouldn't go 'ome if I were you.'

'Just let us out over there would yer?'

'What about our Jack?'

'I'll see 'im when he comes home for Chrimbo.'

'I don't think he's comin' home. That's why I wanna see what the little bleeder's up to.'

'I wanna get out.'

'I'll still be wantin' me telly when I get back.'

'Yer can 'ave yer fuckin' telly. Just let me out.'

'Jesus. You're jumpy aren't yer? You won't get far in that state.'

'I'll catch a rattler somewhere.' He had eight hundred quid. He could go where the fuck he liked.

'I'll drop yer at the station.'

'Nah. You get off. Just drop me anywhere.'

As they drove off the motorway, up a slip road, he got his first sighting of uninterrupted greenery. Not seen any in a long while. And in the first of the fields, towards the far end, he saw a streak of white birds on the grass. Probably seagulls. Probably lost. Then something must have put the wind up – they took off. Altogether, at low altitude, keeping to the edge of the field. From that distance, they looked like they were in for the 800 metres.

'Here'll do,' he said. 'I want out now.'

He walked across the flyover and down the slip road on the other side. Stuck his thumb out and thanked god he'd realised just in time. Patted himself on the back for it. Nothing ever happened and then all this on one day. After so many years of near-escapes and nothing doing – this – an escape in need of more planning. This wasn't the day. There was no aim to the plan. The bullet of it had been fired from a gun not targeted, instead just ricocheting off the empty walls of his limitations. Hitching the lift, his stomach did yeller belly full-on. Full up of cowardy custard, he was too scared to leave but too scared to go home. Knees wobbling, thumb in the air, he didn't even want a lift. He was stuck.

Then he remembered his car. Just two junctions away.

Chapter Four

All day, they'd been looking for Jonathan. Not a proper search, not a drive around or a house-to-house. No. Sitting opposite Charlie in the police station, as if Charlie might produce the lad pronto, any second now. Charlie didn't know or much care where he was, and when they found him, whatever they served him would serve him right. He'd been told enough times too many now.

He left the police station a free man but not a safe one. It was dark and crisp, biting cold, a few stars breaking through the sodium but not many. Stood on the top of the black and white piano steps that raised the police station above the reckoning of the man in the street, he turned to see if the cops had put a tail on him. They had. Crocodile tail. A whole team of traffic wardens setting off for the night shift Christmas parking duty, some with lunch boxes tucked under their arms. After being real policemen, no doubt. So near but yet so. At first trying to figure out which arm of Her Majesty's Charlie's silver epaulets belonged to. The wrong arm. The noose of his tie. His shoe laces still undone. He half wished they were policemen. They could keep an eye on him then. Keep him safe. He could have followed them.

He ran down the birdshit steps of the subway and disappeared into the pee stink tunnel. Before emerging into the frost night air, he was grabbed from behind. It was Smithy, the ugly one. Got him by the scruff and dragged him out of the subway, and Charlie all the time telling Micky that the police had put a tail on him. Then giving up. And Micky giving up dragging him. Over and up to floor 3 of a multi-storey carpark. Floor 3 was empty save for a Jag XJS brand-new and one Vdub camper van. Orange, facing out towards town, the main roundabout and the police station Charlie had just vacated. They must have seen him walk out, been waiting for him. Micky pointed him over to the vehicles and walked three paces behind, not letting on anything.

'Zis yours is it?' Stroking the car.

'What d'you think?'

'Not bad is it.'

The side door to the Vdub opened but just a couple of inches.

'Get yer theivin' 'ands off my motor.'

That was Sammy.

'I quite like these too,' said Charlie, paying more attention to the camper now. 'After one meself actually. Tour America 'n' all that. They've got really big ones over there mind.'

Micky told him to shut it. Charlie was still giving the camper a good going over when his brain caught up with the situation proper. 'I'm not gettin' in this.'

'Aren't yer?'

Micky shoved him up against it. 'Hands up and legs apart.' The metal cold was a comfort. Freezing. Made Charlie realise how hot he'd got. Micky slid the side door wide open.

'Slag,' said Micky, surprised-sounding.

'I told yer she was a slag. I just thought I'd try her out.' That was Sammy again. Dark, deep, a husk on his voice. Charlie couldn't see what was going on, there were curtains up.

'You I meant. You said you'd leave off her.'

'She's crap. Waste o' space. Fell asleep on me.'

'Yer can gerroff him now, Sally, it's over.'

'Yer got 'im then?' said Sammy, his voice clearer now.

'Easy.'

A used condom landed a few feet away, glistening from the street lights outside. Reminded Charlie of the first time he'd ever met them. They were just little boys then. Sammy a real looker, mother's stunner of a boy but quiet and deadly. And then milk bottle Micky with a ginge. Already gone wrong, already on the road to rack and ruin, they'd been sat in the back of a police car, in the pub carpark at the Dog and Dart, their dad in the bar getting a bellyful no doubt. They were throwing empty crisp packets out of the window, sweet wrappers ripped into necklaces of silver foil, fag ends from the ashtray. Charlie'd been trying to start his car, saw the mess they were making and went over. Knocked on the window to have a word. They wound down the window to give him his word and the ginger one a mouthful of chewed-up crisps all over his face at full force. He wondered if they remembered it.

Micky pulled Charlie into view. Sally Tippet was lying there, baring all. Sammy touching her up. She tried to pull the oiled-up red hospital blanket over her but he wouldn't let her, instead resting his hand on her chest. She turned away. Mrs Tippett would have been very disappointed. Sammy smiled at Charlie like he was next and then checked the time on his Rolex. In the dim light, he shone, his eyes white bright, his skin clear as olive oil. Still a stunner of a lad.

A stench of off-milk and, behind Sammy's head, a fluorescent light in the van flickering. Everything fragile, even the girl now turned over, showing scalp through her thin hair, the bony shoulders of a child jutting out of her, like meat hooks.

'Get her out. She can drive.'

Sammy pulled the blanket off her and Charlie looked down and away.

Then the eerie horseshoe clonk of the girl's shoes echoing the emptiness of the carpark as she walked round the van. A spook sound. The scrawp against the concrete certain trouble looming. Charlie thought then and only then how stupid he'd been. He could have legged it in his Hush Puppies by now. But it was too late. They were telling him to get inside. He deserved everything coming to him.

Sammy told Sally to start the engine. Charlie spent a couple of minutes being surprised at the spaciousness, as in those terraced houses that from the front, you just wouldn't believe. His eyes loped from the neatness of the cooker, to the tiny teapot, to the teddy bear with the tiny red ribbon round its neck. To the bits of carpet, same stuff that was in Shirl's bedroom. To the first-aid box and there, he rested his eyes. That was organised of them.

The side door was slid shut with very little of the mechanical grace the cell doors of Her Majesty boasted, this cell a good deal smaller in comparison and a lot more crowded. Sickly perfume came wafting over from the girl and strong bevvy breath from Micky. Intermittent pungent trails of a fishy sex smell had Charlie reaching over for the window-winder retching.

'Leave the windows. You'll get plenty o' fresh air in a minute,' said Micky.

'Are yer takin' me home, lads, coz I'm buggered.' Charlie watched to see if the van turned right or left out of the carpark. Left was home and the van turned right. 'I never said owt if that's what yer worried about. Never opened me trap. I did just what you said.' The van headed through town, the whizz of familiar landmarks flashing past faster than they'd ever gone before.

'We've been your 'ouse and he's not there.'

'Who?'

'Who d'yer think?'

'Our Johnno?'

Micky sat beside him and said, 'Turn it in, Sambo.' Charlie looked away to Sammy in the front seat. Sammy not turning round, a black shirt collar tight against his neck, an overflow of neck flab giving warning of his true thickness. Size. Even in that crowded little space, Charlie felt small.

'Inside job was it? Inside o' the inside. Did yer think we'd not bother? Where is he then? Where's he took off to?' Micky pulled at Charlie's tie to get his attention. Then carefully, like a wife would, did it up for him, but tight.

'I've no idea, lads.'

'Don't lad it or we'll chuck yer out now.' That was Sammy. Not his usual unruffled self. His hair like a baby head, slept on.

'Where we goin' then?'

'To find our tellies.'

Silence.

Sammy turned round and stared at Charlie, smiled, and in a soft voice, like he was giving him a chance, said, 'If he was gonna go anywhere, where would he go?'

'London, I s'pose.'

'Where in London?' Sammy ruffled his hair some more.

'How the Jesus would I know? We're not goin' London are we? This time o' night?'

'Right that's it,' said Sammy. 'Pull over.' They were on a dual carriageway headed for the motorway. The girl broke hard and pulled into a lay-by. Charlie had stopped chewing his lip and was on to fingernails now, biting off as much as he could and spitting, sitting on the edge of his seat. Micky smacked him in the chest to make him sit back. Sit up straight.

The pair of them together – they could come on quite strong just drinking down the Dog. Stuck in a lay-by with them, the job gone wrong, they were terrifying.

Micky turned the light back on. Was enjoying himself. Charlie felt really hot again and loosened his tie, the noose effect dangerous he knew, but he couldn't help himself. Then he went to wind the window down but Micky slapped him off again. Sammy turned round to look at him.

'We'll put you under a lorry eh? See if that gets yer yappin.'

'Oh aye. A great conversation starter that is. Come on, son, give us a break.'

Micky slapped him on his bald bit, hard. To shield himself he covered his head with his arms and for a long time, expecting a repeat attack as soon as he showed face. All he could hear was traffic. In the van, silence. Felt stupid then. Cowering. He put his hands down and looked over to Sally Tippett to see if she'd seen. She was fingering her hair.

Sammy turned again. Every time the man turned, Charlie stiffened and his worries worsened. So worried now, his attention was diverted to bowel control. Sammy made to get up. As if he were going to climb over but instead just reached for a drawer in one of the cupboards. Rattled around in it. Came out with an envelope opener, long and thin enough for a good stabbing. He sat back down and set about picking muck from under his fingernails, long nails. Still silence in the van. Zoom zoom zoom of the traffic outside. Charlie tried for chummy.

'Is Speke out 'n' about then yet?'

'Where's Johnno, Charlie?'

'What was the last you 'eard then?'

'He's done the job, gone back to the service station, dropped the load . . . our load . . . on someone he must have already sized up and then got off in a lorry somewhere. Yer missus won't open the door and the busies are sat outside yer house. You're our last hope so where is he?'

Charlie felt more optimistic now they were chatting to him. Even had the idea the police might have put a tail on him after all. Might drive up any minute and rescue him. Till they turned up, all he had to do was think of something useful to say but what?

Sammy leant forward to search the glove compartment. Produced a black box about the size of a brick. In the dim flickering light and with no passing dazzles from the road right then, it could very well have been a gun. To lunge for the door would be fruitless. It looked like a two-man job getting it on to its hinges. Micky smiled. Charlie reared back in his seat, feeling the trap tighten ever closer, his tie dangling a loose and open invitation to throttle him instead.

'See this?' Sammy pointed the black thing at him and right then, as if on cue, cutting through the silence like the bleat of a lamb on a silent morning, the box rang.

'This is our office see,' said Micky, rubbing his hands together. 'Mobile like.' He was a kid in a den, a girl with a Wendy house on wheels. The excitement of the phone sent him chatterbox. 'And that's the phone. Actually it's her office and our phone.' Sammy stabbed at the phone and held it to his ear, grunting at it. Charlie had seen a mobile phone on *Tomorrow's World* along with talking ovens and three-course-meal tablets. For Charlie, tomorrow was a world that'd never come but here it was. In Sammy's Vdub.

'We'll be with yer in about half an hour. Some unpleasant business to sort out first.'

Micky leant forwards to hear the rest of the conversation but Sammy never said anything else. He took the phone from his ear and said to Micky, 'Barny's sorted. Got a punter with him 'n' all. Says

Harry's Chipper in half an hour an' he'll sort us. I could do with it now. Badly.' Smiling at Charlie. Sally lifted her arm to make all her bangles slide down to her elbow and then looked at her watch. Countdown, it looked like.

'Runnin' out o' time now, see.' Micky elbowed him in the ribs.

'Punter's with him so we can kill two birds,' said Sammy, fiddling with the girl's ear. When Charlie boy comes clean, bingo.'

'Sammy, if I knew where he was, I'd kill him.'

'Who's he posse up with over Moss Side?'

'No-one. He's banned from Moss Side. Has been all his life.'

The girl turned round and smiled.

'What's yer number, Charlie? Yer dog and bone?'

Sammy tapped the numbers into the phone and climbed over his seat to be in the sitting room. Close and right opposite. Charlie's time had run out. Sat with Micky on one side, Sammy opposite, knees almost touching. In a split second flashback, he remembered the very same worry, sitting naked two-up, in the empty baths of his childhood. Scared. Waiting for matron to check necks, knees, nits.

Sammy shouted back to Sally, 'Go slow along the lay-by. Don't pull out till I tell yer.' She started the engine. Sammy did one more tap into the phone and nodded Micky to get the door.

He slid it open with one hand, no problem. Then sat back down next to Charlie. The rush of cold air hit Charlie square on the chin and got him up in a half-hearted attempt to jump out but Micky held him back, an arm over his chest, a grin from ear to ear. Charlie felt his face for a shave, worried, the wire wool of his beard like a jacket, not part of him. He was too old for all this.

'Put him out the door.'

Charlie reared back in his seat, deathly cold now. Sammy smiled and waved the phone at him. ''Ello. Mrs Wilson. Yer old man wants a word. Just gettin' him for yer now.'

Micky stood up, grabbed his lapels and shook him. In two more moves, had him down on the van floor. Charlie felt Sammy's feet underneath him and, next second, kicking his kidneys in. Then on top of him, on top of his legs, keeping them straight. At the other end

Micky dragged him towards the door. They had him held so tight, he could hardly wriggle and trying to just tired him out to weakness. In less than a minute, his head was out the door. Then his shoulders. His spine was set for splitting. He'd be paralysed. Was paralysed. Convinced himself. Sammy was on his shins now.

'Yer can go for it now Sally. Out on the open road. Fast as yer like.'

Charlie went rag doll, was willing to be chucked, his hands over his eyes, protecting himself. Was close to chucking up when he looked and saw how fast they were going, the road not a foot from his head. He didn't care any more. Didn't mind the dying. Anything to get away. His head was frozen to an ice-cube but, inside it, a warm voice. He could hear a nurse shouting, 'Don't close yer eyes, Mr Wilson. Don't close yer eyes.'

'Are yer still there, Mrs Wilson?' Micky poked him in the throat to get his attention and slammed the phone against his head. 'See if yer Mrs knows where he is.'

Charlie opened his eyes but no words came out. Just crying. Last voice he wanted in his head was Hilda's.

'Let's fuck him off,' shouted Sammy.

Micky went for his shoulders and Sammy gave some slack on the legs. Getting a grip for the big push, Micky gave Charlie something to hold on to. More flashbacks. Fighting at the back of the school bus, the emergency exit wide open, big Tugger Thompson trying to push him out. Then the sudden surge of his late-breaking arm wrestling tactic, saving it all up for the last. And then, after two laps round the field, Charlie bursting in first every time. Johnno the same. Pace and panic. A family talent for living.

He grabbed hold of Micky's elbows and lurched back up into the van, butting Micky's mug right on target. Watched him fall back and saw then he had use of a good clean route to Sammy who copped for a big one smack-bang on his yocker, Charlie's reach a stunner. The rhythm of surprise perfect. And he could vaguely remember the van slowing down to a splutter and then . . .

He woke up in bushes on a slip road off the M62. Could barely walk so he sat back down, the light, early morning or evening, he couldn't tell. He just waited. Figured two toes broken, the pain getting worse every waking second, his jaw crispy with dried-up blood, a hole in his head somewhere. Shit everywhere, the smell knocking him out.

He got picked up by the police eventually, one each end. Woke up again to a torch and a nurse shouting, 'Can you open yer eyes, Mr Wilson. Could you just open your eyes.' He slipped in and out of consciousness for three days.

Chapter Five

He'd signed off from the hotel. It was all over. No evidence to link him with the telly job either. But they'd not closed the case. Neither had Micky and Sammy but today was Christmas and Charlie was trying to make it a good one.

He had a new job to look forward to and a good chance the wages weren't heading straight for the one-armed bandits down the bingo. Hilda looked a bit worse for wear it was true, bit withdrawn, lethargic, but the doctor said she'd be like that for a time. Losing her son and then losing the chance to make up the loss down the bingo – she'd get over it. It was no good to keep telling her 'Pull yourself together, Hilda' because, apparently, not recognising the loss *with* her would make her feel more isolated. Charlie told the doctor he'd do his best. It was Christmas morning, a time for trying and a trying time. The day the whole world was put to the test.

It was Christmas, he was drunk and allowed to be. No Jonathan or long uncomfortable silences watching loud telly that no-one wanted to watch but Jonathan. For the first time in a long time, he had the place to himself. Hilda to himself. He opened the curtains but it was still too dark in there. He lit the two bedside lamps that hadn't been used for months because they'd needed special bulbs. Golden Glow bulbs that did for the room what a coat of paint could never do and did for a Christmas pressy too, he'd thought until Hilda tutted. He lit the paraffin stove to remind her of when they had to light it, to make the air all warm with the lamps, to make it look like he really was trying. Up and down the stairs, the whole of the place his, eggshells gone. Coming in from the cold landing to see Hilda lying there, all snug in smell and softness of a paraffin morning, sleepy and, for once, even smiley was a Christmas present in itself. It was a change.

He took her up breakfast in bed. Fried eggs with a crispy brown skirt, burnt bacon, raw toms and toast. Some coffee. Real coffee. They had two coffee makers. Glass jug and plastic funnel and an electric version that did the same thing but with more noise. Charlie went for the jug, always. Said on the packet not to use boiling water but he did. The smell reminded him of his father. That and the sound of keys rattling. The only way to start a day, his father said. His mother hadn't liked it. Wouldn't drink the tea or the coffee. Only juices, blackcurrant. That's what his dad said. Said Charlie was very like his mother, as if saying it could bring them closer together. There was a picture. Didn't ring any bells though. In the kids' home, he'd kept it on his bedside table to wind the other kids up. Them without a mother to look at. His mother looked stern. From the Cameroons. Maybe they all looked stern. Charlie didn't like the sound of the place. Boston was more up his street. New England. That's what the postmark said on the only letter he got off him, 'New England'. Like a new page in an excercise book. When people asked, and they did ask, he said American and for the most part they were impressed. Them that didn't smile, didn't believe him, they were so impressed. Cameroonian wouldn't have struck the same note, he knew that.

'Yer comin' down now?' he said, piling the toast plate on to her empty breakfast plate, in a tone of voice not 100 per cent good mood. He was working up to it. 'Yer comin' down, our Hilda?' Fifty-fifty, it could go either way still. Shirl needed help in the kitchen and he was too drunk to be mithered. Wanted to put his feet up and watch telly. 'Eh, love? See to the dinner?' She looked about to throw up. 'Open yer presents?'

'Oh aye. All two of 'em.'

'It's for the kids though innit, Christmas?' Sitting down on the bed. 'Yer said yer didn't like the way it had got all commercialised didn't yer? Merry Christmas, love.' Squeezing her hand, wanting to pull her closer to him but not daring. They looked at each other. He knew what she was thinking. She was thinking he was being all nice because Johnno wasn't there. Well she was half right but it was more than that. He was almost happy. Near one of those moments. Even

62

thinking about a trip to America. Life in the old dog yet. He was forcing it, so he could get to the moment. Working at it was the only route left these days, and he was taking it.

'Where d'yer think he is, Charlie?'

He stood up and went to the window. Leant against the glass and said with as much restraint as he could muster, 'Could be anywhere, love.'

'I thought he'd come 'ome last night. What if he's all on his own, Christmas day? D'yer think he'll ring?'

'Course.'

'Don't you care?'

'He's me son for chrissakes. Course I care. It's funny really . . .'

'What is?' She was ready to have a go. He was trying his best and she was on patrol. Red alert already and it wasn't midday. 'What's funny?' she said.

'Missin' him,' said Charlie, hoping it sounded genuine.

''As she got the turkey in?'

'She's gonna use that microwave thing.' He moved back to her now and sat down again.

'An' yer don't mind?'

'Don't mind nothin' today, love. Christmas innit?'

'Will it fit?'

'It's only a babby one. Shirl don't even like turkey, she said.'

'Neither do I much,' said Hilda.

'Well, we will today.'

'There's lamb in the freezer,' said Hilda, brightening up a little.

'Shall we have that then?'

'D'yer think Shirl'd mind?'

'Why should she?' He got up and went to the wardrobe to look through Hilda's dresses. Pulled out a cornflower-blue one fit for a wedding, and showed it to her. She looked away.

'She's made all the stuffin' 'n' that, 'asn't she?'

'It'll only be packet stuff. Does it fit?'

'Doubt it.'

'What about this one then? I like yer in this one.'

'Might fit.'

'I'll run you a bath eh?'

'Alright. Alright. For christssakes Charlie. I'll get up in me own good time, OK?'

He didn't want that. He didn't want shouting.

'Dad! Can yer come an' give us 'and?'

He pulled the quilt back so she could get out of bed right away. He was shocked by the blue of her veins. Old legs now, they were. Big legs.

'She thinks we're bein' watched yer know.' Hilda swung her legs out.

'By who?'

'The soash. She's signed off, she not tell yer? Some bloke with a clipboard parked at the end of the street there.'

'I've not seen him.'

'I told her to stop the work, not the dole.'

'Why? So you can sit on yer fat arse all day?' She was just about to reach for her dressing gown. 'I can only do so much, our Hilda. We've all got to pull our weight 'aven't we? I'll go and run yer bath.'

Out on the landing, he looked through the crack in the door and saw her fall back into her pillows, like a building demolished. He wanted to go back and slap her one. He held it together though. Shouted at her, 'Come on, love. Come and see the boy with his pressies.' Then went downstairs without looking back. Without Jonathan there, no-one to answer to, it was too easy to go mad.

It was eerie. Quiet without him. On Christmas morning, he always played his music full blast. The only morning of the year he was allowed. Now all there was, was the telly. Kiddies' tunes. Malcy not interested in his pressies, just the telly. A whole field of Christmas wrapper behind him. And from the kitchen, clanging pans.

'What did yer want me for, love? I'm runnin' a bath for yer mother.'

Shirl smiled. At his 'love' probably. He was only trying to set the tone. Make sure they all fell in.

'Doesn't matter.' Like it did matter. But then, as if gaining speed,

'If she opens her pressies, she'll find somat in there . . . for her bath I mean.'

'Oh aye. Which one?'

'Dad?'

'I'll get her somat in the sales. I've 'ad me hands full lately.'

'Like every other year.'

'Yer know I can't be doin' with all that shoppin'. Come on, Shirl, let's not start.'

'Who's startin'? I'm not startin'.' She started banging pan lids then. Oven door. Drawers shut. Like she was shutting up shop on him.

'And Merry Christmas to you too.'

Charlie closed the bathroom door behind him and sat on the loo watching the bath fill, the water pouring out quietly. He pushed his nudger into the bowl and tried to piss louder than the tap. Wasn't hard. Looked round at the bathroom and saw immediately what Jonathan meant. The tiles, plain white, and then round the bath, white with blue patterns on. It was the same blue they used for the dinner plates in the hotel. Tory blue Johnno called it but it wasn't, it was a classical blue. It was supposed to give the room an Italian appeal, feel, the idea of an ancient Roman bathhouse. But it was more like the lavatories down by the town hall. Specially where the grouting had got mouldy.

The smell of the bath was orange blossom and knocking him sick. He didn't know if he could stand a whole day of being this nice to Hilda. Even though Johnno had gone, it still felt . . . it felt like he'd left his troops behind, keeping guard. He was just about to shout to Shirl about the lamb when he heard the doorbell go. He put bowels on hold, got off the loo and went out to investigate.

In the kitchen, Micky and Big Barny. Charlie's bowels keen to be back over that bowl again.

'Where is he then? Go and check upstairs.' Barny left the kitchen and went up the stairs with loud bangs. He was likely to bump into Hilda coming down. Charlie looked up at the ceiling and then at Micky. Micky in his Christmas M&S jumper and new jeans, looking like what Johnno called a born-again.

'All mended are we?' Micky said, his face a menace of true concern.

'Don't you lot give up? It's Christmas day, lads.'

'Worst Christmas day o' me life. And if your Johnno don't turn up, yours is goin' the same way, pal. Who's she?'

'Gerrout of 'ere.'

'In yer way am I?'

'Dad, who is it?' Shirl had her back to the back door, her eyes going from Charlie to the front room, worried about Malcy in there, the sweat on her top lip in globules, rollers sticking out of her scarf. A perm for Christmas.

'Friend o' Jonathan's.' Charlie did up his belt. He half thought about pulling it out and slapping the little bleeder across the face with it. There were plenty o' pans on the go. Spuds were in.

Micky saw too and turned all the gas off, making the kitchen dead quiet. Charlie's heart fluttered him up to a sweat. He wanted to speak but no noise came out. All he could do was angry eyes. Micky pulled Charlie by the arm, into the front room. 'Where is he, Charlie?' The fairy lights round the window were off and on, in tune with Charlie's pulse.

'I told yer. I don't know.'

'You don't know how serious this is, do yer?'

'Actually Micky, I think I do,' said Charlie, rubbing at the scab on his head. 'But Jesus, Micky. Nothin's this serious on Christmas day is it?'

'Try tellin' our Sammy that.'

Charlie screamed loud then. 'It's Christmas fuckin' day for chrissakes.'

Micky laughed and turned towards the telly. Carol singing choir boys in frilly white collars were giving it their best. 'So it is.' He folded his arms and said then, 'Christmas day.'

Malcy crawled towards him and pushed a big stick of Lego into the back of his leg. Micky turned to defend himself. Then gasped like a mad one, seeing the size of his enemy. It was enough to set him off. Charlie instinctively went for the boy and carried him to the kitchen to Shirley who was watching everything from the doorway, a great worry on her face, the like Charlie had never seen before. He thought he'd seen all her faces but no. 'Don't worry,' he said to her in his best voice. She didn't show she'd heard him though. Malcy over her shoulder, her stare straight on Micky.

'This the sister is it?'

'Me daughter, yes.'

'Very nice.'

'Leave us be and let the little un 'ave his Christmas in peace can't yer.'

Barny came down the stairs carrying Hilda's TV, the one she'd won at Blackpool, a portable that even Barny was having trouble with. When he hit the bottom step, Charlie noticed the back of his head matted with fire extinguisher foam. He'd tried to wipe it off.

'I'm not goin' up there again. She's a fuckin' lunatic.'

'Go and fetch the rest o' the shite.'

'No way, man.' And out the front door he went.

Micky went up then. Charlie looked round for a weapon but found Malcy and Shirl instead, huddled in the kitchen doorway, near to tears.

''Salright love. Don't worry.' He went to the kitchen for a knife.

Shirl turned and saw him with it, hugged the baby tighter and said, 'I'm callin' the police.'

'Don't. It'll only get worse.'

'You're makin' it worse.' And all the tears and sobs of a bad Christmas came then. Charlie put the knife back in the drawer.

Micky had been up and down twice, under his arm the little telly out of Jonathan's room and the next time, his stereo. He dropped it all by the wide-open front door for Barny to pick up, Barny running up and down the path like the robber that he was.

'I've just seen him,' said Barny.

'Who?'

'Johnno.'

'Where?'

'Out there. Where d'yer think? He's fucked off again. So they must o' been expectin' 'im after all?' Looking directly at Charlie who was shaking his head in denial.

'That's fuckin' it, that is. Right, Barny.'

'What now?'

'Clear this place out. All electrics. All pressies. Kiddy's stuff. Everythin'. Lego, the lot. Anything with a plug on it, take. Least they'll be savin' on the lecky.'

'Yer can't do this,' Charlie charged, eyes cracked. 'I didn't know he was comin' home.' Micky pushed him back against the wall and put himself in line for a direct head butt.

'Little birdie tells me yer startin' down the new supermarket ol' Charlie boy? Zat right? You better watch it then, 'adn't yer.' He bounced him against the wall and then left. Walked down the path. Gone.

Barny did the kitchen, left the washing machine and fridge and gathered up all the toys like Father Christmas with a paddy on. When the door finally closed, Charlie was on his own. In a house of silence. Sitting on the kitchen floor. Christmas was over for ever. He'd never live it down. And five minutes late, the phone rang. Wouldn't stop ringing. It had to be him.

'Merry Christmas, dad.'

'Where are yer now?'

Silence. Then, 'Can yer get me mum, dad?'

'Where are yer?'

'Best yer don't know then yer can't say owt can yer? Will yer get me mum, dad, me money's goin'.'

'Get home 'ere.'

Hilda came down the stairs dangerously fast but she made it.

'Zat you?'

'I'm not comin' 'ome, mum. I can't.'

'Well thank Christ for that then.' She took the phone away from her ear, looked at it and then put it down.

Boxing day morning, Charlie called the police. They came round and dusted everywhere for fingerprints. Like the burglars had only left ten minutes ago. Made a right mess. Made Malcy sneeze. Made Charlie nervous. They were bound to have prints for Micky and Barny on file. Bound to have. They did door-to-door enquiries. The whole street knew they'd been burgled now. And him a security man.

Luckily, Christmas day, all the neighbours had been too far gone to see what'd really gone on and in the night even more far gone to hear Charlie forcing an entry. No-one saw. No-one suspected. Lot of people said it was just the sort of thing those lowlife junkie cretins were capable of. No respect these days. No respect at all. And not a couple of hours after the police left, who should turn up but the papers. *Manchester Evening News. Liverpool Echo. Wythenshawe Wanderer. Warrington Weekly. St Helens Siren. Altrincham Leader.* All of them put a picture of Malcy, front page. 'Christmas Present. Christmas gone', 'Little boy woke up to find Christmas all a dream'. The gifts just kept on coming. It was the best Christmas they'd ever had. Continental quilts. Iron. Pressure cooker. New microwave. Toy cars, boats, teddies, Lego, spinning tops, noisy electric things. There was so much of it all, Malcy hid in the glory hole with a set of pan lids. Shirl got a new buggy, hairdressing set, slippers, talc talc and more talc and bath stuff and make-up that wasn't for brown people she said. For Hilda, as well as all the kitchen stuff, everything for the bedroom, sheets, pillowcases, a new teasmaid, brand-new. There was a set of bedside lamps, a reading stand, several alarm clocks and even a hot-water bottle. There was hardly the space for it. For Charlie, a lot of books about England, road atlases and such like. A foot bath. Shaving set. Socks galore. And a present from AAC Alarms. They came and fitted it, absolutely free. After they fitted it, the papers came round again, for a rundown on the appeal. Well it wasn't an appeal but it was now. AAC Alarms had a photograph taken with all the family. All safe now.

He put one of Johnno's tellies on the china trolley at the end of the bed where Hilda liked it. The other in the front room. The strain of not talking had taken tight hold of them all and the relief when *The Flintstones* came on had every one of them laughing out loud. The nightmare was over.

Ten o'clock the following morning, a ring on the door, him and Hilda sat either side of the settee, watching a film. It was snowing like mad out. Malcy and Shirl were sleeping upstairs. He squeezed Hilda's knee. Told her not to get up. At the door, a man and a woman. The man held up his wallet with a picture in it.

'CID,' he said.

Jonathan went to Manchester first. To the street where Wheezy lived but had left, months ago, the lad on the ground floor told him. From there, he drove to Blackpool and stayed in a rather grand bed and breakfast that had its own bar. Not quite hotel since there were no en suite bathrooms or private phones. He stayed half board for nearly three weeks.

There was an English chill about Blackpool that had nothing to do with the weather. It was a living museum for all that should have been done away with, ballroom dancing and bingos, the tat. The hundred and one bad and has-been comedians. The germ of the most diseased areas of popular culture run amok. There was something vaguely manipulative about foisting miles of electric lightbulbs, noise and chip wrapper on an innocent population and calling it tourism. And the tourists, as if they'd run out of ideas on how to have a good time, entered Blackpool, on coaches mostly, as kids to Disney. Clinging to a deluded belief they were in some fantasy land of high-tat chic. Too drunk to notice most of them. 'If all you sell 'em is shite, then that's what they'll buy.' Blackpool was a marketing phenomenon.

What it did have going for it was the sea, the fair and the anonymity. As Christmas crept closer, even these lost their value. Jonathan wanted to see his mum.

He got a bar job and considered offers of work up in Barrow and Aberdeen. Oil work a lot of it, two weeks on and two weeks off. It seemed too limited. What could he do with two weeks off that would justify another two weeks on? It just wasn't enough to make money. What use was money? It bought women who considered a curry and a few drinks fair pay for a legover. It bought clobber and a number

70

of options not open to a man without money. But it didn't, in itself, satisfy. If he could find the right woman, maybe all this would change but his chances of that were still fairly remote. He'd met the whole gamut of them in Blackpool. The travelling slags. The council estaters. The middle-aged desperates. The nice girls who didn't want anything to do with him. After all his life being skint, he had money and couldn't have been more miserable. He wanted a life. The only one on offer – on an oil platform – didn't quite ring true.

On Christmas eve, after the last drink was served, he got in his car sober and drove home. He drove down Lincoln Street but there was nowhere to park. When he drove past his house, he noticed all the lights out. He'd cause a right row if he got them all out of bed at this time. Christmas especially. A time not for the mythical giving and sharing of his childhood indoctrination, rather a time for letting rip, for pent-up anger to be let like blood over the best carpet. No. He'd find a hotel and surprise them in the morning. He had gifts. No man bearing gifts on Christmas day is ever turned away.

The only hotel still taking guests gave him the bridal suite half price, with a full view of the town centre, the old town hall, the lions in the square and the church newly lit-up in amber. There was a balcony. There was snow too. He braved it and stood out to watch the people stumbling home, drunk, singing, loud. Bent over against a wind blowing great smackers of snow at them. Penny drops of freezing water sticky with the filth and grime of a thousand factories. In the artificial lights, they look studioed for a Lowry attack.

There were three bodies on the town hall steps intent on sleeping there. The snow hadn't moved them. What a Christmas day they were going to have. He unpacked his bag and brought out a bottle of brandy. He unsealed and opened it in one twist and then swigged. He put on his coat, walked out of the hotel, over to the bodies, kicked one and gave him the bottle of brandy. It was the only way he could ever have enjoyed it.

When he got back to his room, he drank the booze fridge. He woke late. There was no chambermaid service, hardly any guests and no reason to jump out of bed immediately. His mum and dad weren't going anywhere. He figured he'd wait till around eleven and then go. Mum would definitely be up then. Dad would have done her breakfast. Shirl would have the dinner on the go and all the presents would have been opened. He'd be welcome alright.

He drove down Lincoln Street carefully, these streets not gritted, the slide easy to feel over twenty miles an hour. There was a van blocking his way. Right outside his house. He crept closer and closer towards it and stretched to see if it was his house taking delivery. The back doors of the van were wide open. A new Merc it was, with the sides open too it looked like. He could see a portable television mounted on something. And then he saw his front door was wide open and then Micky. He pushed straight into reverse, turned round to check clearance, revved and, just as he made off, heard banging on his bonnet. Barny had seen him. He reversed fast now, gambling on the ice. But Barny was too big to even try. At the top of the street, he cleared the corner and drove off. His head full of crying but he couldn't cry. He had to drive and think and not cry. He called home to see if they were alright. Alright without him there, his mother said. He drove round Manchester a few times, called in at Doc's but Doc wasn't back from Spain yet. Dylan, the man from the garage, was there. Christmas day for Christ's sake. Johnno returned to the hotel.

He stayed holed up there till the day after Boxing day and then set about making a new life for himself. He couldn't see any way round it. The luxury of no choice was rare and upon him. He had to make a go of it. Not run for it. More 'have a crack' at it. He drove to the Earls Court of the North and sold his car for a song. Right, that was it. He had to make a move now. He bought the *Evening News*, turned to the travel pages and found the ad for the Escape Agency, the god of late flights. He called them. Forty quid, Benidorm, a bargain. Not much more than a rattler to the smoke. Pick up the tickets at Ringway.

Once the plane was through the clouds and the sun of a new day upon him, he was back to childhood again. Giddy. 'Get yer 'ead out the clouds, Johnny my boy,' his dad would say. 'Stop yer dreamin' and knuckle down.' But here he was, up there with the rest of them.

72

Away. Sun. Beach. Birds. And plenty of work. No dream. Spain was for real.

For the first time in his life, he was being carried somewhere fast. There was no stopping or starting and no turning back. Jumping jelly in his stomach, Johnno in the clouds and out of it. No turbulence the trolly dolly said. A perfect flight. A perfect flight chocka with old age pensioners all escaping. About fifty years too late.

Chapter Six

He'd seen her twice now, the first time while lying on the beach, playing chess with Jack, the cheapest pretence at sophistication they could manage. Between moves, they both autoscanned the scene for the talent, someone they knew or trouble. She was at Papa's bar and he'd caught her looking. She'd turned away, immediately. Would she have turned away if it *was* her? He'd knelt up for a closer inspection, but his view was blocked by the icebox man. And then she was gone. Like sand through his fingers.

The second time, he'd just been for a job on a boat. Job? He should have been on the ball for that one. Ready for it. As usual, previous experience was essential. He'd lied to the guy and said he could cook. Said he'd done deck hand work back home but would need some refreshment, time to settle in. For his board and a free trip to the Caribbean, the job was his. 'Congratulations,' said the captain, hat perched fishfinger-style. Of course, closing any deal so quick and so well is a shout loud and clear that the deal is flawed but Johnno wasn't listening. Pleased with his success, he walked the full length of the boat and cheered to himself. He'd made it. He was on his way. The sun was strong that day. He took off his T-shirt and stuffed it down the front of his shorts. Then leant over the front of the boat, laughing to himself. And then felt a hand on his back. Not his shoulder, his kidney space. The hand stroked him. 'Welcome aboard, mate.' And that was the end of that. He got off the boat and felt so down after feeling so up, it was hard to stop the sting of sea juice speed across his eyes.

This was the 'place to be' but since being here, Johnno had not struck gold nor fixed any long-term plans that might help him to. Marbella was the destination for anyone with more ambition than money, because in Marbella there was a lot more money than ambition. You could make it here. Straight or bent, you could make it. Jonathan hadn't made anything except money and not a great deal of it. More than he'd ever made at home but not enough to buy a bar or even a decent car. Surrounded by beautiful women and dangerous villains in the just-born jet-set destination of the rich and famous, he'd been feeling as out of it as ever, the loudness of the wealth all around a constant reminder of his financial impotence and incompetence. A few weeks on a sea bare of buildings, possibilities and disappointments would have been just the job. But no.

He waved ta-ra to his Caribbean dream and looked around the harbour for distractions, to halt the tears, to pull himself together. It might have been her getting into that jeep but such luck was unlikely. And surely just a brain trick, triggered by his disappointment, some ghostly déjà vu of optimism, the gods teasing. But there she was. She had the shoulders and the walk but not the hair. From that distance, it looked like Chas's jeep, but he couldn't be sure. Puerto Banus, Marbella's sailing depot, was a convention for jeeps, high summer. More jeeps than boats. And there were too many boats. Before he could make a closer inspection, the jeep drove off.

Sucking salt from his lips, he fancied nothing. No food. No-one. Not even the long and lithe blondes statuetting the yachts, in their one-piece slivers of costume. His head was tired of the whole confrontation. The glut. The plastic. The fibre glass. The stainless steel stools in the bars. The sunglasses. The Germans. The smell of perfume. The music. *Holiday . . . it could be so nice.* Holidaymakers were tiring on the eyes. On the streets of Manchester, everyone fell into place easily, into places he knew like the office, the pub, the bingo or the market. But these holidaymakers had to be imagined into places he didn't know, might never know. Every street and beach scene was littered with so many human complications, prejudice was more effort than convenience. His sunglasses, hanging from a shoe-lace round his neck, were his shield to it all. And so he put them on, the girl gone now.

He walked round the jetty to see Geoff. Geoff could really work boats. He worked straight jobs for fancy rich blokes and bent jobs for nasty fat blokes and didn't much mind which, so long as the cash matched the risk. He'd worked his way round the globe from Australia and nicked a tall ship in the Far East to sell to some Jew in Israel. Then he'd got his own boat nicked, pirated off the Aegean coast. Was left for dead in a dinghy. Couldn't do a thing about it, he said. He could have been lying of course. Did Johnno want some work sailing round the Caribbean? He'd set him up, obviously.

'No luck then?' He was working on the boat's nameplate with a cordless drill. He noised it back to life when Jonathan shook his head. Geoff signalled for him to come aboard, pointing at him with the whirring drill.

'No. I'm off back up to town.

Geoff stopped the drill again. The nameplate hanging on for dear life, *Tinted Lady 2*.

'Wanna beer, help christen the lady?'

'I've gotta go. I've gotta sort another job out now, 'aven't I?'

'What now then?'

'Site clearance probably.'

'So definitely no go with the Windies then?'

'Yer knew didn't yer?'

'I didn't know for sure, no. But it crossed my mind.' He started the drill up again, laughing now.

'You bastard.'

'Eh, mate?' Stopping the drill and sitting on his haunches, his knees red from kneeling, his skin browner than Johnno's but he still looked white. Bleached hair white. 'You still stayin' up at that slag's place?'

'Yeah.'

'We've got a room on the front, up in town, if yer interested?'

'We?'

'Chas and Jason. They've moved up to Monty's villa up in Mijas.'

'Another one o' yer wind-ups? Do us a favour why don't yer?'

'Straight up, I'm tellin' yer.'

'You know I can't afford a sea fronter.' Jonathan stretched out his leg to kick the boat and rock it, to not feel so small. Geoff up there with tools and a life worth talking about. The boat hardly budged. The water around it was oiled to a rainbow and dark. 'I'll see yer later.' The sun was scorching his back now, hurting nearly. Sunglasses back on, T-shirt out from his shorts and over his shoulders, he turned to walk away

'There's some work with it,' Geoff shouted.

'What work?'

'I'll put a word in for yer if yer interested.'

'Don't fuck me about, Geoff.'

'They need a kitchen fitting. Tiles 'n' all that. Painting. They want it ready to sell. Right up yer yin-yang that, isn't it? What d'yer say?'

'I'm interested.'

'Then I'll see what I can do.' And then back to his drilling.

Johnno waved as he turned and set off for home, feeling just a little more encouraged but not much. There were so many wind-ups, jokers, losers chasing jobs.

There were cabs all over but it was safer to hitch. He walked the tourist route, the only man bare-chested. It was just gone four and the peeps were filling the streets for their evening shopping extravaganza. The streets were so narrow they were easy to fill and, being fond of the squash, a hive for them with more money than dress sense. The clothes were obscene, in every way. Val Doonican jumpers for sailors. Backless bits of skirt for the women. Nothing less than a couple of hundred quid for a pair of genuine Italian sandals pretending not to be flip-flops. He was about to put his T-shirt on but opted instead for the attention. Eyes trying not to look at his arms, well rounded and rock-hard enough to kill two birds with one showing. Costa aggro and holiday romance. He'd been in Marbella for two weeks and, compared to all the other resorts, it ranked last on his scale of value for money, middling for trouble but first for the women. In Torremolinos and Benidorm, like a tramp at a wedding, he'd OD'd on the starters, most of the women not worth a drink but all of them dead certs. In Marbella, the women were on some other level, both financially and socially. But they weren't completely out of the question. There was more shell to crack for sure, but that was all. And they could afford to buy their own drinks. He had the nerve to wink at a few and an occasional smile back reassured him. Because of the opportunities on offer, failure in Marbella was not just inevitable, but motivating.

As usual, he copped for a lift on the back of a bike, a Spanish lad not twelve and not fed very well. The bike not his, it was obvious. He could handle it though. The three-mile road to Marbella was all craters to begin with, that part of Banus still very much a building site and the roads not worth mending till they'd built it. As the town centre loomed, the tarmac began. Only short strips at first until, just a mile away, the road became fast enough for the lad to really hammer it home, just how well he could handle a bike. Johnno tipped him and the kid horned so loud everyone writing out their postcards outside the Correos stopped their pens and stared. Then carried on writing again.

Jonathan set off doing yard-long strides up through the Casa Antigua, wending his way backwards behind the Arab quarter, the neglected walls of an ornate past shoved to the back of the mind of everyone but the poor who lived on the other side of it. Marbella worked in financial layers that followed the ecology of the landscape. In the foothills of the Sierra Blanca, in mini-valleys of peace, lived the peasants. Real peasants with no intention or desire to confront the late twentieth century. They lived in packs of hovels bunched up side by side and back to back, the walls of their life clamming heat into sweat, their livestock living close by, some would say a little too close. Then there were the more worldly peasants who lived on the edge of Marbella. From their hovels, they could see the blank and infertile mountain range offering little but a climb into emptiness and, looking down their tiny streets, seawards, they saw flat-roofed boxes of progress and a chance to escape from their limbo. So near but yet so far. They lived behind and around the old town hall, the sixteenth-century ayuntamiento, and were very well placed to prey on tourists, to hawk jewellery and ponchos, but they never did. They were outdone by the Moros who were hawking for Africa, day in day out and conscientiously. A good proportion of the

79

Spanish peasants were elderly, their children having run off into the din that is tourism. After their layer came another layer of limboed inhabitants who occupied a series of hovels and rented-out rooms, or sold meats or bread or dried fish that stank the place into an oven for a starving cat, and plenty of cats there were too, cats that someone had taken the scissors to, in a fit of temper or a nightmare. This layer was where Johnno lived and was now headed for, past what looked to be the ruins of a Muslim mosque, bombed-out and crumbling away like the peasant life all around it.

They were doing some parts up and in a few months would probably be charging the world just to blink at this lot but, for now, the past was an alley of fish skeletons and beer cans. Up as far as this, the houses were quiet. Stuccoed cottages, squashed in on each other, hid all the grim reality with a flower show. He figured there must be some law for it. They couldn't all be so fond of geraniums. Beyond the geraniums, the even grimmer reality further up was devoid of flower boxes and glossy green shutter paint. Up there, where the slums where, the walls of the cottages were distressed, not Dulux white but faded greens and oranges cracked into veins of antiquity. The window shutters were falling off their hinges and grey with wear, like the little old people that lived up there, hunched, small and just the right size for their duck-down doorways. Up there, the grit of living hung in the air along with the stale smell of dead food. Cardboard boxes drifted the streets like tumbleweeds in a Western. Up there the little peasant kids ate dirt off the street, wrote graffiti on their walls, smashed windows with footballs and ran away, not scared or bothered or even laughing.

The streets of the Old Town were cobbled and too narrow for traffic. Neighbours across the street from one another could talk without shouting. Everyone was living on top of one another. Mavver's was just on the geranium boundary, just inside it. Outside Mavver's, the sign said 'The Rose and Penny House', but even the Spanish called it Mavver's. It was the only place in Marbella where English yobs/villains were actively welcomed. It had a cellar bar where English yobs/villains could do business so long as they behaved themselves, and if they didn't, the landlady Mavver and some of her long-term residents would sort them out, throw them out and keep them out. Mavver knew a lot of stuff and when she didn't know stuff, she did her best to find stuff out. She was Granny out of the Beverly Hill-Billies. She wore spotty frocks, specs and knobbly elbows like guns on her hips. There was something intimidating about those elbows.

Jonathon came out of the alley and was almost at the courtyard that was Mavver's back yard. As he turned to take the entrance, he was confronted by three kids, standing in the archway, one banging his back against the wall, the other two all over him, asking for trouble it looked like. When they saw Johnno, they all stood back against the wall and as was their way, just blinked at him, their great eyelash fans every woman's dream. Spanish kids. They stood as if droned like drunken bees, their arms combing their hair in shyness. It was good to see kids. Real kids *in situ*. He missed them. He missed Malcy. The holiday kids were all stiff, out of their element, hostile even sometimes.

To avoid a confrontation with Mavver, he decided to take the fire escape, which at the very top, opened into Jack's room. He slid back the glass door, fought his way through the nets and looked at the bed. Three of them in it. All out for the count. The two girls, like fairy-tale waifs, snuggled up together at the bottom of the bed and Jack, like a beast, alone in the top corner, his leg hanging off the side, his sheet not covering his ugly bits. The girls were covered except for their legs up to their knees. Gravy brown. At least a week's worth of afternoon sun on both of them. When he walked over to the door he got a look at the face on one. Not much cop. Not very old. One dark and one blonde. He turned the key, turned round and saw the blonde one stare back at him. She smiled. He smiled back, let himself out and, before closing the door, signalled the girl to lock it again. Then he went to his room, just along the landing. Unless there was a door open, the landing was pitch. He fiddled for his keys, got inside and locked himself in.

The room stank. Fags. Sweat. He opened the shutters and then the window. He was confronted by a Spanish woman in black on the opposite side of the street. Not more than ten feet away. She was cleaning her shutters, leaning out, dripping detergent into her geranium pots and not that bothered about it. Too busy looking at him. As if she was still, after two weeks, trying to place him somewhere. Into Africa probably.

He lit a fag and sat on the bed. Then lay down, stubbed his fag out and fell asleep.

He woke up parched. He closed the shutters. Wasn't quite ready for even that much daylight. He felt his stomach. It was all there. He unclipped himself, laid the belt on the floor and sat next to it. He liked to count his money. Laugh a little. Ten, twenty, thirty . . . to figures that got boring. Only at the start of the count was he happy, only then did the laugh come naturally. Fifteen in one envelope. Done. Was it time to go home now?

He'd rung several times but the phone was always out of order. Cut off no doubt. He'd sent postcards, from Benidorm and Torrer, sometimes two a week. Just to piss them off really. Show them what a good time he was having. And a couple of weeks ago, he'd sent a letter, pages of it, telling his mum how much money he'd been earning, how he was planning to get a job on a boat and sail round the world for ever. So what now? He was close to Africa, his spiritual home supposedly. But Africa was starving. It was all over the news. Pop stars were singing for free to feed them. How good of them. He didn't buy it anyway. Didn't buy the roots shit. He wanted some breathing space. His room was grim and grumpy and not likely to fend off the depressions that came at him quite a lot now. His aimless meanderings down the coast were no medicine for a man with a need to do something.

What does a young man do when confronted with so much female flesh he could carpet his room with it, night after night. In Torremolinos, he gets gonorrhoea, used to condoms and bored of it. He gets night work in the long bars, to avoid it. He gets depressed and too drunk. He gets on a bus well away from it all. He gets work in greenhouses picking cucumbers with African Moros, earning five pound a week, chanting prayers for a five in the morning start. Prayers to Allah to help him dry out, keep him on the wagon.

He'd come to Spain to start again and, at the end of the day, make money. He'd started again some six times now, his life one permanent temporary job. He'd gained six months' experience but lost the rest of his life somehow, drifting. And here he was again, in Marbella now. 'Straight or bent, you can make it here.'

He could go home and do the prodigal son routine with a bag of money that wasn't unimpressive considering. But he couldn't see it. Could see instead his room, the washing machine, endless nights down the pub till his money ran out, winter kicking in. He couldn't see himself on that plane. He saw her instead. Wanted to see *her* again.

There was an uncounted amount of notes to get through. Of that, he stopped counting at twelve seventy. He fanned the notes on the floor. If he could paint, if he were an artist, that pattern of his money on the tiles would be something. The tail of a large dead bird. Flutters. Chances. He pondered the fan of notes and laughed again. The kettle was boiled. Still staring at his work of art, he got up to make some tea. His beard was dry. Noisy, unoiled, scratchy at the jaw. Stroking it, he became philosopher. Money doesn't matter. He wouldn't sell his grandmother. He stopped looking at the money. When his tea was poured, he went back to it, his cross-legged count. Eighty, ninety . . . It does matter.

Money had been his only thought, these past few months. Getting it and keeping hold of it. If he had to pretend that money was important, there was no point in working hard and wasting it. Getting money, a brilliant cover for not doing much else, not having a good time. Treating it that way, he'd managed to save up a good deal of it. Perhaps his dad was right. That it only comes to those who have it and don't much need it. He stroked his earring and fanned the notes again.

The sun had managed to slit in through the slats of the shutters to cage the room in surround-sound squalor. A bigger room? A bigger cage. Sea-front apartment? His chances? T-shirts sodden, dish cloth'd to the floor and empty fag packets like cars in a motorway disaster were all over. The sheets wouldn't stay on the bed properly. The bed, a rack of an excuse for a mattress. All this small stuff for such a big man.

The door was thumping. Mavver's thump. She had arthritis and never knocked. He gathered up the notes to a fat untidy bundle. The gaping zip mouth of his belt was just wide enough. He tightened the clasp on his waist. Did up his shirt. The knock came again but louder.

'Who is it?'

'It's only me, darlin'.'

'Yeah?'

'Yer sheets, lav.'

'Already?'

'It's Wednesday innit.'

'I'll leave 'em on thanks.'

'Not after a lady tonight then?'

Maybe he *would* move. 'Nope. And no dinner thanks, either.'

'You've 'ad a visitor. Walks with a stick. Calls himself Smiff like every other cant cams 'ere up to no good. He's in room seven, ground floor. What d' yer want on Sunday. Beef or lamb?'

Just the thought of the stench of roast dinner revolted him. Especially here. Now. The only time when an English yard is fit for sitting in, they came in hordes to baste on the beach. White, goose-bumped, hairy. Roasting. Frying in their sickly sweet oils. Taking away the sea smell. Take away burger and chips. Sammy Smith was in the fucking house for chrissakes . . .

'I think lamb.'

'That's two for beef and three for lamb. It'll end up lamb, I know it.' She sounded disappointed. 'So yer don't want yer sheets doin' then?'

He opened the door and put his head out. What she'd wanted him to do. 'No.' She was trying to look behind him so he opened the door wider to prove he had no-one in with him. No unofficial lodgers.

She looked at his chest, holding a pair of sheets over her own. She

84

was checking the merchandise, it felt like. Wondering what he'd be like on the job, if only she weren't so old. Gone. Past it but still watching. In her other life, a brothel owner from the middle ages. Getting off on the sheet stains. At the facking tea table if you don't mind. Schoolgirls some of them. All night long. In, up, fuck, down and out. Gone.

'You bin in there all day 'ave yer? Day like today?'

Day like any other day. He nodded. She dropped her chin and tutted. Tut, tut, tut.

If yer wanna call names, then fack off somewhere else. Cants. One of her house rules, that was. No name-calling allowed. It ensured his permanent alienation. Which was why he'd stayed really. Jack was mate enough. Jack was going home soon, for a holiday. Said he'd find out if there was still a warrant out for him. Go and see his mum for him.

Mavver couldn't understand why Johnno didn't mix, try harder. Behave more like the villains. She couldn't understand it but she liked him. To prove it, she stuck her nose into his business, his sheets, his moods and movements. It'd be nice to live somewhere with a view.

'I'm off out in a minute.'

'Yer goin' out are yer? What'll I tell this Smiff geezer, if he asks like?'

'Nothin'. Tell 'im I'm out o' town.'

'If it makes for no trabble I will. Can't 'ave one o' me favourites bein' 'ounded can we? Cheeky get asked me to open up so he could see I wasn't lying. Don't worry, san. I never let him in. Just a look I said. Trusts me now see. Like I've always said, if there's owt yer want to know, cam an' see yer Mavver. Now then, take these sheets and if yer need 'em later, you can fix 'em yerself can't yer?'

'How long's he booked in for, this Smith fella?'

'He's on pay by the day. Small bag. Won't be here for long I wooden o' thought.'

After tidying up and making the bed, he went back up to Jack's and knocked the coded rat-a-tat-rat-a-tat.

'Who is it?'

'It's me.'

The door opened. Jack in his bollocko behind it, the girls under sheets on the bed. 'What is it? Is she coming?'

'She's coming. Just two rooms left and she'll be up here.'

'Girls, you'd better go. Mavver's on her way up.'

The girls slid to either side of the bed and bent down, to look for their clothes, the slit on the dark one's backside just visible, the blonde looking round in a panic. Jack went over to the bed clapping his hands.

'Come on, girls, 'urry up. You'll get me evicted.' The girls braved their nakedness to pull up their knickers and in seconds were dressed and ready to go with high heels and handbags clutched under their arms. Jack opened the window and really gently took each by the shoulders and kissed them on the cheek. Then he guided them out on to the fire escape, his fingers on his lips to quieten them. Johnno sat on the bed waiting. He spotted a hairslide on the pillow and figured the girl could afford to lose it. He snapped its crocodile teeth open and closed on his finger and felt nothing, his skin a leather glove now. Jack left the windows open and the nets blew air into what smelt like a perfume factory poisoned by something.

'Bit young?'

'Sixteen and seventeen.'

'They said.'

'They wanted to be.'

Jack wrapped a towel round himself and pulled his hair back to a pony tail. Then searched under the bed for his fags and lit one. He sat down with his back to Jonathan and finding his jeans, counted his money. His snake tattoo looked a mess in his tan.

'That bird you were on about down the beach yesterday, her washin' her feet at the taps?'

'Yeah.'

'She was workin' at Joe's Shed down Banus last night.'

'The bar?'

'Crap barmaid.'

'I was down there this affy. I thought I saw her. Did you get a name?'

'If I did it's gone. I'm off for a shower. D' yer fancy goin' down there later on?'

'Yeah I do. You got any money for me yet?' Somehow, he couldn't see Louise working a bar. He couldn't see Wheezy working anything. But it was worth finding out.

'End o' this week, I promise.'

'Sammy Smith's turned up 'asn't he? Lookin' for me. Some dosh might come in 'andy. 'Ave yer seen him?'

'I heard him. I told Mavver to warn yer when yer got in.'

'D' yer think he's . . . like . . .'

'Dangerous?'

'Well I wouldn't 'ave put it like that.'

'He's dangerous alright. He was dangerous enough with two legs. But then it cuts both ways dunnit?'

'Eh?'

'Well how far's he gonna get on one leg? He's more of a danger to himself now innit?'

Sammy Smith walking with a stick and getting by on one leg didn't sound very promising at all. The nets blew in strong then, high up to the ceiling almost. 'I've got a kitchen job lined up and a flat to go with it.'

'Oh yeah.'

'Mavver said Sammy had an urgent message for me, from me sister.'

'Yer bottlin' aren't yer?'

'No. I was just worried 'bout me sister.'

'Fuckin' 'ell, Johnno, that's the first time you've ever mentioned her. Yer bottlin' it. At least 'ave the bottle to say so.' Jack was big, the biggest man in the house with the biggest room in the house. He did site work and didn't mind his skin turning leather. Patchy brown all over. A football match of freckles all over his nose and a good set of teeth. A grim reaper tattoo on his left arm. A mind of his own and no time for anything but work and women. Straight as a die. 'Who's that off then? The job?'

'That Chas fella.'

'Oh aye.' Jack turned and arched his eyebrow, impressed. 'Yer in there then. He's got gaffs all over the place.'

'I know.'

'We'll get a cab down to Banus shall we?'

'I hope it's her yer know.'

'Who?'

'Wheezy.'

'She wasn't called Wheezy, I can tell yer that much.'

Chapter Seven

Benidorm had been fairly easy. Jack, who'd been holed up there, with some fat Irish girl writing her life story in a villa, way up in the hills, had found him a job at the Hotel Manna to see him through the watered-down winter sunshine. There he'd waited for summer, for the really lively work to begin and for the endless packages of flesh arriving fresh and daily from all over Europe. In the Hotel Manna, he'd waited on some seventy OAPs spending their pensions and winter abroad because it was cheaper to live in Benidorm than South London. Jonathan carried their bags for them, their chairs, their picnic boxes, their suitcases. At lunch and dinner he carried their plates to the table and away from the table. At bedtime he carried the drunks to their beds. And they didn't tip.

Three afternoons and evenings a week, he'd called bingo numbers in the hotel foyer. The prizes he'd arranged in lines, along the reception desk, in order of excitement, radio alarm clocks to wind-up dancing flamencoes. The punters loved him. A born caller, they told him. He had it off pat. Dosi-dos and clickety-clicks, two fat ladies and legs like sticks. His mum would have been proud. But then, how many times had he watched her down the Plaza, while him and Shirl had sat quietly on the stairs, eyes streaming from the smoke. The Plaza was his mother's ruin and the only place she went. Before bingo it had been a theatre. He'd seen *Dick Whittington* there with his dad. His dad for once joining in, clapping, singing, pointing at the stage. Squeezing his little kneecaps to tickle him. Pinching his nose, carrying him piggyback all the way home. He could remember laughing hard. Really hard, lung-busting hard. Because his dad was trying his best to give his son the time of his life, just like all the other kids were having. Just as exciting. Just as nice. Two ice creams. Cilla

Black didn't stand a chance that day. His dad was the star. The one. The entertainment.

The next time he'd gone to that building with the great big pillars outside, he'd been with his mum. On the stage, just one bald head in a shirt and tie, working his ball machine. The women totally in awe of it. Playing three cards a go. His mum six. She stuck rabbits' feet on the end of her pens and marked her card against a clipboard with the Lord's Prayer written all over it. Him and Shirl would sit on the stairs with a string of raggedy kids all keeping the silence of a church, rubbing their eyes. Fighting quietly. Kicks. Chinese burns. Dead legs and arms and ear rubbing. Some kids collected fag butts. The daring ones popped crisp bags when a call was due. Only when someone called house or 'Eee-ahhh' could they breathe. Run up and down the stairs in a frenzy. Beg for Fanta and crisps and to go home early. Lunchtimes during the summer holidays, evenings when his dad was on nights, the place to be was the Plaza.

When all of South London's pensioners were in their beds, bingoed out, Johnno got drunk with Franky, the cook, and very often could be found the next morning by the swimming pool, on a sunbed, freezing. Waiting for the season to start. Waiting for the tug to go home. But the tug never came.

The Costa Blanca in season. The beach a human marketplace. His eye could with ease tune into a scene from the holocaust, a holy mass of burning skin, a great glut of oiled arms and legs mangled into one oven. In a good mood, a David Attenborough mood, he fancied the shores of an African lake in mating season, the females genetically programmed to remain on the sand, end to end, waiting, breeding, every week more and more of them, more noise and more fights, the beach barely visible. Too many people. Using all their savings, Johnno and Jack flew from Alicante to Malaga, and from there wended their way down the Costa del Sol, a similar affair to the Blanca and, in places, still with a severe touch of Spain about it.

On the beaches of course, there was very little Spain left and plenty of work to help with its continued removal. Men perched on tractors created beaches that weren't there before. Peasant settlements were flattened in favour of Meccano outfits. In Torremolinos, it was either navvy work or bar work. Jonathan did the bars, worked all night, slept all day, and shimmied with the women between times.

By July, Torremolinos was comprehensively invaded. Groups of families walked aimlessly round town, each member weighed down with territorial beach tackle like a refugee from a war lost. Those who had come for war paraded football scarves and plastic pints of lager, twenty- or thirty-strong sometimes and good singers too. Besides drinking, throwing up and copulating openly in the discos, they got banned – each ban a medal. In the discos, the bars, the hotels and on the beaches, these warriors spent their holidays fighting natives and Germans and collecting war medals. How long could he last out here? Too many people. Jack and Johnno bussed it even further south to Marbella, a more select resort, word had it. No jobs for bingo callers here.

And no Wheezy either. It must have been her night off. The only bar staff were a man with a shock of white hair, a short tubby girl who looked more like a bouncer and a woman in her thirties who seemed far too busy to mither. The place was half full.

There was a ruffle on the calm of the bar scene before him now. Heads twitched ready for a fight but it was just a fat girl drunk, enjoying a disco that wasn't happening. It was background bar music but she was off her face, on her holidays with Madonna, trying to convince herself and everyone around her, *it could be so nice*. It could never be. Not with her. She spun round fast, her mates embarassed for her, away about her. She was too fat to be gyrating and, just in the nick, Johnno managed to jump from his seat before she fell on him. She fell over his table and knocked all the drinks off. His half-full pint smashed to the stone floor. Awake to the damage, the girl apologised but Johnno ignored her, bent down and went for the broken glass instead.

This was Joe's Shed, a watering hole for the common people, such bars few and far between in Puerto Banus and quite welcome, if only for the price of the beer. Johnno resented paying the prices in the smarter bars but resented more the fact they charged such prices to keep him and his sort out. This financial apartheid barred him from the casinos, the restaurants, the hotel bars and places like Clouds, just across the way, where for double the price of the Shed, you could get a gin and tonic in a glass that wouldn't break on stone but on marble tile instead. He kept out of places like Clouds not for the want of money but for the want of better company than such a waste of money could buy. And still there was no sign of her.

Outside the bar, beyond the fairy lights, a world of yachts, just a stone's throw away – a lob of a brick or a petrol bomb that could crack their parade of wealth into a war zone. A riot if he felt like it. Would like to have seen it. He wasn't the only one. There'd be plenty of takers. From the herd of yobs that patronised Joe's Shed there would be those who would like nothing better than a yachter's life, to be a yachter's wife, bucks fizz and croissant for brekkers, fucking their way round the globe. And there'd be those who'd like to blow the place up. Set fire to it. They all belonged here. In Joe's Shed. The most exclusive place on the harbour. A gold digger's graveyard. No-one with class would ever step foot in the place. It must have been a row of fisherman's houses at one time. All knocked into one now. That was about it really. Not much else had changed. A long bar of shiny wood. Stone floor, stone walls. Tacky pictures of flamenco dancers and, behind the bar, pinned to the tongue and groove, football scarves, notes of foreign money, postcards and posters of tarts with their tits out. And on the floor, half dressed gold-digging women for Jack to home in on, poor waifs and strays on one night forays from Estepona or Fuengirola. Jack went for the pink ones first. The naive. The clean ones, as he put it. Teasers so easy to please and put at their ease, he let them down gently. There would be no champagne breakfast. There would be no yacht. There would be no chance. To compensate for the disappointment, he got them drunk. The one he liked best he took home for a good seeing to. And, if necessary, her mate. And coming over from the marina, there she was, bag over her shoulder, flicking her hair back, digging for that watch of hers, that watch without a strap. It was her. It was Wheezy. Johnno's stomach jumped.

He waited till she was *in situ* behind the bar and then went over to present her with an ashtray of broken glass. She came out from behind the bar and they hugged, for what must have been thirty seconds at least. Both of them thinking up what to say, how to be, how to break it off. She felt so like home he didn't want to. The woman behind the bar, in jeans and short sleeves, short hair and short-tempered, shouted over to Louise, 'I thought you were supposed to be working. We've ran out o' glasses already.'

'I'll see yer later,' she said and left him there, all cold.

Johnno went back to his table. It was empty. Then Jack appeared out of nowhere, excited. 'That one there. I've got her. She's the fittest by far.' He glugged the end of his pint and stood up again. Jar tipped up to his mouth, he scanned the room like a sub with its sights up. Johnno could tell he had his eye on Louise. *She* was the fittest by far. Jack finished his pint and disappeared.

Then Geoff turned up with Chas and a small man who must have been Jason. They all went up to the bar, and lined themselves up like the three bears. Waiting on his drink, Geoff turned and spotted Johnno. Then had a word with the big man who turned and gave Johnno a nod. Baby bear Jason was talking to the woman with short hair. She pointed him into a room at the back. He disappeared into the blackness. Johnno saw Chas hand Geoff some keys. The woman with short hair put drinks in front of them and wouldn't take any money. They talked and, at some revelation of Chas's, they all looked at Louise who was now serving five men all with their eyes on her tits. Then the woman shouted over to her and Louise nodded back. Then the woman left Chas and Geoff to serve some more punters. The two men picked up their drinks and came over. Jonathan, sitting with his back to the window and close to the entrance, smiled. Chas shook his hand and sat down opposite, blocking the view of the bar and Louise. He'd sat down quietly, like they were already good mates, laid his forearms flat to the table, one hand on top of the other and both hands fingered with gold. A gold chain thick enough for the toilet shackling his wrist. After he'd had a good look at the punters out on the patio,

'Jonathan, my san.'

'Yep.'

'Geoff tells me you've had enough o' the labouring.'

'Well I'd rather be doin' somat else.'

'And you've had enough o' slummin' it in that slag's place up the road?'

'Well I ain't desperate or owt.'

'And yer don't fancy gettin' into the films, Geoff tells me.'

'He never said owt about films.'

Geoff interrupted. 'You wouldn't be interested.'

'What sort o' films?'

'Porno films.'

'Yer right. I'm not interested.'

Louise was collecting glasses now. Johnno sat back in his chair to get a better view. Geoff leant forward, trying to get him to pay full attention to what, he supposed, was a sort of interview. Her hair was spot-on, completely unmanaged. She wasn't even trying but she was there. The other girls tried too hard, heavy with make-up and jewellery, handbags and hairspray. Fat. She was light as a feather on all counts. The shorts didn't fit her right, too big. She'd taken weight off. He couldn't make out the real shape of her. She came over to wipe the table.

'Three more beers if yer would,' said Geoff, pointing at Chas and himself.

'This is a pub,' she said. 'It's like England here. You go to the bar.'

'Alright darlin'. Keep yer hair on.'

Jonathan wanted to speak up for her but already and once more, even after all that time, she could make him feel uncomfortable, unnecessary. Like he was encroaching on her territory. She stretched to reach round the whole table with her cloth. Johnno moved his legs but didn't look up at her.

'Well we've cam up with an idea if yer interested?'

He watched her go back to the bar with the glasses and she watched him as she dunked them over the glass washer.

'Wakey wakey.'

'Sorry?'

'Yer wanted work, Geoff said.

'If it's straight.'

'Yer don't mind graftin' then?'

'Course not.' Jonathan was irritated now.

'Good.'

Jonathan watched her preparing a cocktail. She was measuring the spirits like a chemist preparing a prescription, making really hard work of it. Took all the fun out of it for the punter. 'So what is it then? Where is it?'

'Sorry?' said Chas, a touch surprised at him now.

'Kitchens,' Geoff said.

Chas looked like a quiz show host, white curly hair, about fifty, jowls holding on for dear life, piercing eyes and a good Marks and Sparks wardrobe. The only thing that let him down was his missing front tooth and the whistle lisp of a village idiot that went with it.

'Kit-*chen*,' he said, sitting back and folding his arms to get a better look at his new worker. He was impressed with Johnno's coolness perhaps and Johnno made a mental note to repeat this bravura at any future job interview. 'And if yer work out, a bit o' timeshare work.'

'Me doin' fliers? Yer jokin' aren't yer?'

'Bit o' flyin' to start with, to test yer committment. An' if yer good, I want yer showin' the punters round the properties.'

'And I get to stay in an apartment for nothin', Geoff said.'

'For workin'.'

'That's what I meant.'

'So long as there's no bother. Geoff said you were OK in that department?'

'Sorry, you've lost me.'

Geoff translated. 'Yer not on any Wanted posters he means.'

'I 'ope not.'

'Good. While yer workin' for me, there'll always be a bed for yer. Guaranteed. That way I know where to find yer.'

Geoff stood up then. 'Is Jason gettin' changed now then?' The bar was almost empty. Everyone was outside watching a new gin palace sail into view, the size of a three-bedroomed house.

'Yeah, and so am I. Have yer got them keys?'

Louise was at the optics. She released a measure into a glass and then sipped it. She saw Johnno looking. The woman with short hair was counting notes out of the till.

'When d'yer wanna start?'

'Straight away.'

'Give him the keys.'

'What's the address?'

Geoff went to the bar for a pen and wrote it down. Chas stood up and shook Johnno's hand. Didn't say a word. The grip of the shake was warning enough. Chas walked to the entrance, filled the doorway and turned the room dark. Johnno ducked, to look out of the window.

'D'yer wanna come to a party?' Geoff said, handing him the keys and the address. Johnno read it, smiled and stuffed the keys in his pocket. 'Can he come, Chas? To the party?'

'Don't see why not. 'Cept he hasn't got a cossie an' we can't 'ave two Tarzans on the go can we?'

He had his hands in his pockets, shuffling his change, his idiot grin full-on.

'I don't wanna go,' said Jonathan.

'We better go and get changed,' said Chas, checking Geoff's watch, like Geoff's arm was his arm. 'Come on then. Sure yer not up for it, Johnno?'

'Maybe next time eh.' Jonathan finished his pint and scanned the bar for her again.

She'd disappeared. He looked out of the window on to the patio and found her, laughing with a table of blokes. And on the table next to the blokes, Sammy, with his stick. Shit. He spun round the bar for Chas and Geoff. Gone. He looked through the window again and saw Sammy try to order a drink off Louise. He could see her explaining the pub routine and him not happy, pointing at his leg. And then stretching it out to get his hand into his pocket. He looked a right state, pitiful, stiff, damaged. Not a man to meet up with. Louise shuffled from one leg to another, teasing it looked like. He stared at them for ages. Her. Him. The fairy lights of the arch above them. The sheer white of the boats in the distance behind them. The window furry with dirt except for where he'd fingered it. The furry dirt like snow on a Christmas card, the centre of it – them. Unreal. His past. The best and worst of it. Like scrooge being brought up to date, he had a weird sensation of a double déjà vu. Like he truly had been here before. He blinked and the scene stayed the same. Sammy was still trying to give her his money. Then he stood up and began to make his way indoors.

Jonathan went to the bar and asked the woman with short hair where Chas had gone. She pointed out the back and let him through.

He found them in a fridge-cold office, the walls dripping with damp and cracked with paint and age. Jason was still getting dressed up. Geoff was rolling a joint on a desk that had several cameras lined up on it.

'Changed yer mind then 'ave yer?' said Chas. Jason turned round to reveal the skinny chest of a child, ribs sticking out.

'What's he doin' 'ere?' he said sulking.

'He's comin' wiv us,' said Chas.

'What can I go as?' said Jonathan.

'Yer can go as Cheetah,' said Jason. He was pulling up his tights, balancing on one leg.

Chas pushed him into the wall, hard. 'Don't mind 'im,' he said, turning to Jonathan. 'He wanted to go as a girl. As usual.'

Jason carried on pulling up his tights. Geoff handed Johnno the spliff and pulled out more clobber from a big Puma sports bag, under the desk.

'Does he know how to keep his gob shut then?' said Jason

'About what?' asked Chas.

'Us.'

'Fuck me, cretin. He'll think we're fackin' at it wiv each other.'

'I meant . . .'

'Shat it I said. Where's me cossie then, Geoff? 'And it over.'

Jason took an age to pull his gloves on. Yellow gloves up to his elbows. Red tights wrinkled at the knees. Caped in shiny yellow plastic and, with his arms folded, he looked nine years old and ready for his tenth birthday party.

Geoff stood up and Jonathan got into his chair, riding it like a horse, his arm across his mouth, making his smirk more obvious really. 'Yer can count on me to say nowt to no-one about nothin',' said Jonathan, nodding at Jason's knees, sucking on the spliff. They all looked at him suspiciously and then switched to Jason's knees and, still in silence, all of them thinking very hard it looked like, they carried on getting dressed. Maybe Jonathan still dressed and watching, had them all embarrassed.

Chas had every reason to be. With his jacket off, the full extent of his beer belly belittled what at first glance had appeared to be a fair-sized frame. He should have got undressed on the quiet and done them all a favour. Sighting his skiddies when he took his keks off, it was clear there was no wife or woman in his life. No intentions of either. How long had he had them on? Johnno noticed the smell then. Farts and fags and sweaty rags. Geoff was completely bollocko.

'I wouldn't be in 'ere unless I 'ad to be,' said Chas. 'What's goin' on, Johnno? We still ain't got a cossie for yer if that's what yer after.'

Jason was handing Batman his costume, piece by piece.

'I'm lyin' low for a minute if that's alright.'

'Who's out there?'

'Just some mucker from Manchester. It's no sweat, just a drag, that's all.'

Quiet again, for the finishing touches. Chas's mask, Tarzan's oil, Robin's mascara. And at last they were all ready for action, Chas's face fat with menace. 'I don't want any bovver, Johnno.'

'There won't be any. I promise.'

Geoff looked like he always looked. Ready for a swim. Jason, a tart.

'What yer gonna go as then?' said Chas, wrapping his cape round him, his big B on his belly all crumpled and creased, his skin showing.

'Where is it? The party?'

'Mijas.'

'I think I'll just cadge a lift and go home if that's OK,' said Jonathan

'Suit yerself. Have yer paid her for the cossies, Jason?'

'She's not bothered. Old stock, she said.'

'Well come on. We 'aven't got all night. Where are the mobies.'

Jason fished about in his case and pulled the mobile phones out. One for him and one for Chas. Antennae stretched, mouths on the mike, they were gone on it. In Batman land, just like that.

'Jeez it's fuckin' freezing. Can we go now.' Geoff was holding himself, scratching himself like a junkie. Chas was sweating, his mask up, wiping his brow. Only Jason was calm, comfortable, collected. Baby bear had it all sorted. Briefcase in hand. Eyes black with knowing. He was spooky. Even though he had tights on, there was something spooky about him.

In the bar, Katrina and the Waves were playing to a packed crowd. Just the sound but it was loud enough to be live. Jonathan kept on the right side of Batman's cape and Chas swished it about wide and full, beating a path to the exit. Cheers and claps followed him. Johnno didn't look about. He hid behind the cape all the way over to Chas's jeep. Then changed his mind about catching the lift. He watched them drive off to Gotham City and then crossed the carpark over to Clouds, the sister bar to Joe's Shed. The twin sister of shorthair, also with short hair, sat at the end of the bar, counting up her credit card receipts against the bills.

Clouds was for them who were up there and almost everything in there was up there with them. The company, the stools, the prices, the heels on the women's shoes. Only the volume was low, mood music and muttering. He ordered a Tequila Sunrise and went to take it out on the terrace. The woman called him back. Asked for cash up front. She talked like a man and didn't spare him a smile. Smiles galore for the other punters at the bar. Outside, on the terrace, the wrought iron chairs were leaning forward to the tables, as if finished for the night but it was still fairly early. Only just gone midnight. He pulled one away and sat on it. From the terrace he had full view of Joe's Shed and, to his right, the city of boats in the marina. He sipped his drink slowly and made plans for him and Louise. They'd be back together in no time, he knew it. It was one of those pictures he could see. When he saw Sammy the Stick get into a cab, he necked his drink and went back over there, to be with her.

It was just piano music now, to drive the last of them away. As more people left, the piano music got louder. He watched Louise pile the glasses on the bar. Then she spun round the place collecting up ashtrays and debris, like someone was due in. The piano man stopped playing. And then stared at him.

'Af-ri-ca?'

He shook his head.

'Am-er-ic-a?'

He decided not to be rude. 'English, mate. And you? Scottish?'

'Irish.'

'What part?'

'Connemara.'

'Never 'eard of it.'

'It's a soight prettier than 'ere Oi can tell yer. How Oid loyke to be nestlin' in the sleepin' breasts o' Connemara.' And then another tune on the piano. Entertaining himself. He was only about thirty-five. His white hair looked false, done on purpose. So he could stand out in a crowd no doubt. And he wasn't looking to Connemara for his breasts either.

She was drying more glasses, humming the piano man's song and Jonathan wanted her to stop in case there'd been something between them. She folded a teatowel and then grabbed her cardigan from the top of the fridge. She came out from behind the bar, frolicking. He gave her his first wide grin. When they got outside, for the first time in ages, he noticed the stars. Millions of them.

He didn't know how close he could be with her.

'D'yer wanna come back to my place?' Fiddling with the keys in his pocket.

'No. I'm stayin' here. On a boat,' she said, pointing.

100

There were quite a few boats to choose from, arranged carpark-style, row after row. In the sunlight, they looked just like toys, white plastic shiny toys ranked according to size, luxury, style and on the eye, not a patch on the sight of the wide-open sea beyond or the devil-sized mountains overseeing the whole show. In the dark, though, the boats looked menacing. Creaking ghosts. Masts like ancient totem poles watching. No sea to be seen, no mountains lording it.

'That's Ashoggi's launch,' she said. 'He's not on it though. Gone south apparently.' It was a big boat to leave behind. He should have taken it with him. 'A lot of Arabs here,' she said. 'Been coming for centuries.'

'They can afford it can't they? Can I come back to the boat with yer then?'

'Sorry. Security.'

'Well what then?'

'Everywhere's closed now.'

'After all this time?'

'I know. I know.' She was stamping her foot. 'I . . . I don't know what to say.'

'Say you 'aven't got a boyfriend.'

'I 'aven't got a boyfriend.' Taking the mick out of his accent.

'Good. An' 'ow long you 'ere for?'

'I'm working my fare back to England. I lost everything. Suitcase, passport, the lot.'

'Go to the embassy. Ring yer mum.'

'I've been. I know exactly what I've got to do and when it's time to leave I'll do it. But I'm not going home just yet. There's nothing to go home for. I start college again in September.'

'Yerv jus' bin to college.'

'I'm going into teaching.'

'What?'

'Teaching. I've got a place at Manchester again.'

'Do me a favour.'

'What?'

'Come back to my place.'

'No.'

'What's the problem? Why not? We 'aven't seen each other in ages.'

'It's too soon.'

'Two and a half years is too soon?'

'I mean we'll just jump into bed together and I don't want that.'

'Oh right. I see.'

'You know what I mean.'

'Yeah, Louise. I know exactly what yer mean. You mean you'd rather hang around here waitin' for some rich bastard to sweep you off yer feet. That's what all this is about.'

'Johnno.'

She slid her card into the security barrier and buttoned in her number. The turnstile green light went on and she went through. So quickly. So bluntly. The light went red again. The end. He stepped back.

'Well, yer in the right place for it aren't yer?'

'Jonathan!'

He walked off backwards, to get a last good look of her, her cardy over one shoulder. Her hair blowing. 'Yer shoulda just said,' he shouted. 'I'd've gone ages ago. Wouldn't wanna cramp yer style like, would I?' He turned and didn't look back again. He knew she was watching him, all the way, till he slid round the corner. He hid and saw her still standing there, staring after him.

Chapter Eight

In the dark, he'd seen the place differently. A living room of sunglasses, an honorary temple to the God of smoked glass. Nests of glass coffee tables everywhere, breeding and, in dim light, shin-snapping uncomfortable.

In the daylight, the damage was more apparent, a stain on the eye that drew his attention to the sea, time and time again. He wasn't used to looking down on the sea. It usually broke at his feet loud. From the balcony, all he could hear was the din of kids, women laughing and beeping cars that were far away up the avenida. The sea sounded like radio interference. Looking into his apartment, he surveyed his space and tried to own it, for the umpteenth time. His eyes moved from the imitation leather swivel that had done some time with a pump action shotgun over to the smoked-glass music cabinet. He tried to own the shattered floor tiles of brown moody mosaic and then went to the loo for a sit down, taking in the shower room of trees painted green on ceramic water pools in a garden in Japan he thought. His knees either side of his ears, he imagined what it would be like to have a baby. It was his birthday. It was time for press-ups.

Still no Louise. He'd gone back to the Shed the following night. The tubby girl said she'd been sacked and looked glad of it. Try over at Clouds she said. He'd gone to Clouds but the place was full of tossers and closed to the general public. Private party. He couldn't see her behind the bar or waiting on or anywhere. She'd gone. Found herself a meal ticket no doubt.

He was keeping a low profile now. Staying put in his new flat, or apartment as Chas called it. Someone must have partied in it all summer long and, possibly, the summer before that. It smelt rank still, even after a good floor scrubbing. He'd been forced to leave the balcony doors wide-open to let in all manner of UFOs resistant to every insect spray on the market. It didn't feel like home yet.

Still, he couldn't get work much straighter than this, and being indoors, living on-site, it was more luxury than work. And soon there'd be the timeshare stuff. Fliers. He didn't fancy fliers but he did fancy his chances as an estate agent when he finally hit home with a big bag of money. Anyone could be an estate agent. Chas had told him all about it. And with England's property prices going through the roof, he'd make a fortune. All he needed was some capital, some front and a gist of the hotbuttons – the less than obvious selling points that the punters would go for. People bought ideas, Chas said. The fixtures and fittings were a bonus. Showing suckers round timeshare apartments would be a valuable apprenticeship. Johnno was, perhaps, on his way.

No-one but Chas, Jason and Geoff knew where he was. Not even Jack who'd also gone to ground or home or to sea possibly, as a deckhand. He'd been on about that for ages. As soon as the flier work started, Johnno would have to get out there, in the thick of it. Put himself on offer. Hopefully, by then, Sammy would have got bored and gone home. Not that Johnno was scared of him. More struggling with the uncertainty of how to deal him. Or anyone else with recent leg loss for that matter. After forty-two press-ups, Johnno flopped. He laid his head against the tile, still cool and untouched by sun, then rolled over and looked out at the sea. He jumped up, pulled a chair on to the balcony and settled down for a morning's viewing, his eyes once again trained on the taps where he'd first seen her washing her feet.

This was his third day of Sammy- and Wheezy-spotting, voyeuring, perving. Sammy on Tequila Terrace playing cards or playing for girls, getting them drunk enough to blank his leg. He'd seen him twice with two birds, one on each arm, both with tits to die for. Not today though. No sign. Unless it was still too early, or he was way further up the beach at some other bar. Or maybe he'd left for England already. He scanned the sand strip, fast filling up with flesh. The glint of sun glass was everywhere.

The sky was bare. Eye aching blue. Denied clouds, he tried to make shapes of the human clusters baking brown. If he really went for it, he could get them to bunch into flowers, complete with stalk; into windows with frames; into shells. But it was difficult. Bodies were much more difficult than clouds. Too weighty to form any real illusion. But then what *was* a real illusion? That sound of the seagulls laughing at him? He laughed back. Not out loud. In his head, the story of Jonathan's seagull, another suit that didn't fit him. He'd tried to fly higher, smarter, smoother. He was trying for it now. He was up there with the rest of them, a view of the sea, a pocketful of money, a chance to make something of himself. He imagined his balcony gone, to feel that freedom, but it was too heavy and cage-like to deny it. He'd not fly but die instantly.

It was his birthday. No cards, no presents, and nobody's fault but his own. Birthdays always did this to him. His eyes lied and told him he was flying, told him he was going up, growing up in the world, but his birthday bones were heavy as lead and always had been. Since he could remember. His birthday was an anniversary of shame and anger that could, if he let it, send him near-mad. He thought mad because he didn't understand where the sweat came from or why he went rigid with what felt like fear. Even now after forty-two press-ups, his muscles were standing up pert on his arm, shouting, 'Run! Johnno! Run!'

The same fear he felt whenever he was threatened with bricks and knives and husbands. The same fear he felt when the posses from Cheetham Hill drove round the estates marking out new territory, asking him to join up, join in or disappear for good, for his own safety and health and well-being. Disappear from his own life, the star choice of every loser.

On his birthday, he felt under pressure. All day, he buzzed with the nerves of a man about to give a performance. On-edge and always surprised there was no surprise. At the end of the day, always disappointed. His stomach, usually quiet, obedient and well under control, attended these birthdays, an uninvited guest. His gut took on all the stress. He could feel every loop of it tighten and twist into coils so rigid, the stress turned to pain. Only when the day was over did the tension slacken and the gut unravel. He was on the loo again now, his knees up by his ears, wondering what it must be like to have a baby.

And that was it. Birthdays scared him. Clear as a glass of water, his first memorable birthday came back to him. Unexpectedly and suddenly, like a wet-the-bed, he pissed with force as all the pictures rushed in.

He was six. The birthday cake was in the pantry, the candles in a cellophane bag hidden at the back of the knife and fork drawer. He had Matchbox cars, loads of them. The cellophane windows on each new box torn jagged. Dad wasn't home to see him in his policeman's uniform wielding a silver truncheon. Shirl was two then and talking like a tape recorder. He'd hit her with his truncheon several times. It didn't hurt but she still cried. She'd set fire to his Ludo board and, there on the new carpet, another black crater of rubber showed through. They always said that Jonathan was old enough to know better. They broke his spirit and turned him mardy arse. They weren't risking the same with Shirl. So she had the run of the place.

That birthday, he sat curled up on the end of the couch, his policeman's uniform hung up on the back of the door. When his father got home, he'd change back into it and line up for inspection. That was the plan. Mum was in the kitchen washing. Work shirts after a mangle were still dripping off the pulley. The spin drier was broken. There were cuttings on the window sill, dying in the damp. Mrs Johnson had been in three times that day, at it with her neighbouring. Mum wouldn't get involved. Wouldn't return the favours. She got Johnno to take the catalogue back. 'No thanks. Not interested me mum said.' Never never. Not allowed. Mrs Johnson slammed the back door in his face.

He sat watching the racing. Not watching it, staring at it. And through gaps in the clothes horse, kept his eye on the fire that shouldn't have been lit. It was summer. The racing pages were in it now, hissing, drenched in barley juice. Gloom before teatime, this Saturday afternoon threatened thunder, the houses over the back had their lights on already. The fire grunted, close to death. Shirl ran in and chucked her beaker at it, playing skittles with his birthday cards on the mantelpiece. One fluttered down into the fire and, with a big push against the clothes horse, he managed to save it. The clothes fell to filth in the hearth. Shirl screamed at all this and ran back out to the kitchen, to tell on him. He collected up his cars to take them to his room.

Carefully, he picked the rest of his cards off the mantelpiece and took to the stairs, the walls damp against his arm, the air freezing, the carpet smelling of must, the copper brackets that held it down grey with dust. The door to his room was closed. The handle too high. He dropped his load and, on tiptoes, budged the knob just enough to unclick it. As the door opened, so had the gob of his mother, screaming at the mess by the fire. Instead of picking up his load and getting to his bed fast, he kicked in temper every car, until the last one was in. After more kicking practice, he started on his birthday cards, stamping on them, unable to missile them into his room. Mad with himself, he set on each one. Holding the card in his fingers, he began a quiet deliberate ripping. He knew these cards held no value, were worth nothing, would in a day be consigned to the bin. He could rip them to shreds, and lose nothing by it. And then he remembered his mum who'd gone quiet now. She was watching him from the bottom of the stairs. He ran into his room and pushed at the door to stop her getting in. He heard her thumping up the stairs. She pushed the door with such a force, he fell back into the chest of drawers. She grabbed at his jumper and, in a split second of elastic, was in her arms. Still standing, she bent him over her leg and pulled his pants down. He could have moved and got away but he knew not to. He stood there and took it. The smacks usually stopped after five, her anger spent, but she smacked harder instead, faster, like a bully. He didn't cry out even. *She* was crying. She was crying hard, yarling. She only stopped her slapping because she heard the front door go. Dad was home.

If that had been it, he might have got over it. If that was the worst birthday anyone could have, it was easily forgettable. But his dad

107

had come home drunk. He could hear him ranting and raving about his newspaper. Johnno had put all his cars in his bed, piled up in the valley of it, like a stash of treasure, gleaming new metal against a dirty grey sheet. When the creases in the sheet were smoothed, there were road track lines of dirt to drive his cars along.

'Johnno get down here.'

There was a chance of 'another one to go with it', he knew. A yanking. A pushing. The asking for an explanation. He didn't want to give one and couldn't without a blubber which would get him the next smack coming, no problem.

'Johnno get down here.'

He chose the fire engine and got off the bed. Only then did he realise how sore his backside was. His shoulders juddered, his eyes filled, his chest went in and out, his mouth curved itself into a snarl. His dribble ran river from his chin on to brand-new school shoes, still smooth on the bottoms, his most expensive birthday present ever and the one that hurt the most.

'Do I have to come up there and drag yer down?'

And then, he'd not heard her come up, the door flung open. She held her hand out to take him.

'Come on, love. Yer father wants to wish you 'appy birthday.'

And all was well again. Just like that. He didn't take her hand, still sore and sure he was due more comfort than that. But he did follow on and pretend like nothing had happened. Because that's what always happened when dad got home. The house pretended that the day had never been, that it had only just started.

He was in the front room, on the couch, watching the racing, his braces down, his tie undone and still with his shoes on. A bad sign.

'Are they givin' coal away for free now or somat?' he said to his mum, handing her the wage packet. Shirl was wriggling to get out from under her arm.

'It was for dryin' the washin'.'

'I don't see no washin'.'

'It's comin'.'

'I don't see no washin'. What's the point of a fire in the summer an' no washin' eh? Where's the washin' eh? That fire's bin in for hours an' I don't see no washin'.'

'It's comin'. I'm sortin' it.'

'You think we got money to burn do yer? Why not wait till the washin's sorted, woman. Then build a fire.'

Johnno moved back towards the door.

'You stop dead still, my son, or I'll brain yer right there and then, where yer standin'. Now then. Why the fire?'

'It's rainin', Charlie.'

'An' yer think I'd not noticed. Put me mac by the fire an' make some use of it.'

'Why's yer mac so wet, Charlie?'

Nothing. Silence. 'Come here, son. How was yer birthday?'

''S alright.'

'See that. Fire warmin' a summer's day. Brainless these women are sometimes, I'm tellin' ya.'

'I'll put her up in the 'igh chair for her tea,' said his mum, and out she went.

Johnno stood close by his dad, wary but glad he wasn't the centre of attention. His dad didn't even look at him now, never mentioned his birthday again. It wasn't the time for a policeman's parade, he could tell that much. Johnno's two hands travelled the full length of the arm of the couch, his fingers returning again and again to the hole in the vinyl where the foam spilled out. Then, of a sudden, his dad put his great big hand over both his little hands and shouted through to the kitchen.

'And go easy on that housekeepin' coz it's the last you'll see for a long while.' The horse race on the telly was coming to an end, the man talking over it, talking faster and faster to keep up with the horses. His mum came back in.

'There's not even a full week in here, Charlie. What yer talkin' about?'

'It's all yer gettin'.'

'But Charlie, how'm I to manage on this and with no more comin' till *when* yer say?'

'Till some bugger down the labour exchange thinks mugs like me have a right to a decent job. That's when.'

'So yerv lost yer job then?'

'No. I've not lost it. I know exactly where it is. It's been nabbed off me.'

'By who?'

'By someone that can drive better than I can. I had an accident.' Johnno rushed to the window. No van there.

'But you've got rights, love, surely? Or were yer drinkin'?'

'I'll swing for you if yer carry on.'

'So what yer gonna do, lie down and let them walk all over yer?'

And with that, he shot up. He pushed the door closed so she couldn't get out and slapped her across the head, hard, twice. She grabbed at the door to get away and his dad, not bothered any more, let her. He sat back down on the couch.

Johnno went to follow her out but his dad said, 'You stay there where I can see yer.' Pointing him over to sit on the couch with him. Johnno climbed on, tucked his feet up under him and sucked hard on a mouthful of fingers. His dad got up to turn the telly over. There was a war on.

'Get them feet off the couch.'

He sat with straight legs then. His shoes killing him.

'Let's see yer tie them laces then.'

He bent over, untied and then tied his laces again. He'd been tying them on his own for ages.

'Go an' get me bottle.'

Johnno came back in with his bottle of Newcastle Brown, a glass and a bottle opener. His dad took the drink and the opener and swigged straight from the bottle. Another bad sign. Still drinking, he kept his eye on the telly. He stopped drinking and sat forward to listen more carefully. 'Now listen to that, son. Did you hear him? Them lads over there are eatin' death for breakfast. EATING DEATH FOR BREAKFAST. DO YOU HEAR ME?' Bawling his head off. Johnno moved away and went to sit up at the table, his back to the telly and his father. The front room door opened slowly and in came Shirl. 'EATING DEATH FOR BREAKFAST,' and then a swig on his bottle. Shirl got excited and ran up to him, squealing, happy. This wasn't the time. She slapped dad's knee and said, 'Mummy hate you.' His dad leant forward till he was head-to-head with her.

'What did you say?'

'Mummy hate you.' Pointing at him. She knew exactly what she was saying.

'Hilda! Hilda come and get her out o' me sight. Hilda, I'm fuckin' talkin' to you!'

And in she came, her skirt too short now, too red. Her make-up not right, all black round the eyes. A ladder in her tights. Her legs too fat. 'Just look at yer. Look at you eh?' He stood up and dragged her to the mirror. 'I married that. And what for eh? Get these kids out me sight before I lose me rag proper.'

When it was tea-time, mum cried, putting the candles on the cake. She got tears on the cake and Johnno didn't want it then. Dad came in with no trousers on. He'd fallen asleep on the couch and wet himself. He'd gone up the stairs backwards, singing nursey rhymes in an American accent. Shouting breakfast and war but when he came down for his tea he was in baggy white underpants and quiet. He buried all his peas in his mashed potato and blew all the candles out. Made mum turn the radio off and then back on again. And then started talking to the radio, like there was no-one else there. Shirl was in bed. Johnno wanted to go to bed. Mum's hand was shaking, cutting her chop. When dad laughed at the radio, she put her head on the table and her shoulders juddered. Johnno cried then. His dad looked from one to the other, his face getting bigger all the time, and then he exploded. He threw his plate up against the wall and told Johnno to get to bed. Johnno legged it. He sat on the top stair crying and listening. His dad was ranting. He couldn't hear his mum. He heard the plates in the sink. Drawers shutting. Cutlery clashing. Pans being stacked. And then nothing. Just silence. Then his mum saying, 'No, Charlie, no.'

'You think I'm just a friggin' money-bags don't yer? That's all yerv ever wanted isn't it? The money. I come home an' give yer money and yer'd not give a damn if yer didn't see me till the next pay packet came along. I'm right aren't I? AREN'T I? AREN'T I? AREN'T I?' Until she said YES. And after she said yes, she said no no no. He was hitting her. It was the 'no' of being hit but Johnno couldn't hear the hitting. He crept down the stairs and opened the door to the parlour. They weren't in there. They were in the back kitchen. His mum was whimpering, 'No, Charlie.' Dad said it was 'his kitchen', not hers. 'His house', not hers. She was 'his woman, his wife, his for whatever he wanted'. Johnno was in the dining room, the fire roaring now. He was hot, flushed. He wanted a drink of water. And that's what he'd say. What he always said. 'Can I have a drink of water please, mum.'

His mother lay on the kitchen floor, her head on the welcome mat by the back door. Her clothes all open, her skirt up, her knickers cutting into her flesh making big red weals. Dad on top of her. Her eyes closed. From her came a scream to convince anyone she needed tying down. She didn't sound like his mum.

Johnno ran out and up the stairs and banged his door closed for good. He opened his window and threw every single car out, each one landing on the corrugated shed roof like bombs dropping. He pooed the bed that night and never kissed his mother again. Never went near her.

That was the birthday he could never forget, the one his birthday bones, his gut and his heart would not forget and had him, every year, on the toilet. Today was the first time he'd actually remembered the pictures. Every other year, only his stomach remembered. Only his heart. Only his bones. Today it was all in his head, and his water.

Right now, with no-one but sea birds for company, he got the idea he'd been born into the wrong body. A reincarnated mistake. Perhaps he should go up to Mavver's and check for mail, for phone calls, for birthday cards, but instinct told him there'd be no word. No pressie. Nothing. Just Sammy. That's what they'd sent over for him, Sammy with a stick.

He couldn't find *any* shapes in the beach bodies today. None at all. Just the one big idea they were all litter. Mess. He'd like to see the beach empty, in daylight. If he had a big hoover . . . This flat could be a birthday present. The flat, the view, the space. That horizon lining the limit of his wanderings. The fright of starving Africa beyond it. Sky, space, distance, food. They were gifts, of sorts.

Fuck it, he was going to enjoy this birthday. Buy himself a present. Get into the spirit. He thought twice about binoculars. The second thought zoomed in on a child with withered water-wings sinking below the water line to the never-go-beyond shelf of the deep. But breasts from the first thought kept re-emerging and turned those water-wings into bulging possibilities and then decisions about price and weight and carry cases. He could perve to his heart's content then, not have to strain or imagine or even beat himself up about it. He could keep his eye out for Louise. See who she'd copped off with. And there was Sammy of course. And anyway, why shouldn't he buy himself a present?

On his breakfast tray, a tomato, a great melon of a tomato, and some cheese, playing plastic. The bread rock-hard. He drank his coffee and gauged how limiting his view was. True, he could see a long way up the beach, but only outlines after the first fifty yards. On the sea, a raft of lilos and poor men on windsurfers, the worst excuse for a boat he could think of. He slurped the rest of his coffee, pulled on olive-green cord cut-offs and a T-shirt and set off to the shops for bread and binoculars.

For three mornings on the trot, early enough not to be seen by the stick, he'd been out in the town, collecting mini-purchases of independence. His own teatowels. His own pillow-case. His own brush. Coffee, salads, shellfish, eggs, bread. Then a teapot, scissors and Bic razors. Each trip an excuse to come home. Between trips he deliberated and pondered, perved and voyeured from the balcony. He slept. He brushed. Then out again to buy a mop. And a bucket. And then home again. He loved it. Setting out on his mop and bucket trip, he did a flat search for cupboard space. He could not remember seeing the padlock, the size of a pig's heart, hanging from the door in the hall. He would have noticed it before. He re-trod his steps and practised being relaxed and unsuspicious, but the pig's heart beat in his face with a thump, every time.

This morning he was at it again. Bread and binoculars. Out on to the flank of the pavement, and into the sun, alive to the day in a way he never felt back at home, in England. His hair neat, armskin shiny, sun on his neck, like an iron, flattening him.

Try Marcelle's. Across the road, third turning on the right. Jonathan went to the bakery instead and got bread. Then went behind Orange Square and into Marcelle's Audio-Visual Centre and further into it, to the camera section and from there he purchased a box of binocs. Then out, into the thick of it. A coachload had arrived for morning coffee and were out in the square, belittling the orange trees, the sun flashing off their glasses. He was taken in by it, the hullabaloo, the shouts. He felt so part of it, he bought an ice cream. Bobbing out of the square with binocs, bread and a double ninety-nine, he was in a buoyant mood now. The coffee had kicked in. He wended his way through the chairs of a café, empty and full of anticipated business, the waiter placing menus. His balance held firm as he crossed the street gnatted with motorbikes, buzzing in and out of the throngs and the monuments. How busy they all were, on their holidays. Then it was up the Fontanilla to home. Another mission completed without a hitch. A stand on the front to look out to see . . . ahoy there! shielding his eyes from the sun. 'Ahoy there.' Then a pat on his back made him jump and wobble. His ice cream headed to the pavement. Splat. He didn't get chance to mourn it. His face was stuck on Louise.

'How yer doin'?'

He could smell her. Toothpaste. Dressed in a skimpy top that hid only her colour, not outline or texture. Or arms. He smiled. 'Still here then?'

'I'm looking for a room. The boat I was on has been sold.'

'Breakfast?' he asked her, holding the bread up to prove it.

'No. I can't.'

'Sort the room out later.' Pulling at her arm in a sort of apology

'Come on.' Her unmanaged hair was combing itself in the wind. He wanted to be in it. 'Don't leave me to eat on me own. Come on . . . please?'

In the breeze, she sifted the strands of her blondeness behind her ear. Her head swinging, laughing. Hair falling away to be collected and sifted and set once again. Silver pips in her lobes. A pair of empty holes too. They were new.

'OK.' Denim shorts splicing her between the legs. He leant back to get a better glimpse.

'Come on then,' he said. His nipples were on end. Walking across the wind that tickled his lip, he was bouncing a little. She had bags, Puerto Banus clobber bags, heavy on price and light on produce, the string cutting into her shoulder. She was a half second behind him.

'What's in there?' she asked, catching him up.

His arm covered up the label on the box. He turned to look her a warning. He got twitchy then.

'Jonathan?'

'Yes?'

'How far is it?'

'Not far.'

Already he was beginning to regret her. Now that he had her, he knew he was over her. Breakfast over a battle of wits would be a strain. A silent breakfast, alone with binoculars, would have been altogether a smoother, calmer way to start the day.

Louise picked up speed and was soon slightly ahead of him. When he saw the backs of her knees and the wire of gold chain on her skinny ankle waiting for his fingers to circle it whole . . . when he saw all that, he changed his mind again. He caught up and moved along with her, in stride time. And took her suede shoulder bag. And bounced up and down with her breasts. Blocking up the footway, the staircase, the mind, they went up to his apartment together.

'This is rather nice,' she said. She didn't look round, too distracted by the seascape.

'Needs some work. Kitchen 'n' that.'

'The floor too.' Taking a closer inspection now, her nose trying not to screw up. Criticising the place already.

'Just a few tiles need replacin', that's all.'

He threw her bag down on the machine-gunned chair. When it landed, the chair swivelled as if the ghost of the person shot there had upped and left – the spirit of Louise more than it could stand. There was still something there between them.

He went straight to the sink to wash glasses and make drinks. The tiles by the sink were vile, sticky and shaming. They needed smashing off the wall, pronto.

'Drink?'

'Coffee?'

She was out on the balcony, spreading her backside towards him. He put the box of binoculars away in the bedroom, feeling slightly embarrassed about them now.

'I don't s'pose you've learnt how to use a mop yet?'

She ignored him. He moved out on to the balcony with the glasses of coffee. 'I don't s'pose . . .'

'I heard you the first time.'

'So yer not working in the bar any more? I knew that wouldn't last long. What was it? Too much like hard work?' She sat down and took the drink. She placed it on the glass coffee table, pulled off some bread and then cut a tomato, a slightly wrinkly tomato. 'D' yer want some eggs?'

'No, this is fine thanks.'

'So what's happenin'? When yer goin' 'ome? What 'appened at the bar?'

'Questions, questions . . .'

'Forget it then. I don't wanna know.'

'I was just doing them a favour, for a friend of mine. They were short-staffed.' She dug into the pocket of her shorts and brought out her watch without a strap. Looked at it and laid it on the table.

'So where's yer friend now then?'

'She's . . . well she got a job. On a boat. She's gone to Tangiers.'

116

'And you? What are you gonna do?'

'This and that. More bar work I suppose.'

He tried to move another chair on to the balcony but there wasn't enough room. Instead, he positioned the baby of the nest of glass coffee tables. Carefully distributing his weight, he sat on it.

'I thought you were going into banking?'

'I was fooling myself.'

'Well they must have taught you somat useful then.'

He was back in the groove and so soon. Bringing her down. Being sarcastic. In the past, he'd brought her down to quieten her, take the giggle out of her, an irritating childish giggle that she used on people in places where she didn't belong. And he'd brought her down to shut her up, when that mouth of hers rode off into people's lives she had no right poking her nose into. The most embarrassing time when he'd taken her to Giggsy's and, during the interval, introduced her to the band. He'd wanted to show her off to Chunky. She shook hands with them all, which was OK, but then started on them like she was some kind of customs officer. Where were they from? Where was the weed from? He had to tell her what she could and couldn't do, say and couldn't say, be and not be. He'd taught her how to sit sweet and natural and keep shtum. And then she'd got in with her London lesbos and turned on him.

He could see her bristling. She was remembering it all too. He didn't want that. He didn't want to go there. Yes he had been over the top back then but he'd been young then. Just learning. She'd been even younger. They'd been apart for nearly three whole years and they were different people now. Strong enough to be honest. She was woman not girl. But still she used that semi-nymphet nod, that twist of the neck, that half smile half pout. A look to say she was too weak, too young, too beautiful for a fight. A look that said she was special. She'd learnt the art of her womanhood well, keeping the kiddy stuff that was cute and chucking all the hysterical. She was at home with herself, sitting up straight, arms resting on her legs, legs not just crossed but plaited. He wanted to take her sandals off and pull her feet up. He wanted to take her feet in his hands and mould

117

them, massage them. He wanted her feet but she was keeping them to herself.

Gone were the CND earrings, the hair pulled back fierce, the black lines on her eyes, the shine of glycerine on her lips. Gone too was the puppy fat from her arms and thighs. She was lean. Lean, brown and in control of herself. He preferred her like this. He looked straight out to sea and noticed then, that it didn't sound like radio interference anymore. Everything was clear again.

'It's my birthday today.'

'I know. I meant to say. Happy Birthday.'

Then silence. Below them, a fight going on in Spanish. A man and woman shouting. On the beach, a procession of holidaymakers making for the spaces, laying out their wares. Papa's Bar was still almost empty. The sun white now, all the high-rise rabbit hutches in the full glare of it. The blue in the sky unbearable to look at. He left her to find his shades and, once inside, wanted to stay inside. Out of the public eye. Get close to her.

'You know the other night . . . down at Joe's Shed?'

'I've forgotten all about that now. I had no right to expect you . . .'
He wiped the greasy sweat from either side of his nose and put his glasses on.

'I didn't mean . . . I never got chance to tell you. There was a man. Looking for you and . . . well it was quite bizarre really. I was being friendly, asking him where he was from because I recognised his accent and . . . well I'd only just got over the shock of seeing you again. And then a perfect stranger asks me whether I know you? Spooky eh? He made me shiver.'

'D'yer mean him with the stick?'

'He wasn't exactly friendly either. Just over his denial phase I suspect. It's quite common. They go straight into the angry phase after they've come to terms with the loss. Our Toby was the same.'

'What are you talkin' about? Angry? In what way?'

'I asked him to sit at one of the taller tables, so he could keep his leg out of the path of the waiters. It was sticking out, causing an obstruction. He just snarled at me. On the tall tables no-one would have noticed his bloody leg. I thought I was doing him a favour.'

'What did yer tell him when he asked about me?'

'Nothing. I could tell he was trouble. I told him I'd never even heard of you. You'd gone by then so . . . who is he anyway? Are you in some kind of trouble?'

'What?' He stood up and over the balcony.

'Are you in some kind of trouble?'

He turned his back to the sun, raised his sunglasses to his hair and stared into his flat, his eyes scanning the room and resting on her bags. 'You come into some money then?'

'No. Not exactly.'

'Well you must 'ave robbed a bank for that lot?' She looked down at her food but too suddenly. She tried to soften the effect by moving slices of tomato round the plate. 'So what's the story then? Come on, Wheezy, there's always a story.'

'No story.'

She stood up, leant over the balcony and looked to the right, as if to check there was no-one there. The old lady next door never sat out, not since Jonathan had been there. She moved to the left and leant right over to get a view up the avenida, giving him a perfect view up hers.

'So what you up to then? Have you bought yer ticket home yet?'

'Not yet. There's my ticket home.' She pointed to her bags.

'What?'

'I'll be alright.'

'Oh yeah?'

'I'm working. I'll be alright. I'm at Clouds now. It's great for tips.' She smiled him the old baby smile.

If she'd raised the money for a ticket, why blow it? Why not buy her ticket and then blow the rest of her wages? He looked up at her with this question on his lips but before he could ask it, she turned round, leant over the balcony and looked to the ground, her leg between two bars going back and forth, back and forth, banging herself. Hurting herself.

'Tips enough to get yerself a room and some fancy clobber *and* a ticket home to England?'

'Only a cheap room. I was going to try that Mavver's place.'

She sat down and attacked her tomato and bread as if, after all that hard work, she deserved it.

'Yer can stay here for a bit if yer like, Wheezy.'

'Have you got any mayonnaise?'

'No.'

There was so much of them on the balcony. A table full of plates and glasses, a chair, her bag, her, him. And out there, the sea and the people. Yet his eyes couldn't leave her, the fall of her hair, her little fingers, the tautness of her thigh, the muscle in it. She sat up. Found her bag and rummaged around till she brought out a packet of fags, a lump of draw and a tube of suncream. She set about building a spliff, her eyes lidded. He loved her with her eyes lidded. Hated her smoking her doobies, as she called them. Hated the word. Hated the people that had given her the word. She'd not changed at all. She was still riding skid row, treading water till it was time to get real. Still on the spliff. Still on her holidays. Still going to college.

It was a silent spliff. He looked at the glare on the sea and, without wanting to, his eyes kept wandering back to her. He couldn't stop it. She drew diagrams on her knee with her fingernail. She was letting out her scent and it was stifling them both. Speech. Movement. Normal behaviour. She wouldn't look him in the eye. Still eyes lidded, but sunglasses in her hair. Jonathan found a man with one leg setting off for a swim on his crutches. Then back to her knees and down her thin leg to her feet, still in sandals. If she hadn't been there, he would have gone for the binoculars for to see how fast a one-legged man can swim. How could he make his move across the table? Across the land of the balcony. Be still. Wait till the void needed filling. Till the mix of his memory took the thrill too high. Beyond the sea, holidaymakers, sky. Till he could hang on no more.

He reached to take her hand. She stood. Wiped sweat from her hairline and then followed him, into the bedroom. In there, the breath of cold air that braced them, raced them into a clammy clench, body to body, hot and salty. He felt her intake of breath from his chest, as if she'd been holding it since their last. They were suckered together, they moved together. She nuzzled under his arms, her hair soft and feathery in his sweaty fingers, light as the air itself. He undressed her. A hook he removed from its eye. Her shiny cream silk handkerchief top he took away from her breasts, sweaty breasts clinging for their cover. White striped breasts. Breasts white stripe. Tribal. Tribal eyes striped in white paint surprise. She stood there. He never touched but walked round her to sit on the edge of the bed which was so low down he looked up at her now. So tight and so ready, he stood up to lose his shorts and, while he kicked off, she turned around, slow, like a spinning top, waiting for play to begin. And just like a child, she spun to him. Quietly and breathless. Near-naked Louise climbing up on him, her legs smooth up, down, between, right in there and wrapped right round him. They locked necks together, necking swans till he could stand it no more. He found her mouth and planted his tongue inside it, his lips like a baby's hand gripping her lips to never let go, sealing them both together again. His sense of attachment was ferocious and forbidding and unstoppable. His chin already sore from the dribbling, he at last pulled away in a kind of shock at himself, at her, at the ease of her. The strength of her. He felt safe. At last he felt safe. She knew him. She hadn't know him back then, not the first time. But now she knew him. He was astonished. It was like there'd never been a first time after all.

Back down on the bed, he brought her down to him. Just her breasts. She tried to fight this, to claim him with her arms but he wouldn't let her. Just this he wanted, and for the rest, she could do what she liked, he would do what she liked. But he had to have this. He did not want her tentacles yet. Her laying on of suckers. He wanted nothing but her twin white lamps turned on, his hands holding firm the brown wall of her form. Attached by nipple. Feeding. He felt her give in and ooze out. Free. And keyed up for the maximum thrill of her, he dared down with her zip and brought her down flat on the bed, her smell coming at him like a guff of fresh rice pudding. He pulled off her shorts and threw them, the metal button tinging the tile for the start of the performance. The sight of her nakedness, immediate and final. No pants. White stripe. Down hair down there, sad and strokable. A river of hot blood ran right up his spine as he took in the whole face of her body now complete. The mouth of her legs wide open, waiting for him, her eyes in ecstatic glances to the ceiling. And he gave to that mouth all he had given to her other. Her body moving to a flow he hadn't yet set free. She never used to do this. That. Be free as that.

She cried out with the force of an engine starting, starting and re-starting, the rush of fuel moving her bit by bit, her whole body yielding. He felt the suck of her mini-contractions rise up to full bleed and then die. And so he played her again and again, fascinated by the piston movement, the overflow of juice coming away from her. And the spasms that tigered her face to a wrench of pleasure, a pleasure that hadn't ever been there before. An ugly pleasure of mouth wide open and teeth showing. This was Wheezy for real. Her legs wrestling him like a puppy. He was ready to climb on now.

'Wait,' and he dived for his condoms, hoping the moment would stay, was real, would last. He was gasping fast but short. Getting shorter each second he delayed. She rose up for his mouth and he fumbled. She touched him and he fumbled. He pushed her off and he fumbled until, at last, he got the damned thing in. He turned her over and straddled her like the claws of a pick-up, and he worked his pleasure at once, her head in an armlock, his climax a wild yell of pleasure, felling them both to the bed in a heap.

They rolled into a cuddle and rested. Till she started again, a smile on her face tracing pleasure routes missing from his memory. And on him now, over him, giving top and bottom and slap slap together again, their suckered clammy bodies all over again. His exhaustion delicious again.

Before leaving the bed she kissed him on his neck gently and spoilt it all. 'Happy Birthday,' she said, like she'd given him something. Some thing.

She sat cross-ankled on the floor of the shower letting the water sprinkle and splash her whole, her nose running free drips to her lips, her squeaky-skinned legs fresh and just how he wanted her. He got in. Pressed his hand under her jaw and brought her to the right height, the skin on her chin tight and shiny, squeaky against his legs. She needed no more directions. No talking. Just silence and spray and them moving together. A team of two strangers again, giving their knowledge away. He leant against the wall, face to the nozzle, and waited for one more. And then she was gone.

Wrung-out pants, three pairs on the sink. Bra hanging from the taps. Dry. Bright white. New. Must have been. Toothpaste, deodorant and a tube of Spanish womanness, on the mirror shelf. The domestic in him was at first warm and homely to this. But then cold. For Wheezy was back in his life again. He sat on the floor of the shower, knees together and in at his chin. Thinking. He stroked the tickle of the shower spray from his nose and then laid his head bare to it. He didn't know how to be with her now, she was different, more in control. She was real. And strange. She was the best company he'd kept in a long while but he still felt lonely. Somehow, without meaning to, he'd mastered the art of existing in complete alienation. He didn't know how to deal with this. He didn't know how to be with her.

Drying himself, he shivered. Remembering her all over again, from the first to the last. The spliff wearing off. He heard her cough. And then a bang on the door. His gut tightened.

'There's someone at the door,' she shouted.

Glad of the coolness of the damp towel, he wiped his brow, covered himself and entered the fray.

Chapter Nine

In the lounge-cum-kitchen, she shivered wet in her towel, her hair wet grass on her neck, hard and spiteful. She dressed just in from the balcony, in a radiator of warm sunlight. She was exhausted. And worried. Her little experiment had worked out rather too well.

Up until then, Louise was sure that all men wanted women with their mouths shut. Jaws closed tight. Legs wide open. Arms dangling. How many times had she done it with her mouth shut? Eyes shut. Never say never again. How many times in Marbella? Four? Five? And for what? For money now. And why not? The work was neither glamorous nor dangerous. The men were neither glamorous nor dangerous. They'd treated her as a girlfriend and paid for this fantasy of familiarity with enough credit card cash to deserve her.

She laid out her new clothes on the black imitation leather chair. The tissue paper, clean and silky, she folded and returned to the bags, still crease-free.

Before today, she'd been deluded. She'd thought she preferred to be 'taken'. She'd thought the 'being taken', the need to submit, the silence of the screw, the force . . . she'd thought all that the very proof of man's inability to express love, tenderness, open-hearted sincerity. This time she had not been taken. Or bought. Or silenced. She had not been forced by him and she had not forced it on herself.

For the first time ever, she had taken. *She* had taken Jonathan and, at last, it felt rather like being on holiday. A giving up of herself to the unknown. Yielding to the pleasure, she'd put herself in the hands of a man who had no qualms, all the right equipment and was master of the art. With him, she could relax, take and let it all roll over. No-one else had ever come that close. Not even him, first time round. This time round, she had not been taken. Only a whore would ever really know the difference of course.

When Jonathan had made love in the old days, he'd expected nothing from her but the act itself. It was him who controlled her. Him who decided if, when and where and, all that time, she'd felt it her duty to comply. She hated the word duty but that's what it was. To have said no would have introduced the idea of something wrong in the relationship, the relationship such a chain of a word back then. A chain that had to be hung on to, for it was writ large that that's what relationships were for. When there's nothing wrong and the boat is out at sea, why rock it? Why withhold the sex? The silent words of sex were still new to her back then, unheard, drowned out by the banging, demanding, shouting needs of any man who came after her. She wondered then, and she still did wonder, what kind of magic or curse it was that could turn a woman dumb – to a package that must be filled – a tube of flesh labelled 'use both ends'?

Crisp and clean, in her new skirt and top, she sprang on to the balcony into sunshine that nearly took her head off, the attack strong enough to have her raise her arms in combat. After a wet windowless bathroom blowing mould air from the shower, she felt like overdoing all things bright and dry and this play with the sun was just a small celebration of her good fortune. Such play in public cannot last long and so she adjusted herself, leant on the metal rail of the balcony and scorched her arms. She stood back and still and searched the beach with eyes now accustomed but feeling naked without her sunglasses on.

There were people streaming on to the beach from all directions, wearing more clothes than even winter would demand. Hats and shoes and coats and glasses and towels and cool boxes and spades and ghettoblasters and anything to make the going hard, anything to make a *home*. Once sat down and surrounded, fenced and neighboured on all sides, they stripped and waited. Appeared to be waiting for something coming in from the sea. Or waiting to be shot perhaps, each umbrella a target for such potentials. The noise was low-key, as if all in on this secret. She felt a touch dizzy, privileged, a cut above, at home. Completely relaxed. Framed and trapped in a test tube, the Bunsen-burner sun blared and fixed her into a life that was looking up for a minute. She leant over the balcony, not touching. There was quite a drop.

He'd changed a lot and so had she. He'd lost something. Something of his edge. Oh sure, he was good. Very good. He did and always had done macho like he meant it. But he seemed less solid now. Flying out of his own atmosphere, he'd lost some muscle, substance, control. He'd lost his once complete and utter confidence in his right to take her. It had been her choice. Her right. He hadn't paid her or made her. The trade, for once, had been equal.

She knew very little about his life out here and guessed there was little to know. A drifter on the take in the Costas. There were so many of them. Men and women. Women for the taking. But Jonathan, as hard as he tried and as hard as he tried to be, had never come across as a risk-taker, law-breaker, the sort to take liberties with anyone but a woman. He was naturally and sometimes reluctantly giving. Generous. And proud. Without anything to be proud of, he was proud of himself. An achievement in anyone's book but desperately so in his, a man from nowhere with nowhere to go. He was different from the other yobs taking their extended holidays out of reach of the British justice system. He wasn't artful enough for a dodger, not committed enough either to inflict serious damage, or receive wholeheartedly the idea or possibility of any real joy in life. Nothing had been instilled in him and he could instil nothing back. And this is why she'd felt free enough to take him to the edge, to show him that there *was* more. She knew first-hand that feeling of loss. Of looking. She had been there herself. Today the white creases on the sea were talking to her, ushering in a sense of new possibility, of freedom. Yesterday they'd been the ticking clock of the eternally banal, the constant reminder that the nonsense of life was far stronger than its truth. What she had gained, he had lost. He now wore her facility for frost. He was keeping the glass of his eye reflecting out. He thought he was playing the mystery man but he was a mystery only to himself.

Was she growing up now? Was this it? She was blowing up. A strong breeze blew her skirt to a bell. She turned to see if Jonathan

127

was out of the bathroom. It felt like someone had been watching her. No. There was no-one there. She sat on the cane chair and raised her foot to rest it on her thigh. She looked at the devastation on the sole, great chunks of skin missing and in parts so deep there were scabs, soft scabs now after the shower. On the balls of her feet, great white flaps of skin hung loose or were bubbled into a blister. She began the pick. She picked one end of a flap and pulled, carefully, as one pulls wallpaper from the wall, a desire and a need to pull off the whole sheet. From the side of her foot up towards the toes, the flap widening as she pulled, the skin getting thicker as she pulled it away until the sting that warned of immediate blood. And then she stopped. And began again from the heel. Most picks came to nothing. But the best, the thickest, she pulled to the sting. And then she began on the other foot.

She was gaining some perspective now. The world was this big. The beach that long. The sun this bright. The pain that keen. The sex that good. The sex, that expensive. She dabbed at the open wound with the heel of her hand to stop it bleeding. The skin from her feet, curled up into rolls, sat in a pile on the mottled black and white marble floor of the balcony. Like sharings after planing a tree. A pile of her flesh all away from her now. With her feet, she pushed the pile forwards and off the balcony. She then stood up and looked to see if it landed in hair.

Had a thunderbolt from God struck her down yet? Was the selling of flesh such a mortal sin, on par with rape, theft, burglary, murder, blatant and wholesale dishonesty? No. No. No. It was as natural as shopping. No. It was as insidious as shopping, the cost destroying the value as soon as the money changed hands. In Marbella she'd sold herself because she didn't have a passport, a plane ticket, clothes to wear, a place to sleep or any desire to go home very quickly. Because she was an easy thing to sell. She would have gone out for dinner with Marcelle free of charge. Back to his place, free of charge. He was paying for what she normally gave away. Mamoud had paid for his pleasure and been honest about it. Instinct had told her she was wrong to bed down with men she didn't much care for. And now she knew why. It *was* wrong. It was absurd. Ridiculous.

Why should they have her free of charge?

The sun went behind a cloud and, immediately, she was alert to herself. To why she was who she was and where she was. To go home was to go home to Toby. Her big brother Toby. Home *was* Toby. The source of all she had become and run away from. Older than her, he'd fought for it all and all for himself, and because she had legs, she could not complain. Born thalidomide, Toby had taken all of her parents' attention, adulation and unconditional love. They'd fought for him every step of the way. So now he had funds, hard-won compensation for the catastrophe of his birth. He had work. He had recognition. He had every reason to feel sorry for himself. But she had legs. He always said, 'I got the brains and you got the legs.' But there wasn't *any* compensation for legs. Only shock horror they hadn't done her much good. She'd gone to university, but then nothing less was expected of her. Studying economics, she soon realised she was studying herself into oblivion, into a two-bit accountancy firm, into middle management at the local bank. And she stretched her arms up high then. As if on cue the sun came out and the music from the beach rushed up at her. As if the sea itself was trying to get at her.

The beach bar below erupted. A gang of girls was dancing in the sand. Louise threw a few steps of her own on the balcony. And then got into it, stretching her legs wide, remembering her ballet moves, the balance, the teasing of Toby as a child, as he lay there, immobile on the sheepskin rug in the lounge. She danced her tease on tiptoes, on tiptoes he didn't have. And then Cyndi Lauper, 'Girls Just Wanna Have Fun'. Cyndi Lauper, 'Time after Time'. Cyndi Lauper, 'Money Changes Everything'. And she could dance no more now, anyway.

She thought she recognised somebody down at Papa's beach bar. The man who had taken Pippa to Tangiers on his boat. She was sure it was him. His long white hair was unmistakable. And then she remembered seeing a box in the bedroom that held the promise of some binoculars. She went to look for it. On the way there, she was stunned still by someone banging on the front door.

'There's someone at the door,' she shouted.

He came out of the bathroom angry, in his towel. When he saw her, all crisp and fresh, his anger let go and he smiled. They stood and stared their first post-coital stare in the hall, in a pause, and then the banging started up again. He answered it. It was Jason, the dwarf. A stain of a man.

'Do you have to make such a racket?'

'I wasn't sure you were in. I've come to do the doors an' give yer some fliers. What's she doin' here? Or need I ask.'

He walked in and tried to stand quite close to her. She moved quickly away and over towards the balcony. All at once, her sense of safety, security, gone. Not just gone. Bombed out of existence. What had been a private space, a collection of furniture not worthy of calculation, was now, as she walked through it, a perfect picture of a vile and inadequate low life. Insanely, she had considered herself privileged, watching the people on the beach staring up at the apartments. Now, the ugliness that had hardly been there hemmed her in. The grotesque little dwarf had even brought with him tools and drills and everything one could ever need to make the physical environment so very real and fixed. She was surrounded by squalor. On the balcony she felt the slap of the sun laugh at her. She took a deep breath and tried to ground herself. She heard Jason move up behind her. And then the phone rang.

'I didn't know I had a fuckin' phone. Where is it?'

'Bedroom,' yelled Jason, a big noise in her ear, the missing karma she'd laughed away so easily, just minutes ago, now in cheap-perfume nose zone. 'On top of the wardrobe,' he shouted, the phone still drilling through the emptiness of the apartment that now looked not dissimilar to a council flat she'd once gone to, for a party. The furniture plastic, the tables glass, the cabinets and kitchen cupboards designed for an early death.

'What are you doing here, Jason?' she said quietly.

'I'll tell you why I'm 'ere, darlin'.' Loud and clear. He was stood to the side of her now, sharing her view. 'I'm the landlord. Is that OK with you?' He spoke in a squeaky voice, slowly and devoid of any accent, as if he'd developed and designed his tone to cause maximum irritation. A Birmingham sort of voice that begs not to be encouraged.

Jonathan came through looking for a pen and saw them standing close to each other, his hackles immediately alert. She turned an apologetic smile. He didn't smile back. He searched a drawer in the kitchen, found a pen and slammed the drawer shut. And again, before walking out of the room, he looked at her suspiciously. The game would soon be up and so soon.

'Didn't take you long to get yer feet under the table I see.' Jason eyed her with a blatant leer.

'I came for breakfast if you must know,' she said, leaning over the balcony, letting the metal scorch her, brand her.

'And such a fast worker,' he said. She turned. He nodded towards a wet towel on the floor.

'Oh please.' And she turned back to face the sea.

'I take it you've not told him . . .'

'And I don't intend to.'

She could hear Jonathan in the other room, sounding angry. 'I'll ring yer right back,' he shouted. 'Yeah, I'll get everything in one go.'

Jason stood close to her now, stroking his stubbled chin. His nails were neat if a trifle too long, his hands small. Next to her, he stood smaller by an inch, maybe two. 'I'm glad I caught you, actually. I see you've left the boat.' She said nothing, her face intent on the sea, her eyes following the mindless path of a jet-ski. He said, 'It's on again for tonight. Same place as last night but early. Marcelle's got business later on.'

'It's over, Jason. I've finished.'

'They've upped the ante on that film offer. You'd be laughing all the way if yer wanted.'

'Jason, I don't think so . . .'

It hadn't been like this. Dirty, seedy, underhand. Off-hand. It had been civilised. An arrangement. Unremarkable really. And it had started innocently enough. After her room had been broken into, she'd gone to the police to report it. Jason had been stood outside, waiting for a taxi. Instead, he waited for her. He recognised her from the beach and she him and she needed all the help she could get. Pippa had gone. He could, he said, get her a job, preparing lunches for the boat trips down Puerto Banus. And a boat to sleep on. A little cramped but better than nothing. But she wasn't a fast enough worker. The lunches were always too late. So she tried barwork. But she wasn't a fast enough worker. So they sent her over to Clouds. She could be a hostess. Not the air hostess of her childhood dreaming, a sex hostess with the mostest. And Jason was the facilitator – his word.

Louise had always imagined the pimp of a high-class whore in a suit and tie, dealing with the business of entertainment matters with confidence, panache, authority. Jason's approach was more that of a thief in a bank wearing the regulation balaclava. On the day of the first night, wearing mascara and a waistcoat and thoroughly Adam Ant, he'd taken her to Oscar's, a rival establishment to Clouds. Oscar's had been running for some time and, with the advantage of age, was far more successful. She thought he'd taken her there to show her off but no. She was to watch the girls, how they sat, talked, walked and how long they stayed with a client before discreetly making an exit. And then how long it took before the same girl returned and waited for her next customer. He explained that the turnover in Clouds was not so fast even though the fees were half the price. However, the clients usually booked for at least a couple of hours. And every client was investigated for safety reasons. She could have two clients a day and make two hundred pounds, instant cash. He gave her a dress. Toiletries. Shoes to wear. And the one strict rule of the house. On no account must she sit in the bar, holding, actually holding, a cigarette.

She'd seen so little of him, she'd not minded his grubbiness and snidiness. The other girls hardly spoke to him. Or to her. When a customer came through the door, she was always first. So she'd never really got the chance to talk to anyone. In the mornings, he would shout to her on the boat, 'One o'clock start. Don't be late.' As though she belonged to him. She'd only been at it for three days but it felt like a month. It was enough already. No more. Now she minded his grubbiness and snidiness. Now, stood next to him in Jonathan's flat, she'd gone off the whole idea of it. He was the final exclamation mark.

'An' I'll 'ave that pink dress back I lent yer. I can see yer bin shopping. Go a bit mad did yer?' He looked over to her bags, generously strung carrier bags with logos indicating quality. She sneered at him. He grinned teeth yellow with tobacco stain. It was inconceiveable he could ever pass for a woman, his mouth a disaster area. She remembered her first impression, when she'd seen him from a distance on the beach, before she'd had to be grateful to him. He'd been clowning about with Chas, playing glockenspiel on some glasses at the bar. He must have found a tune he could play straight off because he jumped from his stool so he could play it again and laugh properly. She'd been walking towards the bar for some time and, when she arrived, he was still jumping about laughing, tittering insanely. And when he turned round, his white pale chest had startled her and his yellow teeth against a raw red chin had disgusted her. It was the dribble chin of a baby but with a nasty inside to the mouth. He was, in animal speak, a Jack Russell on the loose gone bad. That had been her first impression. He had a skin problem. Had to use factor 20 or something or other, to prevent his skin breaking out into scabs. As for dressing up as a woman . . . he had too much menace about him. Stubble. A moustache. He'd be certified in England just for dreaming the idea up.

'Take it then. It's there, in the bag,' she said.

'Clean?'

'No.'

'Well I wannit back clean.'

'Fine.'

'Yer can drop it into Clouds tonight. Maybe by then you'll 'ave changed yer mind.'

'I won't.'

'It's your shout,' he said. 'But somat tells me you'll be back. They always are. Unless you're goin' home already?'

'Just leave me alone, Jason, OK? It's over.'

The ding of the phone alerted her to move even further away from him. Jonathan returned crumpling paper in his hand. Jason went to the bathroom. Jonathan looked after him in disgust and then turned to Louise with a question on his face. She looked towards the bathroom and sneered.

'You can get all that crap out the bathroom,' he said. Like he'd never been anywhere near her.

He went to the bedroom. Then came back to the lounge. He tightened the towel round his waist again. Body smooth, rich, honeyish. There was a redness, an autumn redness to him, a burnt-leaf glaze across his shoulders. 'Did you 'ear me?' he said. She unglazed her eyes and said,

'What's wrong? Is it him?'

He found some bags behind the leather seat, bags he hadn't unpacked yet. He bent down to one, found shorts and a T-shirt and zipped it back up again. She watched his every move, sat down now, her knees up, hugging her chest, expecting any minute an onslaught.

'I'll make a cup of tea,' said Jason, out of the bathroom.

Jonathan dropped his towel and displayed. She didn't look away. Instead, took some mental photos to browse through later on. For when it was all over. Like hers, his body had something separate about it. He was in control of its muscle, sure, but he had no say in the way it fell on the eye, its possibilities. More defiantly than she ever dared examine her own body, her eyes were all over him with a hunger. Hugging her knees, she rocked herself back and forth and caught the angry glare he threw at her. He knew already perhaps.

She preferred his paler parts, the honeyed coffee of his buttocks and around his . . . the darkness of his centre. There was usually something of the horror movie about a penis but not his. His actually looked like it belonged there. He unfolded his T-shirt and found the armholes. She looked to the shiny posts of his legs and felt calmed by the joyful play of curly hair all over them. And then to his arms and shiny shoulders . . . when his head pushed through the T-shirt, she looked at his face and he at hers. No. He looked past hers. In him, she saw the face of his past, an undisturbed boyhood. She saw the eyes of a child, almost hunting eyes, trying to see what couldn't be seen. A quiver of fear in there too perhaps.

He pulled on his shorts, watching her, then watching Jason wash glasses. Show over, she turned now to look at the sea. Gave him the back of her neck and her hair piled high on her head with grips in, pick-up-stick-style, holding it all together. She felt him come closer. He grabbed at her neck, like she was an enemy. He twisted her head round and kissed it. Felt almost like a warning. And there was Jason watching them.

'So that was Geoff on the phone was it?'

'Yer know it was.'

Jason nodded his head towards Louise, calling for her exit it looked like.

If only Pippa had still been around. If only she had somewhere to go, someone to talk things through with. She wanted to blame Pippa for the mess she was in but she couldn't. And telling Jason she'd packed it all in had been premature to say the least. Well, if she didn't ring home with an SOS it was, and she was unlikely to do that. She could do without the parental interrogations and the rest of the summer paying the price for evading them. What a mess. The walls of the room came at her with a clout then. She was now trapped in squalor.

She gathered up her bags as if to leave. Jason walked to the door and began tampering with the lock. Jonathan rubbed cream into his hands and gave himself a body rub. He looked nervous.

'Louise?'

She was packed and ready to go.

'What?'

'Where yer goin'?'

'I told you before. To find myself a room.'

She looked first to Jason and then back at Jonathan. Then back to Jason who was plugging his drill into the wall.

Jonathan said quietly, 'Would you do us a favour?'

'What?'

'Could you nip to the shops for us?'

'I was . . .'

'Please? You can book yerself in somewhere later on, no?'

The problem: he'd think her twice the slut she was if she went and didn't come back. But a shameless slut if and when she did. She dropped all her bags except one and stood waiting for his money, with her hand out.

'What do you want?' she said

'Get some grub,' said Jonathan, digging into a pair of soiled jeans for notes. Not smiling. Not happy. She didn't look up at him. She walked out of the flat with head down. When Jason closed the door behind her, she took a deep breath and ran down the stairs, fast, banging the sorest parts of her feet down first.

Perhaps Jason wouldn't tell. But if he did then now was the time to plan carefully. First and foremost, she'd need a room. And a job. Now she had experience, now she knew what to expect from men that paid, she could work anywhere. There were escort agencies all over. But they'd be closed now. Once on the books, she'd have enough for a flight in two days. Maybe, just maybe, Jonathan would want to rescue her? Did men still do rescuing? Would he be gallant or mad at her? What sort of sob story would get him to go gallant? She wanted to go home now. She was in a no-win situation again.

She fell out on to the flank of the pavements that led to the beach one way, the esplanade the other. The sun bolded her yellow skirt to summer, frank and simple. In the mirror of the shop window, she saw herself stunning the passers-by, the men walking backwards in a stare. Like a bitch mated, she kicked high before breaking into a near run. Her arms swung high, her head even higher. The sun anointed her. And she could not but wonder at this spontaneous flush of happiness. Lightheartedness. The thought of going home? Of finally deciding? Or was it afterglow?

The rows of palm trees and lines of benches guarded by snap-shotting tourists with too many kids were the omens she needed to keep moving in the right direction. She sat on a bench just in sight of

Jonathan's block, the sea concealed by the raised concrete walk-ways. For a while she could sit and rest, be alone and just watch. But soon, next to her, a grandmother sharing an ice cream with a baby in a pushchair. There was something odd about it. The child. About eighteen months but with the head of a teenager. She closed her eyes. Could watch better with her eyes closed, behind glasses, a breeze of sun oil under her nose, the chatter about her like wake-up birds in the garden. She sat in a daze, eyes open from time to time, the people moving around in a haze. The sun was getting through, boiling her up, when all of a sudden dark. She sat up startled, lifted her glasses and, in her light, the man with the stick and no shirt, a medallion an athlete could be proud of and so much hair on his chest, the tattoos were almost not there.

'Oh, it's you.'

He said nothing, sat down next to her and rested his chin on his stick, a pale wooden stick capped with silver, both ends. With the sunlight back she pulled down her shades 'You're a very beautiful woman you know?'

'Yes, it has been brought to my attention.' She sat up. Looked down at his feet to identify the pretender and a rush of sympathy charged her. He had socks on. He must have been the only man in the Costa del Sol with socks on. And new training shoes, bright white, no label so specially made no doubt. The laces were tied like birthday bows. And bright white trousers starched with a crease to slice bread. Was he blind as well? Could he not see that all this 'new' only emphasised his deformity. She'd noticed this trend at her brother's day school. She felt there was something perverse about broken bodies dressed good as new. Here was an outwardly confid-ent good-looking man with a leg missing, reduced to the clumsiness and fashion sense of a middle-aged ditherer.

'So I'm not the first to notice then?' he said.

'You're quite right. You're not the first.'

'D' yer fancy a drink?'

'I don't actually, no.'

'I was 'opin' you'd walk over to Papa's with me.'

'Sorry. I've got some shopping to do.'

'Shopping eh? Shall I come with yer? Help yer carry yer stuff like?'

'I think not.' She stood up and, in her head, heard the terseness of her words played back to her. 'Listen. I'm sorry,' she said. 'I've got to go now. Have a nice holiday though won't you?' She patted his hand, to let him know that, stick aside, she just wasn't interested.

She was conscious enough now to walk away slowly. She'd been taught to walk slowly among the old and infirm as a sign of respect. At home, she did it quite naturally, even in a hurry. As soon as she neared a struggling figure, she slowed as she passed. As the cars slow for horses. And then a few yards past, she'd speed up again. She did it for the man still sat on the bench making a determined effort not to watch her walk away, still resting his head on his stick, staring at the ground. She moved off slowly as if still in his world and, as the distance between them increased, so did her pace. And then around a corner and gone.

A real spring in her step now and she wondered why. Why the sores didn't feel so sore any more. Was she that glad to have legs? Or was it Jonathan? Or was she forcing her mind into bright corners only. Forcing herself to think positively. Considering her chances of an even marginally successful outcome, she had no reason to be springing the pavements like a child. She slowed to thinking more rationally. Jason had arrived on the scene for a purpose of course. To put a stop to it all. Just the sight of him next to Jonathan had been enough to shake her into saying no. She could go back to normal now. Not go to the escort agency. Ask Jonathan or ring home for a loan. Grow up, for Christ's sake. And with these thoughts, the sun stayed with her, gentle on her neck, with the sea breeze. She was on holiday again now. The end of her holiday. The adventure over, the taste of it to savour for years to come.

These were the moments she liked, what she'd imagined of her holiday. What it was like before Pippa had gone. She liked walking the streets, free and easy, at one with her cosmopolitan counterparts, beach lovers, shoppers, the shrewd rich, the ambitious youth. And the sense of camaraderie here in Marbella was so much more fun, more comfortable than Banus. They were too secretive in Puerto Banus, too quiet with their money, too loud with their wealth. On Marbella streets, the fun was straightforward and honest in its falseness. Happy holidaymakers with miserable children carrying too many toys. Young men in pools of twinkling sunglasses and smiles, loiterers anywhere else but on holiday. Even the smells here, of fry and sun oil, Estée Lauder and leather, salt and sea and exhaust fume – all within her range, reach, grasp. All contrived and contained like a ship in a bottle.

The ground beneath her feet felt hot, strong, supportive, flat and talking back to her, as each foot pounded the soreness of her soles away. As if the ground was laid down just for her, to heal her. Her head was gushing. She was back to childhood almost, recognising the apparent simplicity of life, the certainty. Her future was spread out like a well laid table. The courses served – all surprises. The bill always paid. All will be well and always will be.

'Lady, lady.' She turned round and the man was already upon her. A small shiny black man, with bare chest and a pad of art paper. Animal teeth around his neck. 'Lady. Let me draw you, see . . .' he said, showing her his work.

She walked off. Didn't smile. Didn't say anything. 'Don't get involved with the Africans,' she'd be warned. So Louise ignored them. Every time. She turned slightly to see if he was still following her but he was advancing upon some other victim, not as successful in deterring him. Would Laura give her some work without going through Jason? she wondered. Just for a couple of days?

Crossing the road, she heard another shout. Swinging fast in a dance she spotted the caller.

She waved quickly and then walked on. She couldn't place him. He ran along his side of the road till he was in front of her, was sure it was her and then crossed over.

As he approached he looked her up and down and landed back on her face just in time to start a conversation. Even then he was more interested in her form than in what she had to say, checking out her earrings, the side of her neck, her chin even, before he finally made eye contact.

''Ow's it goin'?'

'Fine. Do I know you?'

'I'm Jack. Johnno's mate. Do yer know where he is?'

'Yes, he's staying up at the front.' She pointed.

'You not down Joe's Shed any more? Me an' the lads 'ave bin missin' yer.'

'They sacked me. Two nights I lasted. Couldn't get the hang of the pints or the money. Not quick enough, I'm afraid.' Realising this would lead to more questions, she added, 'I'm doing a little PR work for some of the hotels now. Drumming up business for the golf courses and such like. Did you want to give Jonathan a message?'

'So yer stayin' in Marbella then?' She could see him making plans for her, on his toes. Hanging on her every word now. Head to one side. The way one listens to a child telling a story.

'Yes. I'm staying with Jonathan actually.'

'So you were his Wheezy after all?'

'You knew about me?'

He was looking away now up the avenida to the beach, his mind on to other things. 'Tell him he's got post back at Mavver's. And I've got his money for him, tell him. He'll need to be quick coz I'm off back to England in a minute.'

'You're going home?' Forgetting herself, she moved closer to him, closer to the sound of the word home. And then remembering herself, she moved away. Calmed down.

'Just for a holiday. See me mam and that.' Then he grabbed her by the arm and pulled her on to the side of the road with him, keeping her close in, away from the cars, like a child. Behind her, a pavement-wide family, handicapped by bags, balls, blow up beds and push-chairs. And a string of real children.

'I'll give it to him . . . the money,' she said.

He looked at her differently then. 'It's a fair amount,' he said.

'Yes?' she said. 'I'll pick up his mail for him too if you like.' And there it was. The split personality of a man deluded. As they all were deluded. He had treated her as a child until the very minute that money was mentioned. In five seconds flat, she'd turned into a scheming hag.

'Right then,' he said, still and very obviously doubtful.

'Well if you think I'm going to . . .'

'No, no, yer alright. I was just thinkin' that's all.' He reached into his pocket all the time looking over her shoulder thinking. He pulled out a wad of notes, counted some out and handed them over. 'He's a jammy bastard tell him.'

After he counted each bundle, she took it and dug it deep in her bag. Nearly three hundred pounds of it. A lot of pesetas. 'I will,' she said. 'What's your name again?'

'Jack,' he said, more doubtful than ever now.

Before she could skeddaddle off, he reminded her about the letter. She walked with him, up into the Old Town, to Mavver's. She waited for him in the hallway. The smell was repulsive, stale grease and beer and smoke. Within minutes, she was treated to a display of vile vituperation – that's how her mother enjoyed describing such outbursts. It was the young Cockney girl, wench really. She was working at the Shed the night Louise had been fired. The two of them had fought, Louise too slow a worker, too lazy a worker, too lah-di-dah all round. Initially, Louise had quite liked the girl. She was funny and, at first, a patient teacher. She'd shown her how to do heads on pints, pull a mix, shake a fancy cocktail on the cheap. She had *some* style in her dress and enough spirit to invite a degree of admiration but she was common and, at this moment, drunk, calling Louise a whore and being held vertical by two bare-chested men who were wearing far too much jewellery. The men didn't believe Louise was a whore but the drunken girl, rather keen to convince them of it, told them about the blue butterfly tattoo under her breast. Louise had shown it to the girl as a way of making friends, as evidence that *she* too had some spirit, and was not just some posh cow from Chalfont St Giles. That she was a rebel at heart.

Of course, she didn't react or respond to this outburst. Not outwardly. As she'd been taught, when faced with 'vile vituperation', the best plan of action was to cut the assailant dead. But the two men who she'd hoped would protect her, wanted to see her butterfly. 'Let's 'ave a butcher's then' was how they put it. Luckily Jack came down and rescued her. Told the men to 'button it' and the girl to sober up, which was good advice for that hour of the day. Then the famous Mavver appeared, a fairy-tale hag with a mouth like a sewer. She wanted Jonathan's address so she could forward any other mail that came. Louise explained where it was but couldn't give the number or a street name. She thanked her for the letter, told Jack to enjoy his holiday and then left. In a hurry. Looking up and down the street for a direct route, her eyes found a group of peasant children on their haunches, eating dirt from the gutter. Normally she took some perverse pleasure in watching peasant children, ragged, running free. But after such an encounter, the sight had a distinct touch of dread about it. There was fear in that street and in the eyes of the peasants, a fear she'd not understood until now.

She'd come full circle now. Listening to the mouth on that girl had brought her back to her senses. She had to get home. With Jonathan's money, she had enough to get home *and* buy presents. Her parents and Nana would, at the least, expect a present.

She walked quickly, away from the peasant streets, straight for the main roads of safety, the desire to get home now, real home, growing at an exponential rate with each stride. There was that African again, trying for her attention. She waved him away more aggressively this time. He shouted something to her. A profanity, she didn't wonder. She turned and mouthed him one of her own and, almost running now, she headed towards Aurelio's tourist office. Aurelio wasn't there. A young Spanish girl with no manners greeted her with 'You want?'

In part Spanish, Louise explained exactly what she wanted and the woman set about making a series of phone calls. Louise studied the brochures and hand-written adverts for rooms, villas, boat tours, yachts for rent. After some fifteen minutes of sitting down, just thinking, the Spanish girl broke out from behind the high desk. All flights to London were full. Holiday season. Full for eight days.

Should she book her in for next Friday? Unless she wanted to go by boat. There was a ferry leaving on Tuesday morning. The price? Breathtakingly expensive. Louise said she'd think about it. Perhaps fly to Bristol or Liverpool, the girl said.

After resting in the tourist office, her panic subsided. She could think more calmly now. To go by ferry, she'd have to endure the coach trip to the port. To go by plane, she'd have to keep a low profile for far too long. Perhaps go up to Malaga, get a duplicate passport and hang out. Leave now. Go back, get bags and leave. What did the girl say? Unless there was a cancellation. A stand by. The cancellations were more likely at night because people got drunk and missed their flight. Yes, she could do that. She could wait at the airport. Go back, have a Last Supper of a lecture from Jonathan and, in response to the onslaught, take the next bus to Malaga.

She sought out a fresh-food shop, vegetables and fruit as well as some fish and cooked meats. She bought all the ingredients for a paella, as inoffensive a dish she could imagine him agreeing to eat. It was that or omelette. And now, with the weight of a decent plan on her mind, she enjoyed the distraction, that fleeting housewife feel. The domestic mundanity. Vegetable ordinariness. The cake of mud under her fingernails. The string of skin on the onion, lengthy enough for a shoelace. The conspirational glances with the other women, turning up their noses at the dried and fly-ridden fish. She made her purchases well, the woman sufficiently surprised at her command of Spanish she threw in extra potatoes, extra potatoes she didn't much want.

Of course, everything was heavy now. Walking back to him and to what he'd have to say. The plastic shopping bags cutting into her fingers.

Chapter Ten

Third World weren't playing loud enough. The balcony doors were shut. On the balcony, Jonathan, ninety-six-degree sunshine blaring, shades on, leg across his thigh, lips cracking, foot tapping but not to the music, not to any rhythm. Every tap a knock-on thought to the next. Jason was indoors fixing locks on. Knocking.

'*Ninety-six degrees in the shade . . . Real hot . . . in the shaaa-aaade.*'

The only words he knew but he sang them with genuine conviction. He didn't sound too bad really, considering. Considering what? He could have been a singer. A Yellowman called Redman Roots jamming it up fine style. He couldn't quite get the Jamaican accent but his Yankee talk was just dandy. Was in his blood, see. *Born in the USA* now, coming up from the beach.

He could lick it up large with them all, given some practice, given the chance. Croon some Lovers with Carol Thompson on his knee, studio stylie. Sly and Robbie backing, bumping bass to beat the soul blood through. He could see himself with a hat, no, with headphones on, eyes closed, finger in his ear, flickering eyelids, smiling at the camera of his thoughts. But the reality was, he'd never have the balls. So why bother thinking on it then? Why squander so much of this valuable thinking time? Well why not? He was old enough to seriously consider his chances in the music business and then, having considered them, wise enough to knock it all on the head. That's all he was doing.

He wanted to get his binoculars out but didn't want twinkle toes to catch him unwrapping them, new. He went back inside to monitor Jason's progress. The hall floor was covered in tools and Jason's much too curly hair, in sawdust. He was bending down, lining up the door with the frame, a lake of sweat down the back of his short-sleeved stripes, his skinny little legs going in at the knees, like a girl's. The hallway cupboard with the mysterious padlock was now open, but not wide enough to see in. Again, he couldn't give in to what would look like childish curiosity. He went to the loo and sat for a while, listening to the knocking. Realised then she'd left all her underwear there. If she'd been serious about leaving, about getting a place, she wouldn't have forgotten her underwear. And how come Jason knew her? Was she one of his whores? They'd stood far too close together for anything less than a working relationship. And he was too thin and small to get a woman like her naturally. And besides, he was a weirdo. Living in Spain, he'd managed to keep his skin as white as a little old lady's. He had arms as thin and smooth as a new set of drumsticks. He was a self-confessed transvestite, but hadn't come out to be brave. No. Quite the opposite. Wearing women's clobber was pitched fairly low on the scale of depravity that is the backdrop of ex-pat life on the Costas and this, Geoff said, pissed Jason off no end. That, and being banned from dressing up when he was on wages. It was a matter of credibility, Chas said. It was Chas who'd forced him to wear a crayon of a moustache to put paid to *any* public display of his womanhood, wages or no wages. Jason, Geoff said, was a born attention-seeker.

Jonathan came out of the bathroom and closed the door, to keep the stench in and to stop any comments about her underwear. Jason was out on the landing fixing the locks on the other side. The music was loud enough to forbid talking. Johnno went into the bedroom to check on his money. To read the writing on his binoculars box. To widen the range of reasons he could come up with, which would bring a man like Jason and woman like Wheezy so close together like that.

With his moustache on, Jason came over like a real bona fide villain, the shell of his nut on the inside rather than the out. It was impossible to tell how hard he really was. His stunted growth and minimal body hair created an illusion of weakness but he was ugly enough and well connected enough to use this illusion to good effect. Had these villains known, as Jonathan knew, that Jason was just a dwarf without a dress, that Geoff was just an Aussie with a big mouth, that Chas was just an ex-car salesman with enough false jobs on his CV to deter the scrutiny of even the most cynical gangsters arriving daily to set up shop in the sun, then Chas's empire-building could have been stopped long ago by someone with no more guts than a girl. Chas had only employed Johnno to add muscle to his 'muscle' story. Johnno was big and black and without the wherewithal to threaten the empire of a two-bit drug dealer. He would not start fights and he would not take over any of the businesses, the timeshare, the whores, the boats. He was no threat to Chas but very possibly a threat to anyone who was. Essentially, Johnno would not beat the shit out of someone who had taken the trouble to give him a flat and a job and was the type of man not to arrange for someone else to do so. Geoff had sounded him out and Geoff had said he was sound. Jason must have fallen into the work in the exact same way but with him being so small, the trick worked backwards.

Jason was no villain and no stud. He ran errands for Chas all day, ran whores for Chas all night and ran up huge mobile telephone bills organising boat registrations for drug-dealers. He always got his hands dirty. Real villains did none of that. Real villains contained themselves. They lived behind electric fences and security cameras. They spent their mornings in bed and their afternoons laid out flat by their swimming pools, cleaning their fingernails. Johnno used to skim their pools for them. Run errands for them. Screw their wives whenever he could get away with it. Another career he didn't want to go back to.

Jason as landlord had been the price Johnno had had to pay for the luxury of a job and assured accommodation. He didn't want to get on with him and he didn't have to either. But without coming straight out with it, he'd never know for sure what Wheezy was up to, what she was all about. Not unless he asked. And he couldn't, no, wouldn't do that. If he asked her, she'd fall straight into the fallen woman routine and hold her hand out for a loan. And if he asked Jason, it would be admitting that he didn't know anything about the woman who'd filled his bathroom with her underwear.

He walked from the bedroom through the hall and back into the lounge. 'Zis bangin' gonna go on for much longer, Jason?' he shouted over the music.

'No. Nearly done now.'

'Yer gonna clear this lot up then?'

'In a minute.'

'What's in that cupboard there?'

'All me tools 'n' stuff. I've nowhere else safe to put them.'

With so many tools around, Jonathan got into a 'work' frame of mind himself and to thinking it was time to make some sense out of the kitchen. To make a start on it at least. Look busy at least. Mark it up ready for the new tile job. He could wash a few dishes and draw the tile plan out in his mind and he was doing just that when Jason emerged, shaking the sawdust out of his hair.

'Got a wench for washin' up 'aven't yer?' he said, smirking.

'You finished?' Jonathan wiped his hands on a brand-new tea-towel.

'They'll be sound now, yeah.' Walking away but insinuating Jonathan follow him. Reluctantly he did, only to see Jason riding the bolts back and forth, checking the keys on the padlock. Proud of his job like.

'Waste o' time if yer askin' me. The locks we had on were alright.'

'Not really.'

'What?' Even with the music blaring, little answers like 'not really' were loud and clear enough to warrant further investigation. 'What did you say?'

'Not really. All the locks needed sorting.'

'They did for what I want. What's the problem, Jason?'

'When they see all this . . .' He closed the door and went out. Then came back in again. 'When they see the padlock, it'll make 'em think twice. Breaking the place'll take twice as long and be ten times more risky. They just won't bother.'

'And who are *they* exactly?'

'The Africans.'

'Sorry?'

'They pay 'em to squat places like this.'

'What are you on about? Who pays 'em?'

'Happens all the time.'

'What does?' Shouting just as the music stopped.

'Timeshare mobs. They stick Africans in, to squat 'em up. The smelly ones. Everythin' bar the camel. Them lot. Know what I mean?'

'But I'm here now, Jason.'

'I know.'

'So why worry?' Jonathan kicked the door closed.

'Normally, they get 'em straight off the boat down Algeciras and then plot 'em right up. The only way to get 'em out is by force, which doesn't always work, or by payin' through the nose, which for us is completely out o' the question. And as for goin' legal, well we just don't have the time.'

'Jason.' The tools were away now, the cupboard door closed. Jason at last turned to look him in the eye. '*I'm* here, remember?'

'This place is top-rent, man. They ain't gonna take you very seriously.' Opening the front door up and checking on his handi-work again. 'We're just protectin' our interests like. They'll be puttin' in entryphones soon but until then, this'll have to do.'

'What d'yer mean? Won't take me very seriously.'

'Well you're hardly . . .' Smirking he was now, biting his top lip in.

'The midget has spoken. I'm hardly what, Jason?'

'Geoff says yer took a bit of a kickin' not so long back. We can't take any chances and, besides that, I think it's only fair to tell yer, there's a kind of war goin' on at the mo. We'd put locks on even if you were dead 'andy.'

War wasn't a word Johnno had a thirst for. He was paying full attention now, reluctantly. Jason was busy with keyrings, not looking up and still not giving much away. 'They might just take a few liberties. Know what I mean? So when you go out, make sure you lock up properly, padlock, the works, OK?' And he handed Jonathan the keys. 'And when yer in, bolt it all up, alright? Use the peep-hole.' Then he stuck his head through the bedroom door. 'She gonna be kippin' 'ere now is she?'

Jonathan set about testing the robustness of the new padlock and the bolts on the door. A whole mob on his mind now. 'You'd better not be takin' me for a mug now, Jason,' he said, leaning against the closed door looking directly down at him.

'Well she certainly will be.' Jason opened the bathroom door and grinned. Then, when the smell hit, closed it again. 'She was 'avin' you on, mate,when she said she was off. How far would she 'ave got without that lot eh? Not very far in her game, I can tell yer.'

'She's not kippin' here if that's what yer gettin' at. And what's it to you anyway?'

'I was just makin' a point, that was all.' Leaving the hall and walking through the apartment, over to the balcony, moving round the furniture like he still lived there.

Johnno had had just about enough of him now. 'I was just wondrin' when Jim'll fix it was fuckin' off? I've got work to do.'

'I'll be gone in a minute. I've got some stuff for yer – from Chas.'

'Well let's sort it and then you can go eh?'

'Just a quick one,' he said, and sat down on the balcony to set about rolling a spliff. Doing it with his legs crossed, his shiny shins cracking in the sun. No tan at all. He must've only given way to shorts fairly recently. Without taking his mind off his work, he said, 'Has the kitchen stuff turned up yet?'

'Comin' tomorrow apparently.'

'So you've done fuck all then, so far.'

'And what's it to you? This is Chas's shout innit? Not yours.'

'He was after a report like. Expectin' yer to be through with the bathroom at least, by now.'

Jonathan went to the bedroom for his binoculars. Dark bedroom, no windows, a bald lightbulb. Under the light, he stripped off the polystyrene, took the bins out of the plastic bag and weighed them up like a villain on a gun. They were heavy, black and shiny. Everything shined in Marbella. The buildings, the bodies, the boats. Jason's shins. And now the bins. The strap was Sellotaped into a polythene bag. That annoyed him. Why do that? Be patient. He figured the hooks and eyes and studs and strips and eventually, but with less zazz than a truly satisfied customer, he threw the strap over his head and looked out into the dark creamy bleakness of the ceiling. He fiddled to get the hang of the focus controls. He threw the box, all the tissue and a book of instructions into the bottom of the wardrobe. He saw in there three blue flip-flops, all odd and different sizes, to fit the Three Bears kind of sizes. Then it was back to the balcony, bins round his neck, like he'd been wearing them all his life.

Jason roached his spliff. Jonathan did captain, looked out to sea and then down to the bars where he got Sammy right away. Sammy with a scar the length of a dress zip, right down his back, wearing long keks, the only one besides the waiters.

'I've got some o' them,' said Jason. 'Zactly the same.'

'What 'aven't you got, smartarse?'

'Did yer get 'em over at Marcelle's?'

Jonathan moved round the balcony. The apartment was right on the end, four floors up and right in the corner. And if he leant right over, he could see right up the Avenida del Mar, which he did, for better sight of the land. He fiddled with the focus again, to look down to the town. At the people milling. Hire cars, beer wagons, motorbikes and taxis and shopping bags and red arms. And there. Louise's yellow skirt flapping about in the wind. And Jack. They were stood close together, shoulders shaking. Laughing, it looked like. He bit his lip and turned round. Jason had stood up to pass him the spliff, blowing smoke up and into his face, which Jonathan could only assume was an accident. And it must have been the cut of a smoke trail that made his eye water. He ignored the spliff and looked back through his glasses and saw them still at it – laughing.

'Liverpool are here,' said Jason, leaning over the balcony, flicking ash on to passers-by and then spitting right after.

'What?'

'Liverpool. Ian Rush, Paul Walsh, Lawrenson, Lee. Saw 'em last night down Banus.'

'What, all of 'em?'

'Most of 'em.'

'Fuckin' hell,' said Jonathan. 'Where they stayin'?'

'The club innit.'

'What club?'

'Marbella.'

'They play golf then?'

'No, football yer clown.'

'I meant at the club, do they play golf? I was just askin' do they play golf, that's all.'

'I'm tryna get a team together, yer know, five-a-side, for a kick about like, y'interested?'

That was something else Johnno hadn't been bad at, footie. With a bit of support and some decent boots for the inter county under 15s, he might have been picked. Jonathan unwrangled his head from the strap and threw the binoculars on the bullet-ridden swivel chair. Then went to the fridge and got a pack of beer out. He bit the metal top off three bottles. Jason jumped for the binoculars and lassoed himself with the strap.

'Put my bins down, shithead, and get on with what you've gotta do.'

'As tight as a duck's arse you are, aren't yer?'

'You 'eard.'

'Chas wants you at the meetins tomorrow. And he wants these fliers round today, in the bars 'n' that. An' I don't mean to be rude or owt . . .'

They stood, big man, small man, staring at each other.

Jason threw the bins on the chair, opened his briefcase, got the fliers out and threw them on the table. 'Chas was wondering if you could do somat about that tat? Yer clobber. Wants yer to make a good impression with the punters like.'

'Is that it? Yer finished now?'

'Nearly. I've got some papers for yer to sign. Tenancy agreements for this place, so if the worst comes to the worst, you've got proof like. You've been 'ere over six months now, Chas tells me?' He fished the papers out. 'If yer get a pull you'll be sorted with these. Sign 'em by the crosses and then I'll get off.'

Jonathan didn't like signing papers, the idea of being rushed, being forced into decisions he couldn't go back on and would probably regret. Was he missing something here? He went for his binoculars again. Had the feeling he was being watched. He looked out to sea first, congested with bodies, lilos, sails, a litter tray of humans and most of them dead looking. Lifeless. Waiting to be taken. Riding the waves. Bait. And on the shoreline, much activity, much running and paddling. Splashing. The born and the unborn, the before and the after. But all of it litter when, as he did now, he scanned further down the coast and in places could see slits of sand untouched by bodies or beach wear. He pulled in closer to three girls, all lay flat, topless, boyishly thin but they were in bikini pants and girls alright. A sight for passing men to cast their eyes over. A gift.

He turned his binoculars downwards and saw Sammy the Stick making slow progress across a bar patio, two drinks in one hand, his stick in the other. He followed him till he reached his table where a young girl of dubious age sat waiting to take the drinking straw and brolly like toys from a cereal box. Then, from nowhere, a bloke of about fifty ran right up behind Sammy and whacked him in the back of the neck, making him fall over and, with him, the placky table, and the placky table next to it, and all the drinks that were on it and there was Sammy flat on his back waving his stick like a madman. The bloke went for the stick and got it clean off him, no messing. After trying to stab Sammy in the stomach with it several times, he settled for beating him round the head with it, the girl gone now, running down the beach holding a shoe in each hand, like she was on for the sprint. Back to Sammy, still lying there, a couple of the waiters trying to help him up, the bloke gone. How embarrassing. Sammy looked up and, as always happens, seemed to zone in, right on his binoculars that must have been sun glinting. Before moving out of sight, Jonathan had got a full-on frame of him. He looked worn-out.

He put the binoculars down, wiped the sweat from his forehead and turned to Jason. He was almost asleep in the chair now. He looked worn-out as well. He signed the papers without Jason seeing and went back to the bins, to follow Sammy again. He was heading back for the town. A gang of lads following on, one of them taking the piss, walking with a limp behind him. Sammy turned, saw it all and turned back, to carry on walking. The lads were drunk or drugged, rowdy, fighting among themselves, hurling each other into oncoming traffic. Sammy eventually sat down on a wall, out of the sun, in the shade of some hanging flower baskets.

'Oy, you.'

Jason woke from his doze, checked the papers, put them in his case and then pulled out his legendary phone, the size of a security walky-talky and getting quite common down Puerto Banus. 'Chas has got one o' these for yer, so he can keep in touch when yer out doin' flyers or viewins.'

'What?'

'It's a mobile phone.'

'I know what it is, smartarse.'

'Jesus, there's no pleasin' you is there?'

'I 'ope he's not expectin' me to pay for it?'

'He's got 'em on special offer. On a trial like. Yer need to go down the Shed and pick one up. The guy that's sellin' 'em needs yer to sign some papers for it.'

'More signin' . . .'

'Chas'll catch yer phone bills if there are any. So long as it's business like.'

Jonathan didn't answer him. He was scanning the avenida again looking for her. She'd been gone over an hour now. Nothing. He sat down and thought, all the time fiddling, fumbling with her watch without a strap. The sun went in and he was glad. He stood up and leant his elbow on the balcony and gave Jason the 'I think you should leave' stare. Sat with his briefcase across his lap like an insurance salesman intent on staying, Jason said, 'She with you now proper is she? Louise?'

'What's it to you?'

'You know she's been workin' for us I take it?'

154

'So?'

'She's just told me she's packed it in. But then, they all say that. They're like drug-dealers. They can't help 'emselves.'

'Why she packed it in?'

'I figured coz she was with you. She was up for it well enough yesterday and the day before that and the day before that and . . .'

'Well it's nowt to do with me.'

'So why's she packed it in then?'

'How the fuck should I know?'

'It's probably me yer know. She doesn't like me.'

'Fuck me, Jason. I wonder why that is?'

Jonathan went in for another beer. Jason got up to follow him. Shouted after him, 'I gets on with 'em quite well usually.'

'How many 'ave yer got?'

'Nine, last count. They come an' go. We're short at the minute.'

'An' is it good money?'

'Used to be. I'm packin' that side of it in slowly. There's more clout in films these days. You only need the girls the once so it makes more sense really.'

'Has she done all that? Films 'n' that?'

'She wouldn't go for it. Got her head screwed on, that's why. The posh ones are all the same. You send 'em out three times an' next minute they've been taken on as a full-time mistress. But the common ones are 'arder to sell. Doesn't matter how hard you dress 'em up, they just don't cut the mustard when it comes to proper entertainment. Not for the likes o' round 'ere anyroads.'

'What you on about? It's all scum round 'ere. As far as the eye can see.'

'Not down Puerto Banus it's not.'

'That's just scum dressed up, Jason. For all that sailing they do, they don't come much shallower than that.'

'Still, they won't buy scummy girls will they? An' like I said, it's 'ard to keep quality merchandise in a place like this. Now with the films, it don't matter where the girls are comin' from. They don't get to do much talkin' anyway.'

'How much was she makin' then?'

'Hundred a night.'

'Quid?'

'No, pesetas, soft arse. Sterling, mate. Sterling.'

'Jesus.'

'If she's still into it and you wanna take her on, give us a shout. She's dead popular. There's a waitin' list for her. She gets loads o' call-backs but we don't tell her. If yer keep sendin' 'em the same ones, they take 'em off yer. An' a different bloke for the first few times breaks 'em in better. She took to it like a duck to water.'

'Really.' He hadn't drunk his beer. He was twisting it in his palm and the condensation round the bottle mixed with his sweat made a squeaky sound. Like a moaning sound.

'If she's into it and yer interested, I'll sort it all out for yer with Laura down at Clouds. It's a hundred for you, one for her and one for Laura. Just make sure you get the credit cards cleared before-hand.

'How am *I* gonna spend credit card money?'

'You don't. They pay cash but we have to put their cards through for a check . . . Laura does all that. It's to make sure the punters are who they say they are. That way, there's no trouble. If you wanna run bitches, you gotta look after 'em. First law of sellin' is to look after the merchandise.'

'Fuck it.'

'You're into her aren't yer?' Jason was walking round him, tutting.

'No. Not any more.'

'I'm off anyway.' Grinning. Pleased with himself.

'Sort it for us then. Sort it with Laura. If Louise isn't into it, I'll find someone who is.' He slung his binoculars back over his head.

Jason gave his new locks one last caress. 'We're not talkin' dinny scrubbers here yer know. The punters want smart. Not any old . . .'

'Yeah, I realise that.' He realised then, that there'd be difficulties. High-class pimp? It didn't sound very feasible.

'You'll see 'em on the beaches doin' fliers,' said Jason, leaning against the open door and, as a parting gift, a trade secret, to help him out. 'If they're skint enough to do flyers, they'll do anythin' usually. Most of 'em. Doesn't take long to sus who will an' who won't. Them on allowances. They're the best. They'll do owt but tell their parents they've ran out o' money. If they can't handle their money they're not trusted with anymore of it. Mad that eh, don't yer think? Givin' yer kids money an' gettin' snotty when they spend it.'

He put his case down then, walked over to the sink, turned the taps on and stuck his head under the water. He slicked back his hair and turned to show Jonathan the face of a girl with a moustache. Somehow, and against his will, Jonathan felt a lot closer to him now. On his side. 'There's a bloke lined up tonight for her. If she changes her mind, get her down there for seven. Then come over to the shed for yer new phone.' He picked up his briefcase, fingered the coins in his shorts pockets, grinned wide and went to leave again.

'Before yer go, Jason. What did yer used to do in England? What's yer trade like?'

'I'm a creeper.'

'Huh?'

'Silent burglar. I'm in an' out without even wakin' the dog. Come's in 'andy bein' small sometimes. See ya down the Shed then later, Johnno!'

It was that easy. No faffing about. No nastiness. No bother. But would she go for it? Whatever, he was on a roll now. The payroll hopefully. The fliers wasn't such a bad prospect after all. Hunting women on the beaches. Fair game. Here he was, a bona fide tenant, with a bona fide job, and now the chance of a right little earner to keep him in a manner to which he would like to become accustomed. After bolting the door, he went straight over to the balcony and scanned the town for her. No sign.

He looked for Geoff's number but couldn't find it. He retraced his steps. The piece of paper with his number on had completely disappeared. Beer pressed down on his bladder.

In the toilet, one hand flat against the wet wall tiles, the grout mildewed to orange, he pissed, nose closed to the stench. The knickers and bras hanging everywhere scared him for a minute. He couldn't look at them. Preferred instead the tongue of a yellow piss stain down the toilet. The polka dot poo on the pan, scatter-gunned since Tuesday. She could clean that up. In the bald light from the neon strip, bald truths. The icing cake lace and frill reminding him of children, the simple white bra like baby eyes, accusing him, watching him. And yet more eyes watching him from the floor, her stepped-out-of-knickers like goggles. Eyes like Mysterons all over the place. He looked up again to the familiar territory of washing hung up and out to dry. And that's all it was. Everyone trying to get through it all, as clean as they can.

He figured the first kill the hardest. The one after, that bit easier. The next, he'd feel next to nothing. The first time, the first girl, would be the test. The rest, just business. If he could offer her up . . . and she was already up to her neck in it, had jumped in, both feet, of her own accord . . . if he could offer her up tonight . . . if he could do her and he knew he could, the rest would come easy. If he scored five times a week, he'd collect over five hundred quid and if there were three or four on the go, it wouldn't be long before . . . then he remembered he had a phone. He had a phone, a flat by the sea, some cash and a bitch in tow. He was making inroads now. Making something of himself.

He went back to the balcony, took up his binoculars and got her right away. Weighed down with shopping bags. Shopping. Women and shopping. Men and work. That's how it had always been and boy did they make heavy weather of it. Just look at her. She didn't know what shopping was. Two bags of it and she was walking like a mule. Now if she'd grown up in Manchester, she'd have been skipping with them bags, glad to be able to go fucking shopping. And he thought of Shirl then, back home. Shirl when she was pregnant with Malcy. The day he'd brought her home, back to where she belonged. She'd been living with that no-mark who could have been Malcy's father but who was too white and scuzzy to be given the credit for him. It was nearly bonfire night and Johnno had been driving his dad's van home. On the seat, three lots of fish and chips to be ate watching the new Bond movie. Which one was it? The van stank of vinegar. He'd been driving along with his hand on top of the food. When he had a woman, he'd drive along with his hand on her tits, and the fish and chips gave him the exact same feeling. And then he saw her. Shirl walking home, in the rain. Shirl, heavily pregnant weighed down with shopping. The sight of her on her own like that had creased him up at first. But even back then, it had crossed his mind she was doing it on purpose. To attract attention. Another woman over-egging the pudding. His mum did it. Shirl did it. They did it just to get noticed. Men on the other hand were proud enough not to be noticed. When in bother, men fuck off.

On that day, you couldn't miss Shirl. Red mac in the rain, her hem hanging. She wouldn't have known her hem was hanging but it was. And she still had her high heels on. The only shoes she had, she said. Eight months pregnant with high heels on? Over-egging it again. He'd driven towards her slowly, knowing she wouldn't want to be seen. Not by him. Anyone else but him. Anyone else would think she'd been born like that. But because he knew her so well, he could gauge exactly how far she'd fallen. Not imagine it or guess. He knew for sure. She wanted him to blank her. She'd turned at the sound of his engine following her and then turned back round again, giving him the option to drive on and ignore her. But he couldn't just leave her with her hem hanging like that, the handles on her shopping bags stretched to busting. The rain pouring. He drove a little ahead, stopped, put the fish and chips on the dashboard and waited. The door opened and the bags were sent in first. Then Shirl. They never looked at each other or spoke. She shut the door, put her seatbelt over her bump and he drove on. Veered left to get on to her estate. Threaded his way down the cars parked both sides and in front of her maisonette, parked up in a god-given space.

'I'll help yer,' he said.

'No don't.'

'Well yer not carrying all that lot in on yer own.'

'I've just carried 'em from the Co-op.'

'Well yer not carrying them any further. Go and get him to help you. He'll be helpin' you scoff it no doubt.'

'He's not in.'

'He is in. I can see the telly changing channels. Go on. Go and get him.'

The path to the front door was down three lots of steps to the side of the front garden. The front garden was a steep bank of yellow grass, littered with metal, wheel hubs, an old dog's basket, and dog shite. The front door had plywood for windows. Shirl didn't bother with the path. She tottered down the bank of grass and at the bottom broke into a run and nearly fell. Jonathan leant over the steering wheel and broke into a bag of chips, all the time watching the front door, watching for him. She went in and came back out alone. She climbed back up the bank of grass, her coat undone now to reveal a short sweatshirt dress, black with cigarette holes in it. Black tights on. She opened the door of the van and picked out the shopping bags.

'What's 'appenin?'

'He's gotta bad back.'

There was no way he could carry that man's food into the house for him. And so he watched her make three journeys down the path with it. And then drove off. His fish and chips he left to go cold on the dashboard. His mum and dad all ready and waiting with a pile of bread and butter and yet more salt and vinegar, the telly on, the gas fire blaring. He left them, got back in the van, went back round to Shirl's, walked in the back door and got her out. She came home with two black binbags and the cot that his mother had bought with her win from the bingo. When she got in, she sat and watched the telly like nothing had happened. Dad made three pots of tea, one after the other. No shouting or berating. Nothing. It was such a good night.

And there she was, Miss lah-di-bloody-dah, making such heavy weather of it, she'd sat down on a bench. Her bags to the side of it. Her leg up on her knee. She was picking something off her feet, chewing gum perhaps. The binoculars weren't strong enough to tell. And then she stopped and put her hands in her lap, in a kind of prayer. Her legs crossed now. Asking for it.

160

He decided to try and phone home. He waited for a Spanish operator to speak English and, eventually, the code. The numbers came to him as numbers he already knew, re-hauled out of his memory. When he rang, an announcement in Spanish. Couldn't make head nor tail. Operator again. All the time waiting, he counted up the money in his money belt. No answer. Then Spanish. Then, please, English please. Right thanks. The phone was barred for international calls.

'Fuck off.'

Then Louise knocking on the door. On his head. He lay back on his bed, listening. He shouted. She shouted back. Back in the hall, he noticed the padlock on the cupboard again. It looked even bigger now.

Chapter Eleven

She was glad to be back in and out of the sun but went for a questioning look on her face, as if wondering what had taken him so long. He held the door while he watched her walk in. She turned round to see why. Did he want her to go now? Immediately?

'What's with all the bolts on the door? Expecting someone?'

'No.'

'I saw the man with the stick earlier. I never said anything.'

'Put the bags down.' She was doing just that when he said it. She turned to look at him. Again questioning. 'Come here.' She began emptying the shopping bags. 'Now. I want you over here, now.'

She walked towards him and, against her will, got excited. She kept her eyes down. He pulled her towards the balcony, as if beating a path. Then he placed her in front of it. Like an ornament, arms to her sides. Over her shoulder, he looked out to the sea, the holiday-makers. Then he stroked her nipples pipping her shirt. Then he opened her up – yanked the shirt right off her. He knew.

'Turn round.'

He pulled all the pick-up-sticks out of her hair and when the curtain of it fell to her shoulders, she shuddered. Breeze on the breasts. She shivered from the inside out, against her will, and she wondered at that. How her body could go to these places without her.

'Over.' He pointed to the baby coffee table, nestled on the balcony next to the wicker chair. 'Bend over.'

Through the bars of the balcony she watched the people making holidays on the beach. She saw a child lick a river of ice cream up his arm. A bald head reading a newspaper. Someone doing a headstand. The African man. Breeze on her nipples again. She waited. She licked salt from her lips. She waited. Hoping he'd melt ice cream any second, minute. Play the game. Give what you can. Make fun. Do as you're told. Skirt up and over now. Pants down. Her white bar of flesh, there for him now. Waiting. A gift as usual, tinged with the sense of loss. Why make her wait this long? She was aching. Worried the ache would subside, would be gone before he . . . but at last. She heard the track of his zip.

The people on the beach dizzied off, became singed at the edges. A heat haze. Or was it tears in her eyes? She concentrated on the sea instead, a sea nearly still. She did waves for it, like she was in it, was it, controlling the rhythm. It was Jonathan in control, though. She held on tight to the coffee table and soon, too soon, it was over. She heard him pull up and beach. Silent. No melt. No nothing. Angry maybe. She knew he'd know but now she knew he knew. She crouched down and covered herself with her skirt. Shy. He, too, was being shy, quiet. She turned round, wanting him properly now but he was fiddling with his binoculars, miles away. He walked in front of her and stood against the bar of the balcony, looking out to sea. Behind him, like a peasant stealing fuel, she picked up her pants and shirt and scurried off to the bathroom.

'What took you so long?' he shouted. 'At the shops?'

'I just took my time. I thought you wanted some privacy.'

Tucking in her blouse, she wended her way through to the kitchen area, back to the shopping. She rummaged to make space along the counter and, from nowhere, a shopping list of white paper fell to the floor like a bird landing.

'What's that?' he said pointing to the floor.

'A shopping list.' On the other side of the list there was writing.

'On the other side?'

'Telephone number, it looks like. Geoff.'

'Give.'

'What's wrong with you?' He went back out on to the balcony. Obviously, he couldn't face up to it. 'Well?' she said, egging him on to get on with it. 'Is everything alright?'

'What was Jack sayin'?' He raised the binoculars to his eyes.

164

'Nothing. He gave me some money.'

'Oh yeah. And what could that be for, I wonder?'

She rummaged for the money in a sulk. The bus plan blown out of the water. The bus to Malaga would be going without her. She was all tired out now.

'He owes it you, he said. Why didn't you tell him where you'd moved to?'

'Why don't you shut up?'

'I'm going. I don't have to listen to this.' She went for her bags. He went for her. Took her arm and pulled on it, like he could pull her back into shape, back to what he thought she was. 'Jonathan!' She was shouting. It was her turn for it now. She wanted the old Jonathan back. She didn't like this one. He left her again. Stunned by the confrontation, he slid back on to the balcony. He lifted the binoculars and set up his store some miles away from her. She emptied the shopping bags and found just one small cupboard clean enough to accept the goods.

He came back into the room and put the binoculars down on the coffee table.

'Giz it 'ere then.'

'Sorry?'

'Me money?'

She went back to her bag, rummaged again, found the money and handed it over. 'What's it to you, Jonathan? It's not like we're going out.' It came out like a slap. She immediately wanted to take it back.

He stood her up straight and held her chin firmly. Then kissed her on the forehead. The loser's consolation prize. He couldn't see inside her any more.

'There's a letter as well, from England,' she said.

'A letter?'

'I went to Mavver's to collect it'

He stopped counting the money, took the letter and moved away.

'Get us a beer will yer.'

Knowing she wasn't entirely welcome was normally excuse enough to pick up her bag and leave. But she went to the fridge and got him a beer instead.

The envelope was quite thick. Inside a couple of pages, one a sheet out of his drawing pad at home. The other a sheet of lined paper folded over. The prison stamp at the top of the page. Dad's writing snuggled up between the lines, like it was being held down.

'Jonathan . . .'

'Shut up a minute.'

It was dated January and read:

Dear Hilda,

What can I say? They read all the letters so whatever I say won't be private. I know how hard it must be, how much it hurts. Have you heard from Jonathan yet? If you do, get him home. You need him with you. Hilda, I want us to marry again. Re-do our vows. Don't ask me why, just say yes. The food's terrible in here and I can't get used to the noise.

Love you always, Charlie. And once again, I'm sorry. P.S. Try and stay off the bingo.

Shirl's letter was a stunner. First the envelope. She'd posted it three weeks ago, same day they'd got his letter no doubt. He read fast and twice. Found more questions than answers in it. He walked as he read and stood on the balcony. Then stared out, straight ahead. He could hear his dad saying it, out loud, still thinking he had some control. 'Try and stay off the bingo, Hilda.' Banged up but still having a go. Well, what now?

Tomorrow, he'd send every penny home to England. Then make another big pile of it. He read Shirl's letter again, for the third time, wanting to get more out of it.

Dear Jonathan,

How's your tan coming on, yer little get. Glad to hear you're having such a good time. Making lots of money. We're always on

166

*pins waiting for your postcards. A letter? What possessed you?
Missing us?*

He wished now he hadn't exaggerated so much. Not exaggerated,
lied.

*As you can see from dad's letter, things have been going pretty
well over here too. The garden's in a right state and so's me mum.*

Trying to disgust him into going home.

*I've got meself a new boyfriend who runs his own business and
there's a job all ready and waiting for you. Building work.*

Carrying bricks. What was she on? His kid sister – trying to set him
up with a job?

*Johnno, we need the money. I'm behind with the mortgage, the
catalogue, the gas, everything. They're threatening to repossess,
Jonathan. We'll have nowhere to live. I've been doing some
agency work but it's not really fair on our Malcy is it? Me
working nights all the time. He hardly sees me as it is. And
now she's gone back on the bingo. You could have sent Malcy
somat for his birthday.*

She could ditch the job and claim benefits for the mortgage. Get it
put in her name but no, she wanted to play the martyr.

*I've only seen me dad twice since he's been in. Since January,
Jonathan. He said he was set up. At first he wouldn't see anyone.
Then he changed his mind. Now no way. He looked terrible last
time I saw him. His shoulders were shaking. I think he's gone
mad. I've written to the governor but he wrote back and said he
was free to see who he liked. Taking the piss or what? Mum's
nerves are bad, remember how she gets?*

Jonathan turned the page over and gave out his best rendition of a proper family sigh.

'Jonathan?' Louise's voice doing 'sympathetic'.

''Ang on a minute.' He didn't look up.

He's out in three weeks. You've had your fun, Jonathan. Please come home.

You've had your fun. He looked up at his present source of so-called fun and recognised, for the first time since re-meeting her, just how far apart they were. They were of a different breed, hers surviving on family fortunes and the occasional delinquency to add excitement to the ever-full bowl of broth. His on matters arising. Skirting the depths of delinquency in a bid to fill the bowl. Morals, as he'd always suspected, were a myth.

He'd been on the slippery slope already but the letter now convinced him. Morals were too expensive a religion to follow. Expensive paintings in a rich man's drawing room. Without an audience, they were useless. A poor man with morals was just a fool in a greenhouse, all the time trying not to break a window. All the time being watched. Well this little slug was on his way out and up the slippery slope. He'd stick at it now, no matter how slippery it got.

She came on to the balcony and he turned away, grabbed his binoculars and did a quick search of the beach for Sammy.

'I've rolled a spliff,' she said.

'Can you cook at all?'

Silence.

He put the binoculars down and looked at her. She passed him the spliff and he lit it. Time to go easy on her. He didn't want her going anywhere now. He tapped the wicker chair for her to sit down. She put her feet up on the coffee table. Her shades on, face to the sun. He passed her the spliff back and sat right on the edge of the coffee table. Then went to stroke her feet. She pulled back. 'Don't,' she said. Then she went back to her doze. She wasn't going anywhere.

'You seem subdued,' she said. 'Bad news?'

'England's bad news.'

She closed her eyes again.

'Not for me it isn't. I really want to go home.'

'What's stoppin' yer?'

'Money.'

'Why blow it all on clobber then?'

'I didn't. I blew most of it up at the casino. I was trying not to look like a . . .'

'Why don't yer take yer shades off, you'll get goggles else.'

'The sun hurts my eyes.'

'Take yer top off then.'

She lifted her shades and looked at him. 'What's my top got to do with my eyes?'

'It's the stripes isn't it? The white stripes look funny on yer.' She undid her buttons, stood up, went to her bag and got out the suntan lotion. 'Yer not gonna stink the place out with that stuff are yer?'

'I've got to. I'll burn otherwise. It's not the cheap stuff. Smells quite nice. Smell?' she said, pointing it at him. He could have smacked her one then.

'I'm sure it does,' he said.

He watched her squeeze the cream between her tits and rub it in.

She rested back to a doze, her shirt loosened, barely covering. It only needed one strong breeze to force it wide open, one small movement. She was teasing him now. Thinking there'd be some mileage in it. Expecting him to give her a loan no doubt. Prostitution by any other name and she didn't think he'd click. He moved the balcony furniture around, got rid of the tables and replaced them with a chair. She sat with her head tipped back, shades in her hair. Jonathan sat forward, put his binoculars on and homed in on Sammy right away – the irritating bluebottle in the bedroom of his sleep. The limper. As quiet and sure as the local sex pest down the swimming baths, back home. The dirty mac. The smell. The scratch of the man's growth against his boyhood cheek and the pineapple cubes all stuck to the paper bag. A bad trade. The end of his swimming days.

Jonathan felt favourite right now. And just as he knew he'd win a raffle before it was drawn, he knew Sammy was there for him, had come to mark his card and to remind him. Whether Sammy knew it or not, he was there to remind Jonathan. To make any further disregard of who he really was and where he'd come from impossible. A limping conscience. Against all the odds and evidence – the new apartment, the job, the chance to make some real money – his gut was shouting home. Shirl's letter folded small to a ball and stuffed in his back pocket hurt. When he rocked back and forth, he could feel it riding over the muscles in his backside, digging itself right in. He'd had his fun. He'd had his fair share of beatings, birds and ball-ache and still had no plan, no future and no idea. There was no future in Wheezy and far too much history to ignore. Jonathan stroked his chin and, for a minute, lost sight of Sammy completely. Watched a girl undo her friend's bra and homed right on the bare breasts, standing to loosen the pull on his shorts. Got back on the breasts immediately. And thought again then, of the man in the mac on the balcony watching schoolkids swim, leaning over to smile at his favourites. Jonathan had been his very favourite.

He pulled himself away from the girl and travelled right in search of Sammy again. There he was, talking to a couple of blokes, stroking a girl's back at the same time, all of them sat up at the bar bare-chested, the girl in an itsy-bitsy. He kept the glasses on them for a while, moving his sights sideways at any sudden movements suggesting trouble. It was like starring in a film but not being it. The distance between him and his co-star unbridgeable now. He didn't care if Sammy found him. Felt sorry for him even. Had Johnno been a ruthless man, he would have, should have enjoyed the sight of the mighty brought down to earth on one foot but he wasn't that heartless. Johnno could afford to be generous. Here was a man clinging on to his dignity by the only means left. His power over women.

'So what sort of business are you moving into then? Am I allowed to know?' She was doing a doze but with one eye partly open watching him. He had to decide if the question was loaded. Sammy pushed the girl off her stool and she fell to the sand laughing. He sticked sand over her and she got up quickly, shaking her hair out. She was . . . He took the glasses away and looked at Louise to compare. She was just as fit. No doubt about that. He looked through his glasses again and this time saw Sammy scanning the balconies, his head moving along towards Jonathan's. Jonathan walked backwards into the flat, a hunter back behind his bush. Out of sight but still facing seawards.

'Timeshare,' he said.

'Uhhh.'

'What d'yer mean, uhhhh?'

'Rather a con, don't you think?'

'And who asked you?'

'The whole idea of a holiday is to go where the fancy takes you, not to the same place, year in, year out.'

'And you'd know a lot about dreaming your way out of a slum, wouldn't you? All some people want is a dead cert. That's all timeshare is. A dead cert. Unlike you, some people wanna sort out where they're stayin' in advance.'

'Well I think ten years in advance is taking things to extremes.'

'Well how does ten minutes grab yer?'

'Do you want me to go?'

'I'm just makin' a point.'

'Well you've made it. Sorry for opening my mouth.' She folded her arms, crossed her ankles and closed her mind off one more level away from him.

They were back on their separate islands now. And everything had finally slipped into place. The teachers, his dad, they'd been right after all. He *was* slow. Running uphill, as he had been, he could never have been anything else. The slippery slopes were for them already up there. To get up there quick, you had to cheat. Scam. Swallow a few principles. He was surrounded by the bent and the bad and a million and one ways to make himself some money. He needed pots of the stuff and pronto and he couldn't see any sense in going home without having a crack at it now. Loud and clear, he'd

171

finally heard the call. She'd been sent back to him for a purpose and he was going to make good use of her.

He'd not made a beeline for this. He'd made serious attempts to take seriously a number of jobs but to what end? He'd tried out a number of career options ranging from builder to mechanic to supermarket manager but each one had required a degree of application or talent he couldn't give or didn't have. Barring the Foreign Legion or putting out fires, he was fucked anyway. This was as good a start as any. And he got to be his own boss too.

A great roar came up from the beach. 'Maggie May'. Rod Stewart. Sung by a huge crowd of men round Papa's place. Jonathan swerved his binoculars to the source of the noise and there was Jason. And there was Ian Rush and the rest of Liverpool. And . . . who was that . . . Walsh? Was that Walsh?

'It's Liverpool,' he said. 'Down at Papa's. Ian Rush is over there.'

'Are you going to run down for their autographs?' Without moving a muscle, not even an eye muscle. He wanted to slap her up then. 'Happy Birthday, Jonathan, Love from Liverpool. Shall we go out somewhere? For your birthday?'

'You've got no money, remember.'

He decided to execute the first part of a plan and not wind himself up with her. Shave off his beard. Get away from her. If he hung around, he'd want her all over again.

'Giz the spliff?'

'What?' she said.

'You 'eard.'

'I think I'd better go, don't you?'

'Listen, Wheezy, I'm just a bit wound-up, that's all. That letter from home . . . like I said, England's bad news.' He surprised even himself, getting a 'Wheezy' out of it.

To the shower. He drip dried across the tiles and when he got to the bathroom mirror, the air pleasantly cold, across the chest, the nipples. Like cutting out the bad, he stabbed at his beard with the scissors, snip, snipping away his old self. *Oh Maggie I wished*

I'd never seen your face. The sink looked filthy with all his hairs in it.

'Louise,' he shouted. He shouted it again.

'Put some music on. And loud.'

He hoped she'd choose one of his tapes. Some black sound he could get his head round. His various tapes done with his own mind in mind. His 'Cottage in Negril'. Nope. She went for Dire Straits. The cissy stuff. 'So Far Away from Me'. Being flash with the CD that he hadn't even shown her how to use. No doubt had one in her bedroom back home. Flash as that. Doesn't know she's born.

His hairs were stuck everywhere, round the taps, in the ridge of the plug, to the sink itself. He had to scrub them off. The beard didn't want to say goodbye. Not at all. He didn't like that, its refusal to go, even under the order of great swirls of water and persistent finger-nails. It was a bad omen. If it don't go, it's not meant to. He gathered up all her bras and pants, opened the bathroom door and chucked them into the bedroom.

He took to the actual shave with a paintbrush of a Bic razor stick. Each stripe uncovering more of him. When he was finished he looked stupid. His face tiled. The top half dark brown and shiny, the bottom, pale, scrawped, dull and bleeding. And lumps. Bumpy. Mistake with a capital M. And no aftershave. Dabbed and swabbed and red-eyed stoned, tiled face and feeling somewhat shaken, having to confront the whole of his face for the first time in ages, he left that bathroom war-wounded and sensitive. So sensitive he could just make out a tap-tapping sound. Someone at the door. Not that fucking Jason again, gassing on about Liverpool. He wrapped a towel round his head boxer-style. Looked through the peep-hole and opened up the bolts again. Bang, bang.

'Yo! Moustaf.'

The two men shook hands.

'I'm just finishing off in the bathroom. Go through.' He looked over to where Louise was on the balcony. She was sat, head back, eyes closed and topless. He put his finger to his lips and said, 'Go in and meet my friend.'

Jonathan went back to the bathroom to check the mistake again. Felt the first cringe of a life as a pimp and tried to laugh it off. His face in the mirror wiped away a good attempt and out loud he said, 'What am I gonna do?' Go out and get some aftershave, some sun on it, some stick. That's what he'd get. Take Moustaf out with him. Next to Moustaf he'd look like a fucking zebra.

He kept the towel on and went back to the lounge. Moustaf was sat on the balcony, quietly sketching out her image. Because of the mix of music and noise from inside and out, she'd not heard him. She looked like she was floating away under two white lilies. She really would do her nut.

'Louise. Meet Moustaf.' He tapped her shoulder and at the same time draped his towel over her.

Moustaf's shoulders were juddering. Jonathan figured on a slap coming, for both of them or maybe just one for Moustaf. She stormed off to the bedroom. Moustaf wouldn't stop laughing. It wasn't that funny.

'How d'yer know I was 'ere?'

'From the beach, I see glasses.' Moustaf picked them up and, unlike most people, instead of putting them on and looking out, looked instead at their shape, weighed them, tapped them. 'The glass keep catching my eye. So I keep look up and then I come close because you browner than them and then I see it *is* you.'

Jonathan got him a beer and showed him how to work the binoculars.

'I gotta go and get some aftershave, man.'

He felt raw, skinned alive. He went back to the bathroom to douse his face with water, once again. He wouldn't go into the bedroom and so stood outside and shouted,

'Are yer gonna cook us up some dinner, Louise? In exchange for yer rent like?'

She opened the bedroom door. 'If you want.' She was playing victim. She'd reverted to type, to what she was like back in Manchester, lost in a world of grown-ups.

'That'd be sound. Me and Moustaf are goin' out. I'm gonna get me some aftershave, for me birthday like.'

'It looks awful,' she said, and shut the door.

'I'll be bringin' Moustaf back with me.' No reply.

Moustaf was working the glasses like a professional now. Jonathan got him another beer.

'What yer lookin' at?' Moustaf didn't answer. He was too engrossed. 'I can't sit out there any more, it's too hot.' Nothing. 'Can I have a look at your drawings then?' Moustaf patted his sketch pad as an invite, without taking his eyes from the glasses.

Jonathan looked at the pictures thoughtfully. He'd like Moustaf to teach him a few things about drawing. How to do faces for a start. He could never get the look right, the expression. No matter how hard he worked on all the separate parts, the whole never came out right. He flicked through the pad and then back to the image of Louise. 'Can I have it?'

'You like?' asked Moustaf, finished sightseeing now.

'Yeah, I do, only you 'aven't done her butterfly.'

'Let me finish and then you can pay me.'

He sat down to finish the job. Louise emerged dressed from the bedroom. He looked at her very briefly and then carried on sketching.

'Louise, meet Moustaf, a friend of mine. Moustaf, meet Louise.'

She gave a forced grin and plotted herself up in the kitchen area. Moustaf smiled, shrugged her off and went back to his pad.

'What's for dinner then?'

'Omelette.'

'You will stay for some nosh, Moustaf?'

He nodded but didn't look up from his work. Louise set about peeling potatoes.

'We'll be about an hour or so,' said Jonathan, pulling on Moustaf's little bag to tell him to up and move. Moustaf ripped out the page and took the pad and pencil with him. 'And Louise, if anyone, and I mean anyone, including that slag Jason, if anyone comes to the door, don't say a word. I'm gonna lock you in so they can't get in.

OK?' He picked up the shiny new padlock off the kitchen counter, a fistful of keys, a bottle of beer and then left.

She set about slicing the potatoes. And then some onions. And then she got bored. She might have been back in the bedsit with Jonathan, once again without the means to sort herself out. Once again, dependant on him. It had been just as boring with him then. There was no spirit about him. No depth. No ambition. Sex was all there was and now even that was a no-no. She'd laid herself bare for him on the balcony and what did he do? Go for a shave. She'd been so worried about what he'd say and yet his only response was to withdraw. What a man. Still, she could call home now if she wanted. She could escape if she had to.

She went out on to the balcony and took up the binoculars. The beach was beginning to clear. That was because the shops were opening. That's all they did. Shop and tan. She couldn't see Jonathan and the African. She looked around for his picture. She sat down in the swivel and examined it closely. What struck her was the arch of her back. He'd sketched her in profile and, from that angle, she looked to be struggling away from something. Her lower back curved to a hollow, forced in on itself. Strained but agile. He'd lined in some muscle. It was a back under stress and not at all sexual. Even her breast, though it was too large, too out of proportion for her size, it wasn't curved to a sexual swell. No nipple definition, as if he was being polite. Her face rounded, full but the nose straight, like a ramp. She couldn't quite make up her mind if he'd captured something of her. Or if she was reading more into it than was there. She'd look at it again later.

She picked up the glasses again and went on to the balcony. The sun had gone round now. It was less scorching but still warm out. *Relax, don't do it, when yer wanna come.* She hated the song. She swung the binoculars seawards and fell on a man full stretch on his lilo. When the major wave swelled, he disappeared. And then reappeared again some distance to the left or to the right. The lilo was red and looked, just for a second, like her lost suitcase.

The binoculars were heavy. Her wrists were tired from chopping the veg. She couldn't hold them to her eyes now. She couldn't stem the tide of tears that came without warning. She left the balcony, took off her skirt and went to bed. She lay there, crying. For a good while, crying. She was in no fit state to call her mother. If she did, there'd be an international incident. She sat up to calm down. Then told herself to lie down, take deep breaths and concentrate her mind on getting home. This was no holiday any more. Locked in Jonathan's flat and cooking him dinner. She'd fallen for the oldest trick in the book. Whore to mother in one foul swoop.

When she woke, she swung her legs off the bed and stretched, making an arch in her back. All the problems came rushing back in. When she stood up she felt a pain in her toe, like a pin prick. She looked down and found a small strap belonging to something under the bed. She pulled at it and found Jonathan's money belt, stuffed to the gunnels with money. Rolls and rolls of five-thousand-peseta notes. With the money that Jack had given him and all this, he could so easily lend her the money to go home. So why hadn't he offered? She stuffed the belt under the bed and just then heard the front door open. They were back. He came straight into the bedroom, found his money belt and immediately counted off the bundles. Then he smiled at her. Looked at her legs, clicked his tongue and walked out.

She dressed, dusted herself down, finger-combed her hair, wiped her brow and went into the lounge. She gave them one of her widest smiles. As soon as Moustaf had gone, she would confront him. She was ready for him now, after the rest. He offered her a beer and she took one. The cold fizz on the back of her throat was fantastic, a wake-up call. She took another long long swig and both men eyed her curiously when she finally let the bottle drop. Moustaf turned the television on.

'It's all in Spanish, man.'

'Yes,' said Moustaf, not entirely seeing Jonathan's point.

'Yer won't understand it. You don't speak Spanish.'

'No,' said Moustaf still not seeing Jonathan's point. He changed the channels but wasn't happy with any of them. He opened the drawer beneath the TV and found video cassettes. He took one out and waved it at Jonathan.

'No, no,' said Jonathan getting up and taking it from him. He put it back. 'They're shite anyway,' she heard him say. He closed the drawer and looked over at her, stood at the cooker now, oil splashing her arms.

'I'll take yer to work after, Louise.'

'I'm not going tonight.'

'I thought you said . . .'

'I've changed my mind.'

'About England?'

'No?'

'So how do you intend to . . .'

'I'll talk to you later.'

They went back out on to the balcony to take it in turns with the binoculars. Waiting for their dinner.

They all ate hungrily but Moustaf took the biscuit, all the biscuits, and then left. She'd put too much oil in the omelette. The eggs were so heavy they wouldn't move in or out of her stomach. They were just stuck there, in a huge ball of fat. She retched. Another drink might just do the trick. She downed two more beers and Jonathan came back from the bedroom to catch her finishing the second bottle.

'So talk then.'

'I . . .'

'You need the money right?'

'But couldn't you just lend me the money? I'll send it back to you?'

'If you knew the number of girls that have said that to me.'

'But Jonathan, you know me . . .'

'Louise, I don't know you at all. I know fuck all about you.'

'I know you kn–'

'You don't know me. You'd like to think you do. You probably tell yerself you do and believe every single word of it. But you know nothing. You don't care about anyone or anything but yourself.'

She felt sick. Needed the bathroom. But he was mid-speech and she didn't want to spoil it for him. He'd obviously been thinking about it for some time. His sentences were all disjointed, not connected and there was very little passion to match the meaning of what he was saying. He didn't look mad enough to mean what he was saying.

'I've decided to take a leaf out of your book. I'm gonna look after number one for a change. In exchange, I'll give you a piece of advice. *You* look after number one. In the shit or out the shit that's all you need to know. And you're very good at it when you're out the shit so it's just a matter of adapting really. I can't see it being a problem meself.'

And she locked herself in the bathroom then. He didn't know what to do. What would a real pimp do? Break the door down and drag her out by her hair? He couldn't do it. Not right off anyway.

'Louise.'

Silence.

'Louise.'

'I'm not goin' back to work for him, Jonathan.'

'You won't have to. Work for me.'

'Why can't I work for myself?'

'You tell me? It's your game.'

'I could ring my parents.'

'Well go on then. Ring yer parents. Why the fuck don't yer? I would.' Silence. 'Well?'

'Because I'd never hear the bloody end of it. I already owe them five hundred quid.'

'So then you'll have to earn yer way home like everyone else does. And Louise, don't make me the monster. You were 'appy as Larry till yer spotted my bag o' money.'

And then she came out, eyes staring straight at his, bloody mindedness written all over her. 'And just think,' he said, trying to take her hand, 'in a couple o' days, if you don't go out spendin' it, you can buy yer ticket home and not worry any more.' She pulled away and stood with her arms folded. 'Listen, after a couple of nights, you'll be sorted right? You can stay here till yer plane goes and no-one'll be any the wiser.'

'So you don't mind?'

'Why should I mind?'

'I thought you'd mind.'

'About what?'

'You know what.'

'I'm sorry, you've lost me.' It was like erasing a blackboard. Like she'd never happened. She hadn't really. He didn't know her after all.

'So you don't care?'

'Why should I care?'

'I thought you'd be . . .'

'Louise, if I could make the sort o' dosh you've been making, I'd be first in the queue.'

'Would you?'

'Maybe. If I had to I would.'

She went to the fridge and took out some water. She drank it straight from the bottle.

'But I don't have to really, do I?' she said, after a really long swig.

'No yer don't. And if I was you, I'd be campin' outside the embassy day and night screamin' blue murder till they got me home.'

'I mean.' She bent down to put the bottle back in the fridge and without turning round said, '*You* could lend me the money.'

'And your parents could give you the money. And afford it too.'

'My parents aren't rich you know, Jonathan.' He was surprised, stand-back shocked a little, to hear her shouting. 'They're not wealthy.'

'They're not scratchin' their arses either. Yer mam's a solicitor isn't she?'

'She's a legal secretary. A glorified typist.'

'That's not what yer told me . . .'

'I was lying.'

'And all them great big trees in yer back garden?'

'One apple tree.'

'And yer dad?'

'Struggling. Jonathan, he was made redundant last year.'

'Jesus, it's violin time already is it? Struggling to pay for next year's Caribbean holiday is he?'

He walked off and away from her then. She shouted after him, 'They've given me so much already, I can't keep asking every time I run out of money.'

'So how were you intendin' to pay me back then?' And then too long a pause to fill with any truth but she tried anyway.

'Out of my grant, next term.'

'I've seen you on a grant, remember. Sounds to me like you 'aven't got much choice, Louise, have yer?' He lifted the glasses to his eyes but didn't look out. His eyes were closed.

'But . . . I don't want to do it any more. What about us?' She knew, as soon as she said it, the answer to that question had been covered. She was just digging herself in deeper. 'Right then,' she said. 'So no loan.'

'Louise, if I hadn't got that letter, I probably *would* have lent yer the money. I'm not a pig. Yer know that. I just don't see why I should . . .'

'Fine. Fine. It doesn't matter. Two more nights and then I'm out of this place. I'm quite capable of looking after myself so don't you worry about me. Number one it is from now on. You were right. It's time I learnt.'

She sat shuddering on the couch, lip quivering. He went over and gave her a hug. 'I don't think that yeller skirt's a good idea. Yer look like yer goin' off on a picnic. What else 'ave yer got?'

He picked out the pink dress from her bags.

'That's Jason's. It needs washing.'

'I can see him in it yer know.'

'He gives me the creeps.' She was stood, thumb in her mouth, like she was waiting for her school uniform to be ironed. Slapping it on thick now.

'It's true. There's somethin' about 'im. Wear it. 'S'not all that dirty.'

'I've got a little black dress. A new one.' She darted towards her bags.

He stopped her, cupped her chin in his palm, kissed her and said, 'You can save that one for later. Put this one on, I said.'

She pulled away and stared a comical hatred at him. A cartoon of shock. Enough disgust in her expression to make him feel really uncomfortable. They were miles away from each other now. Miles away. He revolted her. The hairs on the back of his neck went up. He stood back, stunned. She took the dress to the bathroom and closed the door behind her. When he heard the shower pipes humming, he tried to get in. He'd changed his mind now. But the door was locked.

The buzz of Banus disguised a million and one unwholesome deeds and everyone there knew it. How clean were those yachts? They shone now in evening orange and pretended the innocence of toys but she knew the menace on the faces of their owners and much of what went on inside those cabins, once the bars were closed. When away from home people behave at their worst because they can get away with it. Jonathan was back to eyes shut again. Wouldn't look at her.

On one side of the quay there was Clouds, out of the sunlight dying anyway now. And on the other, Joe's Shed, soaking up the last of it. They were to go to Joe's Shed first to hook up with Jason who would no doubt be sat at the workers' table, deciphering the *Sun* with his index finger.

Before them, a glut of human traffic still shopping and, behind, the same, the air full of perfume, bewildered people out of their routine and in the mood for a holiday. Laughing falsely and sounding almost in a panic, the women were too keen to be shopping, the thrill of overspending already wreaking its havoc. There were hardly any men walking. Mostly sitting on the edge of bars, smoking and drinking or, if not doing that, working. She could see the piano man from Joe's Shed putting baskets of condiments on the tables outside. She stopped walking suddenly.

'What's up now?' he said.

'Nothing,' she said. He'd been planning this all along. Had worked it so she'd be his and not Jason's. She'd been blind not to see it. Groups of shopping women were splitting up and walking round them to join up again in front. She could have been doing that. She could have been out shopping with her mum.

Off her own back, it had been fine. But now she felt manipulated. Rushed. It didn't feel so natural to her. She didn't feel that hungry for this job any more. Didn't have either the drive or curiosity to move her forwards. Now it was just for the money. And money just wasn't enough.

Marcelle's sports car was there, waiting for her. Marcelle wasn't like Mamoud. Mamoud had been genteel. Over genteel in deference to his English Lady. Marcelle had screwed enough English ladies to do away with the manners and pussyfooting. Of all the ones she'd had, Marcelle had been the worst. French with no English. No pretence. No respect. No partnership. With the others, the unspoken contract had bonded them, made the deal palatable. But not with him. Yet he'd been her only call-back. She should have been pleased since a call-back was recognition of her skill to thrill, but no, not from him. She'd wanted Mamoud to call back but he never did.

She looked away and ahead over the marina taking in as much as the eye could see. Like a hoarding advertising cigarettes, the boats were plastic, the sky untouchable, the mountains, home, reality unreachable.

'Come on, we're late, what yer starin' at?' He was pulling on her arm, walking her fast through the tables and chairs to the bar entrance.

'Jonathan?'

'What's wrong now for chrissakes?'

'We could go for a meal, to a club, anything but this. I could send you the money as soon as I get home.'

'Louise, if that's what you want.'

'So you *will* lend me the money.'

'If that's what you want.'

'Why change your mind now?'

'I ain't forcin' you into this. I need all the money I can get for me mam but if . . .'

'It's OK. You keep your sodding money.'

'Louise!'

'It's OK.'

The men were playing in their Sinclair C5s, out on the quay. Driving straight at each other and then swerving at the last minute to avoid a collision. Jason got out of his when he saw them. The man that sold the dinky cars and the mobile phones didn't want to play on his own so he got out too, and went through to the bar. The warmth of the sun on the back of her neck was the last stroke of friendship she'd remember. Really remember. The rest would all be a daze.

Jason stood at the bar with the phone man and signalled that she go to the table, the table with the newspapers on. Joanthan took her over and, in seconds, Jason joined them.

'You're late.'

'Tough,' said Jonathan.

''Ang on 'ere a minute, Louise. I wanna introduce Jonathan to someone. I'll have a drink sent over for yer and then I'll go over to Clouds and sort it all out. What d'yer want?'

'Brandy,' she said, not looking at him but around the bar which was still nearly empty. A group of lads were quietly drinking in the far corner, either ending a session or just beginning one, it was hard to tell.

'Right. Brandy it is. Is she alright?'

Jonathan looked down at her and she smiled up. 'Yeah. She's alright.' He left her there reading the paper. Jason took her over a brandy. From the bar, Jonathan watched her sup it too fast and wondered if she was OK, if she was going to go through with it. He went back over to her.

'I won't be long. You alright?' She nodded and smiled again. Putting on a brave face. He'd seen the very same face when he'd had her in the study room at the university library. Anyone could have walked past and seen through the glass but she'd wanted to please him. Her brave face had ruined it.

'Mr Charlton, this is Jonathan.'

Jonathan quite liked the man. Straightforward. Scottish. Made a joke about a Scotsman selling mobile phones but Jonathan didn't laugh. Something to do with inventions. Said he'd made a fortune in Scotland, selling his little car to the golf courses. Sinclair the computer genius had invented it. It ran on a washing machine engine but not up the high street as he'd been hoping. Just right for getting from green to green though. Did Jonathan want a go?

'No thanks. I thought the whole idea was to walk round the golf course,' he said, 'for the exercise.'

Jason butted in. ''Ave you got that phone for him then, Reg?'

Big belly, big thick moustache, shiny gold buttons on a navy blue blazer. His cheeks were spotted with deep red blots, like someone had flicked a paintbrush at him. Blood busting its way out all over. Little berries growing on the side of his nose. Mr Charlton drank from his pint, moved the glass out of the way and put his case on the bar. Jonathan quite fancied a mobile phone.

'Quite 'eavy isn't it?' he said, not putting it to his ear but weighing it up, the way Moustaf had weighed the binoculars.

''Ave yer tried carryin' a phone box on yer back lately? Now that's what I call heavy, big man.'

Jonathan smiled, remembered Louise and looked over. She looked dreadful. Ill. She'd lit a fag and put it straight back out again.

'Where do I sign?' he said, pen poised at the ready. 'Hope this isn't gonna cost me owt?'

'No. I just 'ave to keep records of who's got what. Right sign there and then . . .' flicking through some pages, 'there.'

'Yer stayin' for a drink, Johnno?' Jason was trying to be his mate now.

'I don't think so. It's dead in 'ere. I think I'll get off. He looked over at Louise again. He wanted to take her home now. He moved the forms closer to one of the lights behind the bar and began to read. Couldn't be bothered. Signed in the two places and gave the papers back to Mr Charlton. He was hanging on there, waiting for them.

The man finished his pint, knocked back a short, ripped off the duplicate pages, pushed them over the bar and said, 'Read the warnings before yer start usin' the phone. OK?' And Jonathan looked at the forms more carefully then, moved to a better-lit section down the bar and searched the paper for the word 'WARNING'. He took the forms to the gents with him, the light in there really strong, his bladder bursting. He pissed his way down the page, holding the form in one hand, himself in the other.

He couldn't find the word warning but got it nevertheless. He remembered the credit card check. When he re-entered the bar, she was gone.

He was in slow-motion, the action moving too fast. He went outside and ran round the place to sight her. Nothing. Found Jason sat at one of the tables, shouting down his phone. He ran over to Clouds and spoke to Laura who told him to sling his hook. Louise wasn't there. He ran back to Joe's Shed and Jason was still on the phone.

'We've got three up at the Club, two down at Chester's.'

He pulled on his arm but Jason waved him away. Mouthed 'Chas' and pointed at the phone. God was on the line.

'I think we're bang-on about our Reg yer know. Yer know what he said? That his landlady was a Catholic. I told yer didn't I? Told yer he'd come up with some excuse.'

Then a long pause. Then . . .

'No, the conference is done and dusted. He wants it for some party. It's just propaganda like. If we do it tonight we kill two birds. They've paid a deposit 'n' everythin'. And we've fixed the match for Sunday if yer into it? I'm gettin' a team sorted, aren't I? I told 'em it's for charity like. You'd think they were fuckin' pop stars, 'onest to god.'

Shouting his head off he was. Walking about, making sure he was seen, heard, in the way. People dodging past him to get into the bar.

Jonathan wanted to ram the phone down his throat. He kept a lookout for Louise, but nada.

'Listen, I got Johnny boy in me face 'ere. Better go. See yer later.'

'Jason. Where is she?'

'Gone, mate. I sent her over to Laura's with Reggie boy. Clouds, over there,' he said pointing.

'But I thought we were gonna . . . Reggie? She was supposed to be goin' with Marcelle. That's what she told me. Who the fuck's Reggie?'

'Yer phone man. Something came up so Marcelle had to pull out.'

'Where's he gone with her? Phone 'im on his mobile.'

'I just have. He's turned it off.' Jonathan was stood over him now but Jason wasn't worried. He put his feet up on the chair next to him. 'She'll be alright. Don't fret. They often tank 'em up with a few drinks first. Oil the wheels like.'

It was just a game to him, a joke. Jonathan spoke calmly. Cool. His 'in control' tone. 'Did you do a check on his credit card?'

'No need. We know him. Listen mate. I've gotta go. Go and try Clouds. She might still be there.' He jumped up and looked at the screen on his mobile. Jonathan had left his on the bar and only then remembered. He went in to get it.

When he came out he said, 'I've changed me mind about her now.'

'She's not *yours*, Jonathan.'

'Isn't she? Well she ain't fuckin' yours.' He pushed the table over and the vinegar bottle smashed on the tiles. The smell was sickening. The thought of her with that Reggie. He was wasting time and it wasn't his to waste now. He wanted to run but didn't want to show Jason how desperate he was. He wanted more than anything to rub the little get's nose in the vinegar glass. He was back on his phone again now, walking away, a finger in his ear. Nothing registered with him. Not Jonathan. Not the vinegar. Not Louise. Nothing but the money.

Jonathan walked quckly across the quay and in seconds, sighted her in the carpark. The car seat belt across her pink dress like a

Thunderbirds uniform. Her head was lolled to one side. She didn't even look awake.

The phone man was looking behind to reverse. Jonathan ran fifty yards through dust clouds to catch them but they were gone.

When he went back to find Jason, to pummel more information out of him, he'd gone too. There was nothing else to do now but wait.

Chapter Twelve

The tide had washed most people off the beach, that and the shade, the cool. Those still left dotted the sand like tics on a beast. A few stragglers, early drinkers, were lounging at the bars. Some local lads made a gang of themselves along the water's edge. They lived here, all the time. Were born here. They knew the sea, its strength, its daily habits, its fish. That's why they ambled so close to its edge, not as a romance, not as tourists. This was their street corner. They were in training shoes. A wave comes, they know how far to jump back, how far to move forwards. They laugh or poke fun or strike out for more aggro. They wave-dodge, mid-banter, mid-swipe, mid-holding their ribs and laughing out loud. This was their sea really and their day was nearly over now.

He wondered if she'd be up to going clubbing later on. She hadn't looked well, up for anything at all, let alone . . . Maybe his mind was playing tricks though. Feeling sorry for itself. How would she dance these days? She walked well enough but how would she dance? How long would she be? He should have waited for her. Stayed down there. The part that he was, he'd fled the scene, in a panic almost. Got a lift on the back of a bike and nearly died in a head-on. Omens rushing at him thick and fast, he'd even run up to his flat in a panic. Why?

So friendless now, sat alone on his balcony, watching seagulls, he thought of his budgie, Tiny, remembered buying it a mirror and a bell from the jumble sale. Remembered the noise it made. '*Waiting and waiting, nose to the grating, eyes firmly fixed to an oblong of sky.*' Not bird brains at all. The gulls were squawking, doing Hitchcock to make him feel uneasy, get him jumpy, jumpy enough to think about his dad. Or was that an excuse not to think about her and what she was up to. '*I think I'd be wary to keep a canary, in case*

189

he should suffer as keenly as I.' He'd let his budgie go. His dad whacked him, mum blanked him, Shirl didn't care and the teacher said he'd as good as murdered it. It was the teacher that taught him the '*Waiting and waiting, nose to the grating.*' 'Dead in a day,' she said. 'Gobbled by a cat,' she said. 'You'll go far,' she said, on the day he left school. They said that to all the kids. It was the Manchester way of telling them to fuck off.

He'd crossed another line and he knew it. He'd been after work and, from that work, money. He'd always assumed that was the way. Work then women then wife and kids. But it wasn't like that at all. It was all about money. The wife and kids could be missed out completely. An unnecessary expense and a lifelong emotional drain. Of course he wanted kids, but not the house or the wife to go with them. Of course, if he never married, he'd for ever be alone. And he didn't fancy that much, either. But still, he didn't want what his father had had and couldn't imagine why so many did. And to think, after all that hard work, after a life of grime and time spent watching other people's valuables, he'd landed himself in jail for the crime of just being there. Just watching. But then, it was his father who'd said that the sinners who burn longest in hell are those who stood and watched the innocent burn in theirs. A security officer watching tellies get stolen was hardly hellfire and damnation material but perhaps God saw fit to punish bullshitters without mercy too. Six months in prison without any telly would do him good. It would be interesting to see what sort of welcome Mrs Thatcher's world of opportunity had in store for him when he got out. And it would be Johnno paying the mortgage now. Johnno who could barely contain himself now, looking forward to the opportunity of confronting his father with, 'Have you not found yourself a job yet? I mean a decent job. It's about time you played the game and paid your way, my father.' Dad on the dole without a pot to piss in. It served him right.

He dug in his pocket for her watch without a strap and watched the seconds go backwards they were going so slow. He took off his earring. Fingered the loop. Battled with it being omen or junk. Had he come full circle now? A gull flew in so close he could see the

whites of its eyes. He felt loose. Not in charge of himself. Get a grip.
Go the loo.

He stroked the bumps on his chin. He could have lent her the
money. Easily. He'd let her go out working on the scum of his
meanness. Was that Sammy on the hobble over there? He raised his
binoculars and saw it wasn't. Was it that shitehead keeping him in,
banged up? Was it Sammy had him running up the stairs in a panic,
back to his cell, back on the loo? He couldn't stand it. The watching.
The waiting. What did Jason say? That looking after the women was
the first law of the jungle. Well he didn't like it. Didn't like it one bit.

He looked down at himself and decided to change, another one of
those new man changes. Stick with the timeshare. Do selling. Get
good and go home and run his own shop. Estate agent? Shit
landlord? Whatever shit he turned into, he'd at least have the
stomach to smell it. He'd go and buy some new clothes now. Ready
for the meetings tomorrow. Do a proper job. Look smart. Get Big
Man Chas to take him seriously. Take those fliers and hand them
out, in the bars. Now was the time to look sharp. He had a job he
wasn't taking seriously enough and if he worked it right, he could be
something he could own up to. Tomorrow, he'd send all his money
home. Take *her* home if he had to.

God must have sent Sammy over to impress on him the weight of a
conscience just as Wheezy had turned up to tempt him. Why else
were they here? They'd turned up on the same day and unknown to
one another, had talked. As his dad always said, there is no such
thing as coincidence. All this was meant to be. The ugliness and the
beauty of his past like ghosts sent in to warn him of his future, to
help him make the right choices, to tempt him into badness. Sitting
up on that balcony, watching all that sea, with a bag full of money, it
wasn't too hard to turn the devil of that job down now. It wasn't a
job. It was money. Just money. He wanted Wheezy back now. He
clenched both fists and, when he opened, saw the perfect imprint of
her watch without a strap in his palm. He couldn't stand it. He'd go
and find her. Get a fucking strap for her watch. He'd seen the logo
for it on a shop down there. He'd walk the beach way and drop fliers

on the bars. Sammy wouldn't be walking the beaches with a gammy leg. And he caught himself then. He had to admit that he was scared. Scared of Sammy Smith.

He slid some fliers under the back of his money belt and then left. He ran down the stairs and stamped on every third one, loud, heavy. At the bottom of his flight he collided with an American tan pair of English doves, fluttering. Huddled together on the stairs. Right there. The male told Jonathan to watch himself and moved his bird out of the way in case the African tan rubbed off on her. Jonathan reared up at him to scare him and then carried on down the flights, jumping on every third stair. The last stair was for his mother but he jumped over it.

Out into the cook of the streets, the light near dim now, the air glinting with jewellery and shiny arms, bronzed. White white clothes, in the distance, like flags, moving along in drunken droves. Earrings and smiley faces from all angles. He was sweating, moving too fast. Making people look at him. He could hear shouting drunks off the beach. He slowed his pace and walked close to the walls. He chose a new bar, Vivi's, just at the beginning of the Old Town, right on the main drag where, if Sammy wanted to find him, he could.

Flowery sofas Lego'd the side of the dance floor and, down the bar, a curve of stools. Chrome leg-high jobs. Leather tops. Like midgets with no heads. Michael Jackson playing. Later on there'd be bottoms spilling all over them stools. Office girls in gangs of tits and arse, screaming drunk. Squashing and squidging from one buttock to the other. Sliding on and slopping off. There were two climbing up there now. They thought they looked sophisticated. As if they didn't get stools like that at home. On their tall stools with their tall drinks made taller by blocks of ice and umbrellas to make sure they had a ball, they sat and flicked ash and compared lines around their tits. And they were going topless tomorrow to get rid. Made sure Jonathan heard all about it. He could dig that. Could dig the little one getting her tits out, no problem. Could dig the fact she'd want to feel a breeze on her nipples. He always did. He drank two beers, paid and left leaflets on every table and window sill. He gave the girls one each. Then he went to Tonio's Tapas bar. No English staff or beer. Spanish telly and no welcome for tourists. He could have a quiet think in there. The old men in caps and ten o'clock shadows, drinking schnaps and brandy, ignored him. For a minute, he likened himself to these peasants, these men whose town had been stolen from them. Real men getting away from the blare of foreigners just playing at being alive. He could smell the toilets every time the swing door swung open. He might have been back in England, in the Tap room at the Shire Horse. Tonio didn't thank him for the tip. He liked that too. He liked not being welcomed and he liked not being asked back. He decided to make Tonio's his local. He left through a side door and wended his way down an avenida of pink pavement, newly laid with vacant squares of soil waiting for their perfect arrangement of flowers to arrive. Everything real was dead, dying or about to be killed off. The glare of the contrived landscape was taking its toll now. He ran to the beach for a sight of the sea and, even in the dim, it rushed at him with the salve of an Optrex bath.

Now was the time to be out with a girl. The sun blast gone. A cool breeze. He could be sat at one of the beach bars with her now. With her, laughing. Playing chess. Back then, they'd played chess for hours on end. They could have been in the sea, paddling, chucking splashes at each other. Or having a meal. Or in a park, canoodling. They could have hired a car and driven home, the slow way. Through Toledo. She wanted to go to Toledo. See some El Greco, she said. They could have been anything they wanted to be.

Now he was striding down the beach as a worker, dropping fliers on bars where they looked at him as scum and perhaps hadn't heard that there's scum and there's scum. Ten minutes along a newly created industrial strip of a beach, dark and grainy on the eye, too flat to be real, he heard a familiar voice. A Scottish voice. Instead of carrying on with his walk, he veered towards where it came from. The bar was round with a straw hat on, wooden stools on poles driven deep into the sand, all around it. Behind the counter, above the plates of fruit slices, innocent strips of killer tape flapped in the breeze, catching flies by the dozen, a whole graveyard of them already massacred. Sticky drinks, lime wedges and Pepperami sticks were a feast for beach flies with no dead sea life to tuck into. It was a false beach for them too. Jonathan ordered a bottle of lager.

The man telling the story had his back to him now, his audience, four men, all mad for it. He was in long shorts. Not good. And socks. Not right. Not round these parts. Alright for clowning about. The man was talking with his body, throwing back his hair in a fury. Could do with being cut, that lot. Lunging forward, the man got close to his audience, to say something quietly. And then, like a child, danced backwards, as if the sand was too hot, his feet hardly touching, his arms waving windmills. The men laughed and laughed, their eyes fixed, dead on him. By the time Johnno was drinking his beer, they were holding their ribs, roaring, falling off their stools to hold themselves better. And the Scottish man stopped then. Johnno hadn't caught a word of it. All quiet, the men were reduced to wheezy laughter and the Scottish joker, with his head to the sky, quietly guzzled from his bottle. He leant on the counter and wiped the wet beer from his lips, his face serious. Johnno felt stupid for not getting him sooner. It was Billy Connolly.

He ordered another beer. The barman was Spanish and, like Jonathan, not in on the joke. There was no-one else there. Just the four men and Billy and a barman in T-shirt and jeans with boxes of produce still to unpack, shelves newly built and waiting. Of course Johnno wanted to go over. He wanted to meet Billy, shake his hand. Have a laugh. But he couldn't. They'd not even noticed him. If he kept looking over they'd know exactly what he wanted. He didn't feel cool, waiting around for an invite. It should all happen naturally to work properly. So he walked round the other side of the bar where he had absolutely no chance of meeting Billy Connolly. He tied his laces that didn't need untying and he didn't finish his beer or leave any fliers. Before his back was turned, they were all roaring again. Jonathan looked back, wary now. Were they laughing at him? Were they pointing at him? Someone had buried a man in the sand, right up to his neck. On his head, bread for the birds. Six seven eight gulls like planes in a queue, circled and took it in turns, to feed and take off again. So Billy thought that was funny did he?

He walked down the beach, angry at his own shyness. Ashamed of it. He couldn't help himself. Freddie Starr had spoken to him once, in La Cepa's, Fuengirola. He'd felt so proud. He didn't even like Freddie Starr, flash git, but if he met him again, he'd be just as proud second time round. So sick but so true, because in the face of fame, he was too aware of how small he was, how unnecessary, how far he would never get to go.

He dropped the rest of the fliers in an abandoned castle moat and then buried them, his foot kicking and pounding the sand over, a dog on shit-cover duty. Then he got closer to the sea for an easier time on the legs, cramp imminent. Should he take off his trainers and paddle? He looked around. Very few people about, a group of girls eyeing a group of boys. In the sea, a lone jet-ski and a couple of windsurfers, a yacht the size of a house and a couple of heads bobbing. The sea was dark blue, darker than usual. Jewel blue and looking cold. No paddling. No fizzy waves between the toes. No tickles. No sinking feeling. Just pound the sand and go.

He'd not walked all the way before and felt the three miles on the beach as ten on the shin. He bought a very expensive bottle of water and drank half. The other half he poured over his head and swilled his face and soaked his T-shirt to a mess.

Only place he was fit for now, was the Shed and he didn't fancy it, a team of drunks on duty outside making more noise than they knew. Some in fancy dress, Batman and Robin again. Keeping the Shed to his right, just in view, he marched off shopwards. He passed Clouds and looked in there. There were two girls sitting together laughing. Their faces went straight when they looked at him and then they went back to laughing again. Laura was stood behind the bar with her arms folded. There was no point in asking her again. And he'd gone right off the idea of doing any real shopping. These shops weren't right for him. Not busy enough. Smelt too much. Smelt too much like her, all perfume and leathery. Up in Marbella you could look and not be looked at. Here the shop assistants camped out in the doorways, bored and poised to jump, the ding of their doorbells sounding eerie, sinister in the quiet.

He settled on the cheapest strap they had, bearing the logo. The best part of twenty quid was about as friendly as he thought he should be given the circumstances. She was worth more, for sure, but it would send out the wrong signals. As for men's clothes, there wasn't much choice once the Italians were ruled out. They were ruled out immediately. More style than required. And anyway, he didn't think they'd welcome trainers and dirty laces on their beige carpet runners. Or let him try on. And the clothes were so sharp, they weren't fit for wear and tear. A choice of stripey or fucking stripey. He bought one shirt. Denim. Fifty quid's worth. A very fine shirt. A fucking stripey shirt. A safe shirt. An American shirt.

After three times round the same block, his feet sore from the cobbled street and unwilling to confront any more glass shops and staring faces, he was just about ready to find her. He left the main arena of activity and walked towards Jo's Shed, the hand-painted sign on varnished wood proud and naïve and sad in a way. Against the plastic glass frontage of Banus – shops and boats, restaurants and bars – it looked to be clinging on. A miserable boast of the past still standing. Jonathan lingered before going in. Wondered whether to casually order a drink or just wade into the din, guns at the ready, demanding. A drink, he decided.

He didn't look about him in the bar, not even at the gymslip German serving, her tits almost out of her halter. He went for gin and tonic and bought a packet of fags. The man next to him got up to leave and so he took his stool and settled down. Sat right the other end of the bar, staring straight at him, was Sammy.

He nodded and Sammy nodded back, all civilised. In a blue check shirt, his eyes black and blank, skin brown as Johnno's, he'd been stacking the sunbathing in, big-style. Was that why his eyes had lost their bite? Why they were dead? Was that all there was to it? Sammy over on his holidays, recuperating? Johnno debated whether to go over. It was all he could do to break into his packet of fags.

He sipped his drink, got a book of matches off the Frau and lit up.

Never had a fag come in so handy. It helped. Got him to thinking that if Sammy had come for him, he'd have brought some muscle to make up for his foot. Wouldn't be dining and dancing the girls as he was now, the girl sat next to him, on call it looked like. Paying attention. The cigarette was making him dizzy. Johnno necked his gin and got ready to go. Sammy jumped off his stool immediately. Johnno put his fags back on the bar. The piano man struck up a Randy Crawford fly away number. A calming number. A fight was inconceivable, surely. There was space for it though. Johnno looked round, saw he was out on a limb, everyone gone outside now. Sammy had his stick all sorted and was making his way over.

'Y'alright there, Johnno,' as he approached.

Jonathan emptied another fag out of the packet. 'Fine yeah. And you?' Grit in his teeth.

No answer. Sammy walked past him, over towards the gents. Johnno watched him swing his leg out to walk, the bad foot like a weight, a mind of its own he could tell. Sammy Smith without a foot wasn't Sammy at all.

The walk to the loo was a long one. Johnno stopped watching and, once again, picked up his fags to go. Sammy yelled over, 'I'll just have a slash and we'll talk, yeah?'

'Right,' he answered. Sammy's girl shook her head. A warning. He used the back exit of the Shed and ran to the road for a lift. He flagged a taxi in the end.

He jumped out, outside the post office. And there was Moustaf, in the square, dishing out his charm still. A puzzle of a man who could turn hot to cold on account of the price of a bottle of aftershave. But then, Moustaf could live for a month on that, six months even. Jonathan had offered him money. For keeps, food, whatever, but Moustaf pushed it back at him, digusted. He'd take it alright from strangers. He'd sketch a stranger, for a fixed price, give them the sketch and then ask twice the price. For my wife he'd say, or for my babies. He always got more than what the punter wanted to give. If no-one bought his sketches, he'd beg, hold his hand out and beg for the money. His wife was in Morocco. He must have sent all his money home because he lived and died in his shorts, threadbare cheesecloth shirt and an African tooth necklace that his sister made, he said. There were millions of them, on the pavements, all over the market. He'd take money from strangers but not from friends. Wise? To beg or bitch? What would he have done? If she'd been begging, would he have been more generous?

He shopped quickly. Didn't try on. Just held the clothes against him and paid. Hated it, the work, the looking for the right size, the choice, the disappointment, the sales staff following him around. He stopped off at Vera's for a beer. Full of strangers. White and drunk. Just arrived. Of course, it was Saturday. His birthday. He went home, hoping she might be sat outside the flat. But no. He bolted the door.

Through the glass, he tried to make out the ink swirl of the sea. Then he spotted some legs and arms in white holiday garb plodding up the shore. Their arms entwined. They were trying hard to be smoothly romantic, their feet fumbling heavy in sandy weights. They were burdening each other with all that summertime expectation but the beach was black and cold and heavily against them. In the end they split up to make their walk to the prom more efficient. Then they went out of sight. He fiddled with the window catch to open his way out on to the balcony. And there he waited. And waited. Snoozed until a campfire party on the beach got going. Youngsters. Guitars and tom-tom. And then, rising up to him, to stab him, the softness of 'My Lady D'Arbanville'.

At around one o'clock, he was falling asleep again, in his chair, the sea a black bedcloth not warming, not helpful at all. The smell of chips strong. Voices on the beach. Running sounds. He lit a cigarette and inhaled. Stood over the balcony he looked up towards the town for signs of a taxi. The lights of Marbella twinkled Christmas back at him. False gloam. Electric. And then the sea came to him. A smile. And then a freak blow of wind to make a shell of his right ear, and through him went that thunder of being. He shivered. She should have been back hours ago.

And then came the banging. Someone banging on all the doors

down the corridor. Doors opening and closing. It was the devil's last shout. They came for her and what had he done? Nothing. And now they'd come for him . . . Something had definitely happened to her. She was gone and Sammy was here. Sammy was in the house. He'd called for heads and got tails. He'd been given the choice and he'd chosen wrong. And now the devil was upon him Bang. Bang. Bang. There were people shouting up the corridor. A babble of German and Spanish and English. Like demons awoken from their graves in the sun. At night this babble struck him to the bone of his being, to a dread so intense, he could not believe he wasn't dreaming. And then he heard Sammy's voice. Jonathan. Jonathan. He stayed still till the banging came at last to his door. Heard Sammy singing, 'Jonathan. Jonathan. Wakey Wakey Jonathan.'

If it hadn't been so late, he would have let him in. If he hadn't been waiting for her, he would have let him in. If ifs and buts. He listened still. Sammy was working his foot through the door, booting it and booting it but to no effect. A police car drove up and parked right in front. Five minutes later, Sammy was climbing into it. Johnno was cold now but he stuck it out on the balcony. The least he could do was suffer a chill for her. Then the guitars on the beach played out another Cat number he didn't need to hear. The one his dad really liked.

Chapter Thirteen

At last a cab rolled up. It was gone five. He hung over the balcony to gauge the state she was in. The cabby had to help her out and prop her up against the wall. Then he drove off.

He ran down to get her. She could walk but only just. He had to half heave her up the stairs.

When they got to the door of the flat, she suddenly came alive and elbowed him out of the way. Then, unsteady on her feet, made for the balcony windows. He'd closed them to keep the bugs out. She fell forwards to the glass, only her forehead holding her up. He looked out and saw what she saw. The tip of a tongue of fire bobbing up on the horizon, deep deep red, a slit of fire on the sea.

'Louise, what's wrong?'

'Nothing,' she said, but she sounded almost in tears.

She looked all in. Her teeth clattering, as if cold but she was red hot. Sweaty forehead, the lot. Bit o' Spanish gyp no doubt.

'I . . .' She lifted her arm up to her face. 'I feel really tired.' Then she started chunnering to herself, like in a dream.

'Well it's five o'clock in the mornin'. I'm not surprised. Where've yer bin?' And then wished he'd not asked. He pulled her from the window and her head fell to her chest, like her neck was broken. He lifted it and looked at her. 'You look horrible.'

Still chunnering.

He pulled her towards him. Took her in his arms and rocked her, her cheek against his breast, her arms dangling. He felt then, the full release of her, the full force of her little body against him. She reminded him of Malcy, middle of the night.

'You weren't wearin' that when yer went out, what's going on?' She was in a blue dress with a lacy collar. Looked terrible on her.

She didn't answer. She was breathing in deep, giving it all her concentration. Maybe she'd had too much sun, all in one day. Too much drink? She was gone. Gone gone. He looked out and saw the sun a red headlight now, out of its sea, turning it blood. He should have taken her straight to bed, but no. He wanted her with him, watching the day come in. Silent and compliant. He slid the window back. Some air would do her good. If she was sick, vomity sick, she could do it out there, not in his bedroom. He walked her out on to the balcony. She wasn't rag doll but nearly. He sat down and laid her across his body. There *was* no air. The heat was still in from yesterday. She didn't look comfy but she didn't complain. No twitch, groan, nothing. He hummed his 'My Lady D'Arbanville' to her. He couldn't get the tune out of his head.

The blue was coming in now. Baby blue, the stars all inside out and gone. Night and day. Like a double-up anorak. And to his right, on the other side of the Esplanade, candy floss pink streams of cloud, not heavy enough to be around for long, like her maybe. Then birds, black against this backdrop. They were flying in streams, in the same direction, so quiet, so very quiet, like they were carrying secrets. He watched the sun all the way up until it turned banana. All this time, he played his lips across her hair, to a rhythm, as if driven by some someone else working him from the inside out.

There weren't many times in his life he'd felt like this. How often had he had that feeling of togetherness without communication, no levels to measure, no blame now. A clean slate. A new day. Just him, her and all that out there. He arranged her fingers into a comfortable climb up his muscled arm. Those fingers, brown as they were, still spidered foreign against his skin. So small and delicate. And then, just then, he became wary again. He was trying to see her more. Not just see her, see behind her. Why *was* she in this state?

He looked away and out instead. The sea had turned from black plastic mac into a swimming pool streaked with dark, dark streaks that could have been schools of fish travelling down the line for brekkers. The air was thick but without smell, no food in it, no sun oil in it, no distractions on the hint of breeze that came not quite often enough. He felt different. He felt what he thought other men must feel, with their wives, with their family. He dug in his pocket for her watch and strapped it on to her wrist. Got the feel of a wedding ring from it. And then he carried her to bed. In his arms. She was light enough to throw in the air and catch. But he wouldn't do that. Not now. She was sound asleep now. In the bed, he stroked her hair until he was.

He woke in fine fettle. Didn't jump from the bed as usual. She was in it. He had work to go to but he didn't want to now. She was snoring. Snorting from time to time. He felt her. She was sweating. Down the legs she was sweating. And snorting again now. Louder. Like some grunting lion, warning him off. He got out of bed.

Went straight away to the balcony like a homefire burning. He surveyed the beach and the early-up bums lying on it, still dressed. He considered his options for the day. He'd have a look see. See how the big man Chas operated. It was supposed to be some kind of privilege to work directly with him, that much he'd gathered. He could go and see what sort of job he'd be turning down. Give his new clothes a show. He strummed the bars of the balcony, from one end to the other. Making a bet his dad was doing the same, across the bars of his cell window. He laughed just thinking about it. The funny side of it. His dad, banged up for a robbery. Tragic but funny all the same. He'd send mum the money today. And then he remembered it was Sunday.

He set about his shave. It was like returning to base, shaving. But for the bumps, he was pleased with his new face now. Remembered himself. Then remembered Sammy. But he wouldn't be out the clink till lunchtime at least and only then if he was lucky with a full wallet on him.

It was time to go home and he knew it. All signs were pointing in that direction. Even her. He splashed himself with water. 'Pull yourself together, man.' He splashed and then laughed. Felt mad for a minute. Out on a limb. He stared at himself to fix some reality. That walk down the beach had given his chin some colour. One more day and he'd be done all over. Mustn't forget to tell her about Billy Connolly.

He took his clothes from their hangers and lay them on the bed, quietly. She was dead to the world. Still dressed. He thought she'd have woken and stripped off at some point. He got close to her face and breathed all over it. To see if she was pretending. No. Dead to the world.

He enjoyed the getting dressed, for the first time in a long time. Today, he would measure the impact of his new image. One advantage to being different from the mob was the joy of having some impact on it. He could never be one of those suckers on the beach out there, one of a crowd, doing whatever the next man was up to. There weren't that many down there yet. Ahh . . . Sunday. Even on their holidays they stay in bed longer. Even holidays can hold on for a lie-in. How many for lamb at Mavver's today? Dressed and ready to rock, he clapped hands. Yes. Let's go. Before leaving, he looked in on his sleeping 'what could still be' wife potential and smiled. Her snoring had got louder. Slightly off-putting. He'd leave a note. Tell her to clean up. Tell her he wouldn't be long. And not to speak to anyone. He'd lock her in so she couldn't go anywhere. So no-one could get to her. So Sammy would know to clear off. So Jason couldn't take her. It wasn't safe to just leave her there. He felt bad, snapping the padlock on. It was a serious lock. He'd explain when he got back. To do it in a letter would make her nervous. 'Locked you in.' Nah. She'd be alright. He'd phone.

In the shop windows, he checked his physique, the difference it made when he pulled his shoulders right back. Checking to see if the slim cut of the suit showed up his money belt – ridged out in any way. The mobile phone spoilt it. Too bulky. Made him look lopsided. The fall of his jacket, no flaps in it, was supposed to hang straight as a ruler.

He hoped he didn't look too new, too smarmy. He wanted to come across as someone naturally in tune with his own good taste. Hoped she'd approve. She'd tell him straight. Had been straight enough about the disappearing beard, no messing. He liked that side of her, the stern side. And then how she was that morning, that childish side. He liked that too. He remembered the note asking her to clean up and reminded himself to ring her. Before she got on to scrubbing the kitchen tiles. They'd be getting hammered off next week. He stopped now, to give himself the full frontal in a shop window. He looked good. Would he still be here next week? He couldn't really see it.

The bus dropped him off in what appeared to be wasteland, just scrub and bushes and brown earth, not soil or fine enough for sand, not soft enough. He could see the hotel, a white box, standing all on its own. Unusually so. The Spanish didn't go in for solitary properties usually, that luxury of isolation. They lived in clumps, as if there really was safety in numbers. From where he stood, the place looked like a carpark, the windows just open black spaces, narrow and regular and all around. How to get to it, that was the next question. His shoes felt tight now, his feet hot. He didn't want to take his jacket off because then he wouldn't be the full picture, give off the full effect. He'd be like any other git in a T-shirt. But he soon gave in. It was too hot to pose.

Along the road, he saw a small sign, like a flag stuck in the dirt. He hoped a sign for the hotel. He headed off, trying to walk with new professional determination. He wasn't going to like this job, he knew that already. But he was stuck now. It was a money job and he needed money. Or he could go home and start over. He could take her home and make it up to her. She'd be back in Manchester soon, as a student. He could try that one again. They could live together. He wanted her again now. For the second time, he really wanted her again.

He followed the gravel drive till he came to a group of bushes, flowering pink and yellow, not pleasant, pungent. He rounded a bend and came out on to more gravel laid thick, new. There was the entrance to the hotel. Over to the right, in the grounds and facing out to sea, was Chas. And a couple of serious-looking business men. And then, the reflecting light taking him by surprise, he saw another man in a leather jacket – around his feet lots of boxes and in front of him, a camera on a tripod. Not a photo camera, a movie camera, it looked like. How the fuck could he wear a leather jacket in this heat? Not cool. Not cool at all. That cheered him, considerably.

He'd gauged his new image perfectly. The impact on Chas was fantastic. He seemed nothing less than proud to introduce him. Stood up to welcome him to the table. He was looking quite smart himself, boyish with his curly grey locks shining almost yellow in the sun. He wore a striped shirt ironed with some authority, and beige trousers that no end of ironing could improve on, his big belly not quite in tune with his puny legs. Masses of creases round the groin.

'This here's Jonathan Wilson, one of my new boys. This here's Matt Delaney, he's in charge of finance, my laundry man. He's also very good for the punters. He knows the lingo and knows how to spot time-wasters. And this is Gerry, he's one of our satisfied customers, the proof of the pudding as they say.' The men nodded hello to him. Knew not to bother shaking hands.

Chas pulled a chair over. The man with the camera had wandered away, down towards the beach. Jonathan kept his eye on him. He kept stopping his walk to look for something. Then got down on his haunches, like he was looking at angles, behaving like some big time movie director. 'That's Marcelle. He's filming backdrops today, some scenes to stick in the videos.'

'Videos?'

'Yeah. I told yer. For the punters.'

They were sat under a palm tree. There were quite a few palm trees around the place. Palm trees that were meant to be there. The hotel wasn't. The tacky placky tables and chairs just finished the place off. The patio floor was top grade tile mind, the grouting sound, shimmery in the sun.

A waitress came out with a pot of coffee and only four cups. In perfect but forced English she said she'd bring an extra cup. The three men sat forward for the refreshment and Jonathan, feeling something of a fraud, joined them. They were talking about bumping up the red sales more than the blue. Cool-down periods. Stuff like that.

'So what 'appens?' Jonathan asked Chas this, but then looked to the other men, for answers. 'Today, what happens?'

'Matt talks finance. Gerry talks benefits. They get a free drink, a free pen and a video tape. Matt shows 'em charts of property values going up, I get their defences down. I tell a few jokes, put up a few objections and Matt 'ere talks some sense into me. Shows everyone how stupid I am. It works. We've done it twice now. The difficulty's been gettin' 'em to the meetings. Which is why we've given 'em an exclusive invitation to one of Marbella's top hotels.'

'But we're not in Marbella.'

'Near as damn it. Don't matter anyway, once they're 'ere, what they gonna say? When they see the vid, that'll cheer 'em up. First time we've got the vid stuff together. Jason's s'posed to be 'ere with them by now. Where the little bleeder's got to, I can't think.'

They carried on talking between themselves then. Chas punched numbers into his phone but he couldn't get through. Jonathan was sweating, wincing at the heat coming off the white building. There was nowhere to go, except to the beach, where the film man was.

'Is he Spanish? The film man?'

'Nah, French. Done a lot o' work in the States. Told us what kit to buy 'n' that. He owns the audio visual shop up in town.'

'Oh right. I'm with yer. I got me binoculars from there.'

'He's got some kit I tell yer. Fuckin' amazin' what yer can do these days. Gonna put Hollywood out o' business eventually.'

'What is?'

'The video kit. Any bugger can use it. Do what yer like these days. Cheap as chips. Marcelle was sayin' it's already got out of hand over there. The States like. Kids makin' their own snuff movies and whatnot.'

'Snuff movies?'

'Where the killin's for real. The actors snuff it on screen. Dead popular apparently.'

And all the men laughed. Jonathan watched Marcelle sizing up his shot. No. He already didn't like him anyway. Without all the nonsense, it was clear the man was bad news.

Over to the left, over the men's shoulders, Jonathan could see the vast spread of shit-coloured high-rise that was Fuengirola. Where the punters were coming from. The other side of the hotel was still being built, diggers still there. Not open for resident guests yet, Chas said. Which was why he'd got the place so cheap.

'What time's the coach due?'

'Soon. Very soon. There should be some punters from Marbella 'n' all, assuming you got them fliers out like I asked you to.'

'Yeah. So when they arrive, then what? What am I supposed to do?'

'If you 'ang on a minute, I'll go through it wiv yer. All in good time eh.' Talking to him like a child now.

He turned his chair to look at the sea and seethe. The men carried on talking, Chas saying he'd tried to speak to Jason but his mobile must have been out of range. But he was sure everything was on. And would they take lunch at the Club before they went back. What time was their flight? Delaney asking what the hit rate had been so far. Delaney saying there were quite a few rich peasants knocking about, these days. Specially from London. Sold their council houses and come out with grands. Made Jonathan think of his dad again. What a loser he was.

Marcelle was making his way back to the table. When he reached, he didn't even nod. He dragged a chair, sat down and tried to pour coffee. The pot was empty. Jonathan smirked and turned away, back to the sea.

Just inside the foyer of the hotel, there was a noticeboard announcing the first of a series of timeshare meetings for that month. In his new cream strides, wide but straight, a chocolate-coloured Ralph Lauren T-shirt and a beige jacket hung neatly over his arm, mobile phone in his mitts, Jonathan looked the sort of person who might use such a hotel. He felt very comfortable walking into it. He got nods off the staff. Respect.

'Now then,' said Chas, adjusting his shirt collar and tightening his belt. 'We're expecting about thirty on the first run. I want you to stand here and greet them in, shove 'em a marketing pack, OK?'

'You've dragged me all this way to 'and out brochures?'

'Hold yer 'orses. After the show, I expect at least one couple for an immediate viewing. We may get two, I dunno. You go back to

Fuengirola with 'em. Keep 'em sweet on the coach. Tell 'em about yer own gaff. Make 'em out to be . . . yer know the ol' game. Take them to the properties and show 'em round. I'll give yer the keys and directions later. It's dead easy to get to. Right on the front nearly.'

Jason turned up then, panting. Wiping sweat with one hand, holding a briefase and a big plastic bag of videotapes in the other. He was in full *Hawaii Five-O* costume. His gold medallion had swung round his back, the disc banging him between his shoulder-blades. He turned round and saw Jonathan standing there. Caught his smirk and put the briefcase down. He swung his medal round to the front, embarrassed.

'How'd it go? Give those to me.' Chas took the videos.

'Sorted,' said Jason

'What, all of it?'

'Yep.'

'Go back up to town and case it. Delaney's takin' it back with him.'

'All of it?'

They walked away then, out of earshot. Then Jonathan heard, and got the feeling he was supposed to hear . . .

'Did yer bring the brochure packs?'

'Yeah, they're on the steps, round the side.'

'Good.'

Then they moved even further away, well out of Jonathan's earshot.

Chas opened another button on his shirt. Well stressed out. Sweating.

They kept walking away, further into the foyer, Jason yapping in Chas's ear, ten to the dozen. Chas looked back, not at Jonathan, out to the grounds. Jason opened his briefcase on his thigh, took something out and gave it to Chas. Then took something else out. A tape it looked like, like the ones in the bag. He turned, looked at Jonathan and laughed. Chas had his eyes to the ground now, hands in his pockets. Like whatever Jason had told him, had calmed him down a bit. He was watching his feet, each foot doing a little dance, like he was putting out fags. He was thinking hard. Then he nodded. And then Jason turned to leave. As he waked away –

'I'll see you later. Couple of hours eh?' Chas shouted after him with debt in his voice, this time. Whatever Jason had done or said, had clearly impressed him. Jason waved as he walked out, past Jonathan, smiling.

Louise awoke to noise. A banging noise. Head banging. Rage rising. But plotless. Almost. She had to escape. That was it. Escape. Go home. Now. Money. Phone mummy. Escape money. Plan. Find phone. Hang on a minute. Think before mummy. Her head lay still on the pillow, thinking.

Then she sat up, swung her feet round and cried out. Between her legs. She joined her hands together and wedged them between her legs, to get air between her legs. She'd been slit with razors. She lifted her dress. A strange dress. And a strange pair of pants she had on. Not hers. The dress. She hadn't seen this dress for weeks. It was from her suitcase. She pulled down her pants and looked, lying back, straining her head for blood. Nothing. Nothing but noise. A banging noise. Razor cut noise from her legs. Acid inside her. Lemon in the eye noise. Her stomach throwing up. She watched it move, her rolling tum, turning over. Peristaltic waves. Tightening her muscles to spasm. Her body was in some desperate hurry to get somewhere, her mind gone. Lost. Trying to remember. A sunrise. Nothing after that. Not much before it.

'Jonathan,' she shouted but it came out weak.

She got up, walked legs wide apart to the noise. A banging. 'Who is it?'

'Is Jonathan there?' The noise stopped.

'No.'

'Where is he?'

'I don't know. Who is it?'

'Friend of 'is from Manchester. I need to catch up with 'im. It's urgent, love. Have yer got keys for this lock out here? Can yer put 'em through the letterbox?' He was clattering the letterbox, trying to look in. She stood away from it. Looked at the bolts on the inside, undone. She wanted to bolt them up but didn't have the strength to reach that high or bend that low.

'Well 'ave yer?' Getting angry. Slamming the letterbox down.

Standing there, outside the bathroom, she remembered the conversation with Jonathan. Him refusing to lend her the money. Him dragging her down there and into the bar.

'D'yer know where he is or what, love?'

On the baby glass coffee table, just inside the lounge door, the fliers advertising the timeshare meeting. She took one and shoved it through the letterbox at him. It all went quiet then. He'd gone. She turned the key in the door and tried to open it. Still locked. Locked from the outside. She was a prisoner. That bastard had locked her in. She went to the balcony. Slid the window open. Stepped out. The sun took her head off. Shock. Throw up. She ran to the bathroom and threw up green. Her stomach desperate to come out of her mouth, the spasms unbearable. She staggered back to the bedroom. Looked for the phone but it was back on top of the wardrobe. She could hardly reach it. Couldn't reach it. She slid down the wall, and sat leaning up against the wardrobe, thinking. Trying not to vomit. Not to cry. Her legs wide open. She pulled her pants down, down to her ankles, for air. She wanted her mum now.

What had he done to her? The money. From where she sat, she could see under the bed. Had he left a note? She felt her hair. It was still there. For a minute it felt like she'd lost it. Just calm down. Calm down. Bananas. Electrolytes. Would Jonathan have bananas? A gut certainty there'd be no bananas. A gut like she'd never felt before. She fell out of consciousness then. Was awoken by the door. Metal knocking the wood. She stayed frozen to the wall there. What would he do to her now? When she heard the bedroom door whinge open, she stayed perfectly still. Breathless. Saw no-one. Seen by no-one.

Then, a couple of minutes later, she heard a voice, a man's voice, Scottish. The man who sold phones and dinky golf cars. Then moans. Her own moans. Louder. The volume went up. Then 'Oy you! Hold her down . . . well make it look like yer 'oldin' her down.'

211

Then nothing. Then the same thing again. The man's voice talking. The moans. 'Oy you! Off her.' Then nothing. Then the same thing again. Then nothing. Then she heard keys jangling. A door whining open. Then nothing. Then the door whining closed. The cupboard in the hall. Then more television. She was sure it wasn't Jonathan but not sure if she was awake or asleep, dreaming or listening. She felt sick again, shivery.

Then came lots of men's voices. And more moans. The volume getting louder. She could see pictures of the men in her head but their voices were coming from the living room. Was she dreaming? When she tried to see the faces of the men, she couldn't. Only their bodies. She didn't need to pinch herself, the cold that clammed her skin, the vomit rising, the dry mouth told her all she needed to know about whether she was dreaming. She could see the men now, properly. In her head. Saw them coming down on her, the sound effects louder and louder. Coming from out there, out the door. She had to get up, and go out there. She had to get up and go out there. Were they out there? No. The noise came from the television. The noise went quiet then loud again. The laughing. She could remember the laughing now, and could hear it now. The tape was in her head. She had to get up and get out there.

She tiptoed to the door. It was partly open. She came out of the bedroom, into the hall. She could see into the lounge, from there. She could see the back of Jason's head. She could see her suitcase, standing centre-stage in the room. Like some joke, like some tease, there was her suitcase. She banged her head against the door jamb, madwoman style, bang bang bang. She was there alright. She was all there. Her red suitcase. Her suitcase.

Jason was leaning forwards, to the television. He was wearing the pink dress. His arm was going ten to the dozen. On the television, her. In the villa. The French man's villa. She remembered there being two couches but on the television only one. She was on it. Legs walking in front of her, back and forth, back and forth, but there she was again, on the couch, naked. A man holding her arms up over her head, another one getting on top of her. A man wearing a ghost of white gown and silver mask, lying on top of her, pushing into her. When he got off, 'You're in goal.' Jason was leaning forwards, pushing himself back and forth. Her head fell against the door jamb. She watched as another one got on her, this one black and completely naked. Men talking in the background. They were noisy. Marcelle telling them to clear out of the way. Clear shot, he said. Clear shot. Three times. 'Move the table! Move the table! Get out of the way!' He could speak English, perfectly.

'Now, see all these here.' He swung the bag of videotapes at him. 'Label each tape and then put them in the presentation packs, along with a brochure and pen. OK? And keep one for yourself.' Like that was a treat.

He did up his shirt buttons, leaving the top one open. Then straightened his cuffs. 'To be honest, they're not that good, yer know. We haven't got a handle on the editing yet, Marcelle's gonna sort that out. But the punters won't know no different. If it's all amateur looking, it'll come across more real to 'em. Make 'em think they're not bein' 'ad.'

'And are they? Bein' 'ad?'

'What d'you think? Liven up lad.' He looked him up and down then. 'If you don't mind my saying, you look smashin', son. Just the part. I was wonderin' if . . . if yer fancied a trip to England next week?'

'What for?'

'Bring somat back for us, some paperwork. Can't trust the post with deeds and the like. I'm buyin' some more property yer see, well, me bravver is.'

'I hope yer not . . .'

'It's all above-board, honest.'

'And why me?'

'You got anythin' better to do? It's a there and back job, no 'angin' about.'

Then they heard the wheels of the coach on the gravel. Chas crumbled, was in a right state. He pointed to the room where he wanted the punters to go and set about adjusting his shirt and trousers again.

'How do I look?'

'You look fine,' said Jonathan

'Not too scruffy.'

'No, casually smart I'd say.'

'Get goin' then . . . start doing up the packs. Come on, lad, you're me marketing man now.'

He piled everything on to the desk at reception and then packed each folder with a tape and the *Your Dream Come True* brochure. In the top right-hand corner, there was a picture of Chas, smiling, like Mr Butlin. The reception girl picked one up and flicked through it, then laughed. Jonathan flicked through to see for himself. The beaches looked like Paradise, empty and not Spanish. And the women lying in their beds eating breakfast! Well they weren't like the women now approaching the hotel *entrada*, women from the bingo, grannies and grumpies, wrinklies and frumpies. He thought of Louise then, in bed. Poked his head round the door to see if there were any men coming. The men were in groups, standing at the bottom of the garden, taking in the view, smoking. Hands in pockets, shuffling change. Getting into character.

As each 'guest' entered, Jonathan bid them good afternoon, gave them a presentation pack and sent them off in the right direction.

By guest number twenty, he was doing it mechanically. Not even looking at them. The din died down as the last stragglers waggled through. He turned to see how many were left – about six or seven. When *they* were all in, *he* could go in.

He was counting how many he had left when he saw the stick and the blade carving scratches into the wooden bar across the door. The white trousers. The quiet. The silent scream again. Short black hair, white shirt, white jacket, brown face, big eyes, smirking, like he was really glad to see him.

'You there, Sammy!' As cheerily as he could. The man in white wasn't cheered though, instead moved right up close. Too close. Stuck the blade of his knife right on his foot but luckily Johnno had gone for expensive and not been swayed by the comfort of deck shoes. The blade wasn't sharp enough. He moved away quick but Sammy grabbed his arm making him drop all the brochures and boxes. Sammy stabbed at a brochure with his stick like a litter man and, using it as a cover so reception couldn't see, he pulled a gun from his inside pocket. He had stick and brochure in one hand and a gun in the other, trained right on his balls.

The reception girl shouted over, 'It's time I think. They're starting,' and then set about shining up the already shiny wooden reception desk. He watched her, not the gun. He was immobilised. Needed directions. He looked down at the gun to see if in fact, it was real. None of it felt real. The barrel was shiny, quite narrow. Quite powerful-looking aimed at his balls like that. It did look like a toy gun but too finely sculpted, too heavy-looking. Sammy had moles on his fingers, with hairs standing up on them. He couldn't take his eyes off the hand, not the gun, the hand, the fingers. Saw past it for a second to the false foot in a shiny black shoe, then back to the hand and then back up to see a face with a question written on it, which he didn't know the answer to.

'We'll go and watch the show, shall we? You lead the way, I'm right alongside yer.'

They were the last ones in. Chas was slotting a video into the tape machine. The peeps were already bobbing up and down, trying to get a view.

'Now, ladies and gentleman. Thanking you for taking the time to come and join us here today . . .'

'Now then, shithead. What you got for me?'

'Eh?'

'You 'eard. How much you got?'

'I don't know what yerron about, Sammy. I've got about six, seven hundred quid. If yer that ribby, yer can 'ave it.'

'If yer don't behave, Freddy Pontin over there gets it.'

They were stood by the back door, away from the hubbub, no-one aware they were there except Chas who was trying his best to come over professional. The telly was on now, the music, Spanish. Everyone standing up to get a better view. 'If I shoot, you get to keep the gun. Get me? Now then shitface, what gives?'

He sounded desperate, plotless, which wasn't the Sammy Smith of old. Like he'd been practising his speech but didn't really believe in it. Reaching out the only way he knew how to, but not sure what for any more. Maybe to prove he could work, on his own and with one foot gone, a gun. He felt sorry for him for a minute. The gun had already lost its power. He'd pulled it like an ace but it had blown up in his face. It was time to take control of the situation.

'Yer wanna talk business yeah?'

'I want what's mine.'

'Well you won't find it in here. Let's go.'

Just inside the door where she stood, there was a glass coffee table, small and square, the smallest of the nest. Speed was of the essence. She looked at the table and looked at Jason's head and made the connection. She threw it down on him with such force, she missed, intending to hit him splat with the flat of it. Instead he got the edge. Split his head wide open. The blood-let a relief, almost a celebration.

She could, she thought, hear footsteps coming up the stairs. But no. Her attention went back to the head, the blood, the TV. Though it happened quite quickly, it wasn't that quick. She could remember every detail but nothing of the night before. Nothing of what she'd seen on the screen. The impact of the glass, she wouldn't forget. She saw the wind of her weapon separate his hair into starshape strands. Saw it all through the glass of the table. Saw his hair stand on end long before the glass embedded itself in his head. She saw the crease in his skin when his neck flipped back and she could still hear the sound of the crack, the snap.

She yanked the glass from his skull and felt the slug of his flesh glug away from it, the end of the coffee table smudged with salmon paste, hairs streaked through it. He slumped like someone unwilling to fall but fall he did, off his seat, to the floor and then, for the first time, she saw his eyes. Light glinting off them. They were like jelly, not glass.

She saw the same scene play out, over and over, again and again, for about thirty seconds or thirty minutes. She was still holding the coffee table. Her arms aching. The television quiet now. She thought, maybe, that the men had been watching her. She looked but nothing. Just blue. A sheet of blue and a crease of white pixels chasing the screen like some mathematical sea on a fast fast tide. She looked back to the body. There was a movement. Head movement. No. Just blood from his ear, dark black red, treacle-like, leaking on to the tiles to congeal. Some of it was seeping into the rug, turning pink hessian to a sanitary towel. He shaved his legs, she noticed.

She put the coffee table down. Went to her suitcase. Opened it. Everything was still there. Most of it. No basque. No bikinis. No bath bag. Her address book was there. Even her traveller's cheques. The clothes that were once all her world, now just a snapshot. As though she'd worn them all out. Not part of her any more. Nothing to do with her. They said nothing about her. Except that once, at some time, she had a little white dress? Was that her, was that hers? It was, she knew, but from some other world now. She picked up skirt after top after T-shirt after skirt and threw them down again. Picked them up again. Smelt them. Smelt her. Would like to have climbed in the case and stayed there. Locked inside it. She closed it. And went to bang it with her fists but was too exhausted. Instead, she saw a torrent of tears land on the suitcase with a dash, with a soft and silent dash, like the saddest ever squirt from a broken water pistol. Anger squirts.

The anger was cold though. Not the hot anger of frustration, the anger she knew. This was freezing brain anger. Below-zero anger. The release of it, the vent of it requiring movement low and slow. Quiet. Methodical. To raise the temperature gradually. But then, without her permission, her body went into spasm. She vomited. She moved fast now. Wiped her mouth and gurgled like a baby. Then tore the dress off herself. And every stitch she had on, to fall down foetal on the tiles. Crying like a baby after a slap now.

She stayed like that till she steadied her breath, till the sweat from her face stuck her fast to the tile, till she heard a noise, a high-pitched ringing noise. Coming from the briefcase. Alert again, she heard doors banging along the corridor outside. Phone ringing. She lay still, dead still. As if to move might make her more visible, seen, a target again. The floor was the only hiding place.

How long she lay there, she couldn't tell. Till the taste of vomit woke her. Till the pull of her face on the tile opened her eye and forced her to see out of the room, over to the balcony, to the aching clear blue sky. Till she was forced to open her legs to give air to the sizzle of razor cut between them. She was forced by something, someone, to open her legs. And let in the air. She was raping herself. And when she sat up, she saw her suitcase again, like some dream mixed in with the real, she remembered and was awake. But trapped. Locked in. Her head bleating an alarm, a beep . . . her brain trapped with it. A high-pitched sound like a bird trapped, a scream. She shook herself but the noise was still there. From outside her, not inside. From the briefcase on the chair. She went over to it and, for a flashback, saw it was daddy's. Exactly the same as daddy's. An excuse of a briefcase. Not like mummy's, all leather with lots of compartments for folders and papers and bundles and books. This was a box and in the box – open the box and take yer pick – the screaming bird and so she flicked it open to set it free in the air. And the noise blared at her quite loudly then. Shocked her. It carried on ringing. She picked it up and pressed the red button. And listened.

'Jason, I got Delaney here tellin' me you was gonna be meetin' him private like. What's goin' on? You better not be creamin'. You get my drift? I'll break yer bleedin' neck if you are, d'you 'ear me? . . . Well say somat. I want you down here now. It's all gone fackin' pear-shaped. The nigger's facked off 'n' I got Delaney sittin' 'ere pickin' his arse waitin' for the money. Where the fackin' 'ell are yer? Bring that money down here NOW. An' I mean all of it, alright? Every last soddin' penny alright?'

'Hola.' She was re-adjusting herself now. There were humans out there still going on, talking, making calls. She was awake now.

'Who's that?'

In Spanish, she rambled.

'What the fuck are you sayin', woman? Habla ingles? Habla ingles?'

'A liddle.'

'Where in Christ's name is he? You tell 'im this is no fackin' time to be out on the shag.'

'No entiendo.'

'You take a message?'

'Message si?'

'Tell him we need the money down 'ere OK? Delaney won't go to the Club for it. Bring money si?'

'Ahh money si?'

Then shouting at her. 'Tell him to telephone the hotel.'

'Hotel?'

'Si Si. Me batteries are dead tell him.'

'Dead. Si.' She saw the blood puddle then, the size of a puppy wee puddle. She put some magazines over it.

'Me batteries.'

'Oh, oh, oh, no entiendo, no entiendo.'

Then quiet. Pause. Then someone else on the phone. He gave her instructions in perfect Spanish. Tell Jason to phone Chas at the hotel.

'Adios.'

Where was the money? There was another case stood by the television, a steel one, all metal. Like the one Marcelle had had, for his films. It was more like a safe, strapped over with a chain lock. She found Jason's jacket and searched the pockets. Credit cards. A bunch of keys. She felt hot now. The keys cold. She put them on her forehead and breathed in deeply. Then back to his pockets. A wad of pesetas and another of sterling in his inside jacket. The keys on the table there. She tried them all and then tried them all again. There was one key nearly fitted and then bingo. She undid the strap lock and then tried the keys again for the smaller locks. Eventually, she got it to open. It was full of money. Sterling and Spanish. Shit. She rifled through the layers and underneath, lining the case, found blocks of hash, ten, eleven, twelve blocks wrapped in pink hessian cloth, much the same colour as the dress she'd been wearing. The same colour as her Volkswagen.

She sat back on her heels to think. To slow down. She looked at the body again. She had to get rid of it. She remembered the padlocked cupboard in the hall. It was open. She prayed out loud it was big enough to take him. A wardrobe of a space and deep. There was a rail and on it clothes, collecting dust off the floor, all crumpled. She recognised her red jeans. Most of it she didn't. There was some Lurex. A wet suit. She was exhausted. How could she drag a body all that way?

She had to get the job done and quickly. There were boxes of tools and tiles to move out. On auto pilot, she set about the job like a worker, employed mindlessly. Till the cupboard was empty enough. Then she moved everything out of the runway, coffee tables, bags, another leather chair. Then, by his flesh-cutting silver stilettos, she dragged him, in shifts, to the cupboard. She lay the wet suit down and made sure his head was on it. She used finger and thumb to close his lids. He looked 'at peace' as Nana would say. Till she bent his legs up tight, so she could shut the door. Then she shut the door. Her father would have wanted her to do all this, under the circumstances.

She opened her suitcase again, and put the money in it. The metal case she locked and took to the cupboard. His legs flopped out. She threw the metal case and a corner of it hit his head, right between the eyes. His face had gone blue she noticed. She folded his legs up again and shut the door. Looked for the bunch of keys, found the right one and locked it. Silence.

At last, a sit down. The buzz of the TV screen blue. She pushed the rewind on the video. Waited. And there it was. The show. It seemed more acceptable watching it backwards, like she was erasing the truth in some way, saying it didn't happen. She sat glaring till it stopped, her eyes aching to stay open, tiring at the screen. Then she played the tape from the start, her bare feet in a blood puddle, not caring now, not really there at all.

She saw the one couch. The coffee table. The couch centre-stage, still. Not moving. The man sat her up on the couch but she slumped.

He sat her up again. It was a girl. Not her. Just a girl. Tricked. A trick is a trick is a trick. Tick tock. Trick. Trickety dick likes lipstick. TV. Powder puff. Blind man's bluff. Not her. Not alive. Dead with progress. Not dressed any more. Stark naked. Rewind. Rewind. Do the trick again. Do it again. Do it again. The battle to watch and not to see. Blind man's bluff. The Emperor has no clothes. She has no clothes. Rewind. Rewind. Rewind. How many times can she watch and not see? Watch and not see? See. See. See it. But she couldn't see. It wasn't her.

'Yer weren't this pissed when we left, come on, buck up, me lassie.'

He was shaking her. He opened her dress at the front. Took a sly peek. Then shook her again. 'Come on.' Then he peeked again. Like he was doing something he shouldn't. Then lost his patience and manhandled her dress off her shoulders. Yanked it off. She was smiling at him. He touched her. She went to touch him back. 'So yer awake then are yer? Wait there.' And then he was gone. She fell to the side again. She fast forwarded. Stopped when he came back into shot. He sat her up, bent down to her breasts. She put her arms round his head. He was on her breasts for some time. He put her hands down. Sat her up and said, 'Just you 'ang on there, darlin'.' Then got his phone out. Dabbed a number. Then spoke. She was reaching out for him.

'D.S. Monk here. Can I speak to Channings please?'

'Yeah. I've been in and had a look. What? Yeah. They've got the black kid sittin' on it, I reckon. No sign o' philanderin' at the villa.' He looked around the place then, up towards the camera. He poked her to wake her up. She woke up then and looked to the ceiling. The camera must have been in the ceiling. Must have been. She tried to remember what the ceiling had been like from the first time. But she couldn't. The polystyrene was falling off Jonathan's ceiling. Something else he'd have to see to.

'What?'

'Yer know, I'm not sure. I've still no' met Frenchie yet.' He stabbed her in the stomach and she sat up, eyes wide open. 'They wouldna be usin' the darkie though, would they?'

He knelt down. Moved her legs apart and sat between them. All the time talking into his phone. She looked asleep but with eyes open. Didn't look like her. Wasn't her. It was someone else. He took off her shoes. She looked now at her feet, the blood glue between her toes, the smear, the period gone wrong, so wrong. Her stomach doing period pains, and bad ones.

'Well I guess tomorrow's as good a time as any.'

He ended the call, jabbing at the phone. And then carried on undressing her. Laid her down.

'I knows your game, darlin'.' And then he set to. Huffing and puffing. But then doors banging. The man looking up at the camera worried. The camera swerving off, up to the ceiling. And then Jason's voice. 'Get the fuck out of 'ere. I can smell it on yer, pig. Fuck off, go on. There's a good boy. Go back to Scotland Yard and tell 'em yer fucked up. Literally.' The camera swivelling round then, to follow him. The man getting his clothes. Jason in a bright green dress, pushing him.

Then Jason shouting for someone to come down. Then lots of clothes and costumes walking past the camera. Then, in turn, Jason introducing them. Batman. Robin. Robin Hood. Superman. A gorilla. Dick Turpin. A Grand Wizard from the Ku Klux Klan. A large silver stick. Spiderman. A black man. A naked black man. His face and her face. The only faces. Like he was being punished too. And her. Her the only girl. Only her face. Body. Her. The skin, hers.

'Maximum ten minutes each and start with the nigger. When we do the other edits we'll have him as the main event. Get 'em all at it. Now then, lads, share and share alike and keep her face pointing out. We need to see her face. It's pointless else. Right, after the nigger . . . can someone explain to him where he's supposed to go . . . right then. After him, it's you Robin Hood. You're on first. Marcelle, yer ready? Shoot.'

In the carpark, Sammy drilled the gun into his spine, hard. It really hurt. Jesus, there was no need for that.

'Sammy, what's goin' on eh?'

'In the taxi, smartarse.'

Jonathan looked around. The place was deserted. Except over in the trees – there was Marcelle with his camera, aimed directly at them.

'In, I said.'

The taxi man was reading a newspaper. Johnno got in the back and Sammy followed.

It was boiling inside. He put his jacket on the floor and his presentation pack on top, to protect it. Then wound down the window. Sammy told him to wind it up again. 'I wanna see you sweat for a while.' He had the gun trained on his balls still. It was still hard to take it all in, take it seriously. Sammy tapped the driver to go and, reluctantly, he put down his newspaper. They were away.

'Sammy.'

'Just take me to yer stash for starters. Papers, everything, I wanna see.'

'Sammy, yer've got it all wrong.'

The driver reversed fast across the gravel and skidded. Enjoying himself.

'Shut it.' Sammy jibbed him in the shin with his stick. Ripped his pants and got through to his skin. He could feel blood pouring. He looked and patted his leg. It wasn't much. He'd shut up now though. Sammy leant over. Like he was going to kiss him. But instead dug the gun into his groin, then closer to his balls, dug in hard. Jonathan pressed himself up against the car window. Couldn't breathe out for a while. When he did, 'Yer want me alive don't yer?' He looked out the back window and saw Marcelle watching them, camera on his shoulder. Just standing in the drive, watching.

'That depends.'

'Yer off yer 'ead, Sammy.' It was easy to see how these snuff movies came about.

Sammy picked up the presentation pack, rifled through it with one hand and said, 'Done pretty well for yerself considerin'.'

'Oh aye, that's why I was stood on the door, Sammy.'

'Yer the best dressed fuckin' doorman I've ever seen. And what's this?'

He pulled the mobile phone out of Jonathan's jacket pocket and threw it out the window. The taxi turned on to the main road, heading towards Marbella. Sammy tapped the driver on the shoulder and pointed up a track, a track going nowhere. The driver turned sharp, just dodging a head-on with oncoming, and, in a low gear, rocketed the taxi up the drive. The road went up steep for quite a while and then curved round into a hill of bush and waste, toilet paper type of waste. It stank. Sammy told the driver to stop. Then got out and now had his gun out in the open. He waved it at the taxi driver. The man got out with his hands in the air, having watched too many shit movies. Sammy pointed further up the hill. The taxi man started walking. Then he got his stick out of the car, stabbed at Johnno's leg again and said, 'Now drive.' Johnno got out. Coughed. Coughed a lot. Like a fit on him. 'Shut that up.'

'I can't 'elp it.'

'Shut it.'

'Sammy!' And that set him off coughing again. He looked up the hill and could just see the white shirt of the taxi driver. He was too far away to see if he still had his hands up.

'Sammy, get a grip,' he said, sitting in the driving seat. 'What the fuck d'yer think I've got, for chrissakes?'

'Two fuckin' legs for starters, now drive.'

Down the hill quick and out on to the main road towards Marbella. Another dig in the bollocks with the gun. He screeched to a halt. Coughed again. A coach overtook them. Beeping its horn loud. 'Sammy! Will yer pack that in?'

'A bullet in yer bollocks won't kill yer. Did yer know that? Ever thought about that fact before now? Now, take me to your place. I'm dying for a cup o'tea.'

'What 'appened to yer leg, Sammy?'

'I paid me debts with that, Johnno. I was gonna pay 'em with a lorry load o' tellies but . . . well, you're gonna tell me all about my tellies over a cup o' tea, aren't yer?'

224

'What, yer mean someone took yer leg off for a few tellies? I can't believe it.' Johnno was surprised enough to smile and forget that Sammy didn't have a leg and did believe it.

'You'd better believe it, sambo boy. Because you owe me two legs now. Call it interest.'

'I've got yer money. Not all of it. But I can get it. I can get it for yer.'

'Good. I hope the work's not too demandin' coz I'm gonna do to your kneecaps what my creditors did to mine.' He spoke in a robot tone. Like he'd been practising his speech, all day, every day. 'And I put my life on it that these Spanish butchers up the hozzy will be just as cack-handed as them back home. So drive good, Johnno, coz you'll not drive again.'

'I've got five hundred quid and I can get loads more really quickly. Just leave me legs out of it, Sammy, please.'

'Five hundred quid? A drug-dealer like you? Look at yer! Do me a favour.'

Johnno couldn't figure that one out. He'd gone to great lengths to look snappy, done a good job, he'd thought. 'Sammy, you've got it all wrong. Wires crossed somewhere.' They were at traffic lights. A middle-aged couple gone fat together, bored of each other, crossing the road. A flock of gulls flew over, screeching. Like they were laughing. 'Sammy, listen to me.'

'Drive. I've been waitin' more than six months for this one. Now drive.' And poked him in the ribs.

'You'll have to wait a bit longer. Look. Traffic lights.'

'Drive, I said.'

Jonathan looked at the gun and went back to his driving. At least now he knew that Sammy was thinking in the short-term. He couldn't find that much money that quickly no matter what. Unless, of course, Chas helped him out. He could pay it all back later. Dreams of taking Louise home were out the window.

'Look, about the tellies, I'm sorry. I hit someone, didn't I? Turned a motor over. Yer must've heard. Yer must've known I'd 'ave to get off.'

'Yer not expectin' me to come round to your way o' thinkin' are yer?'

He moved into top gear and drove on. Sammy leant over and frisked him, up and down his torso. Found the money belt. 'Stop the car.' He pulled over, slowly, gently. If he made a run for it here, there was nowhere to go except in people's houses, up alleys or down towards the beach. Just play it out, he thought. Play it out. He lifted his T-shirt. 'Get it off.' He took it off. Sammy unzipped the pouches, flicked through the money, unfolded the hardback section and unzipped the pouch to his passport. 'I think I'll keep hold of all this lot for now. Drive on.' Sammy undid his own shirt and wrapped the belt around himself. The gun between his legs, pointing upwards to the car roof. Jonathan kept his eyes on the road.

'Put yer foot down.'

'Where we goin' exactly?'

'You're takin' me to where it's all at. To my compensation fund. Whatever you wanna call it.'

'You want me to take you to a stash I don't have?'

'We'll 'ave a good nose round and see then, won't we?'

There was no more talking right up to the town centre. 'I don't know where to park.'

'Where d'yer normally park?'

'I don't. I 'aven't got a motor.'

'Course you 'aven't. Park there, next to that jeep.'

'No parking, it says, look.'

'It's in fuckin' Spanish. How'm I s'posed to know that. Park . . .'

'No, Sammy, it's in English too. Look up there, look.'

'You 'eard.'

'You'll get a ticket. They're mad on it round –'

He stabbed him in the leg with the gun. The more he messed with it, the less threatening the gun was. 'Sammy, let's go and have a drink down Papa's. Talk it all through.'

'You fuckin' moron. D'yer think I was born yesterday? Yer flat's locked up like the Knox and I wanna know why.'

'It's to keep out the Arabs. That's why.'

'You fuck with me one more time and I swear . . .'

'Did yer come over 'ere lookin' for me or did yer find me by accident? He was trying to line the car up, so he could reverse in, next to the jeep. Chas's jeep.

'Yer little sister put me on to yer.'

'Shirl?'

'How many you got?'

'Where d'yer see our Shirl?'

'I met her on a visit up the nick. They wouldn't let her in. Yer dad didn't wanna see her. I 'eard her give her name and thought dik-eye. I know who she is. I took her out for a slap-up. She needed it, skint as fuck over there, your lot. She's well sick o' you, I can tell yer. Likes her scran mind. Her bein' a nurse, she's soft on one-legged fellas like me see.'

'. . . Sammy . . .'

'Just park will yer. What's wrong wi' yer?'

'Sammy?'

'And she's a great little worker.'

'What?'

'She's stopped wiping arses for a livin', Johnny boy.'

Jonathan was still reversing but badly, on purpose badly, letting a whole parade of holidaymakers get past. Sammy was looking for something in his jacket pocket. Pulled out a wallet. Out of that some photos.

'She's got great tits 'asn't she, eh? And the arse. Now there's an arse.' He went through the photos in quick succession, not stopping on any particular one. Jonathan, from where he sat, caught just flashes of flesh. 'Not many get the full house but she's got the lot. There's somat about black chicks does me in, yer know. The shine I think. Comes out good on film and look at her there, she's a right poser isn't she?' The photo under his nose. Shirl smiling, bright red lipstick, shy. 'Done it before though 'asn't she? Look at this one she gave me.'

He'd stopped but kept the engine running. Sammy kept the gun between his knees. It was pointing upwards to the roof of the car but with a slight tilt, aimed just right for an own goal. Just within reach. Sammy had the photos fanned like playing cards, maybe twenty, thirty of them. Running his finger along to find the joker. Now was the time to make a move. But moving on a man with a gun not two hundred yards from a beach bar and now, in front of the car, women with kids, tiny kids with wispy blonde hair and buckets and spades . . . it wasn't the move to make. As soon as the pavement was clear . . . 'I sent a couple into the nick, for yer dad, cheer him up like. Well he hasn't seen her for ages so . . .'

Sammy found the picture he was looking for. Shirl still at school, in school skirt and nothing else. 'The lab technician took that one. Turn the engine off then. Let's go for that cuppa tea eh?' Jonathan looked in his rear-view. 'He's the father of her kid yer know. But no, yer don't know do yer? I forgot. I'm the only one that does know, she said.' Jonathan turned the engine off. 'And guess what?' Sammy put the photos away and got comfortable with his gun again. 'They're all the same, women, aren't they?' He aimed the gun and said, 'Right then! Let's go see what you've got for me.' He opened his car door to get out.

Jonathan turned the key, whacked the gear stick into second and took off. Sammy nearly fell out but managed to save himself. Jonathan concentrated hard, searching out clear routes down the pavement, then on to the road. Committed overtaking suicide a few times and then got himself down a side road. Sammy screaming. Sammy scared. His stick too big to manoeuvre.

Johnno drove straight into a carpark. Sammy all the time, telling him to slow down, pointing the gun at his head, pulling hard on his new T-shirt, getting it all out of shape, making him madder than ever.

As soon as they got to the ticket barrier, Sammy spotted the cameras. Hid the gun under his leg and went quiet. Then, past the barrier, out it came again.

'I'm gonna fuckin' do you. Get the fuck out of 'ere. Go on, drive out of 'ere. Or I'll do yer.'

'Do me.'

He drove screech-fast round the carpark, down to the lowest level. Sammy still pulling on his T-shirt, digging the gun in his ribs, digging deep enough for bruises. The gun jolted as he drove, riding over his ribs, back and forth, in the valleys of his bones. He stopped the car. To stop the pain. They were alone, in an empty corner. Jonathan flicked his arm and slapped out with a fist into Sammy's face. Then jumped out quick, all the time knowing the gun was trained on him. By the time he'd got round to Sammy's side, Sammy was coming out the car, with his gun in one hand, his stick in the other, his foot and his aim all over the place. His foot looked heavy. He clicked the trigger. And so Johnno just went for him. Got him by his armpits and shoved all his weight at him, up against a concrete pillar. They were about the same size, maybe Sammy was bigger, but not quick any more, not quick enough. He kneed him, took the gun and coshed him around the head with it, four, five times. Then just chucked it away, as useless. Then took his stick and threw that away. Then started on him. Boots, butts, body blows. Sammy had his hands up, trying to defend himself. Trying to move out the way. There were cars driving past, hooting their horns, a security man walking towards them. But Johnno wanted to finish him off now. Got him flat on his back, straddled him, butted him one last time and then got up. Finished him off with a few kicks, up between the legs. Even though he was done-for, down and out, a few last kicks. Then he found the gun again. Then sat down on his stomach, hard, to wind him. Then straddled him, face to face, watched him for a second, playing dead. Hardly a mark on him. Sweat. Blackheads. Eyelids flickering. Maybe a bruiser coming up there. No blood though. Good. He didn't like blood. His eyelashes were flickering. Thick eyelashes. He opened him up. Using his finger and thumb, he opened his eyes, as if bringing him back from the brink. Then he brought the gun round. Aimed it right between his yokkers. Right between his wide-open eyes.

'Don't,' said Sammy, 'there's a bullet in it.'

Jonathan looked at the gun differently then.

'With my name on it?'

Not as dead as he was making out. His hands suddenly shot up, one in his ribs, the other went for the gun. Knee on the back, right on the spine but not strong enough. Jonathan was heavier, firmer. Had to hold on to the gun now. He'd get shot else. They fought hand-to-hand, Sammy trying to lever himself out and not being too careful given the gun was supposed to be loaded. Jonathan fired. Nothing. He knew it. Sammy lay still. Sammy the sad bastard. He wanted to ram it down his throat, so he did. He coshed him across the head with it and then, holding his head straight, rammed it down his throat and pulled on the trigger, again and again and again. Nothing. Sammy curled up his legs. A few more kicks to deaden him.

He unclipped the money belt and yanked it from under him. Took the photos of Shirl and his wallet from his inside pocket and threw the photos in the bin. Wrapped the money belt round the gun and turned to leave. Then remembered his jacket was in the taxi. Got in the car, bent down to get the coat and, in the windscreen, caught a glint from the cap badge of the security man, still there. Waiting for cops to turn up, no doubt. Hiding behind a concrete pillar. Jonathan took the keys from the ignition and shut the car up. He'd be a lot safer on foot. The security man came out of his hiding place and shouted Spanish at him. Pointing to Sammy on the floor. Like he was complaining about the mess. He was big. Bigger than Jonathan. No gun on him. Not a cop. Definitely not a cop. But acting like one. Then he heard the crackle of his walky talky. He made to go. But the security man stood in his way, right there, facing up to him. He was about to give himself up when the man suddenly backed off, backed away. Wouldn't chance it. Fuck it, what now? He went back to the car, got in and drove away. Straight through the crash barrier. Windscreen like broken ice. With his hand wrapped up in his jacket, he put the window through.

There was no point in going back for her. It was time to go home.

Then Marcelle shouting, 'Clear shot, clear shot.' She stopped the tape. Went queasy with the wiggle of her toes sticky with blood. She moved to get off the chair but then the gouging razors started up again. She'd been gouged out. With her eyes, she followed the trail of blood out to the hall, black against the brown tile. She was cold again, sick. She looked over towards the balcony. Then to the kitchen area. Saw the note. Whimpered getting up. Making herself not whimper. Not now. Not yet. She read the note. Clean the mess up it said. Clean up, it said. She looked round. Scratched the scab off her arm. Felt the trickle of blood between her fingers, rubbed the blood into her skin and out loud, said, 'Of course, clean up.'

She showered and dressed just to her underwear. She found a plastic carrier bag. It still had mud in, from the potatoes. In it, she put the video and her bloody clothes. She'd tried to record over it but with no joy. It wouldn't work. If she chucked it, someone might find it. Someone might fix it, play it. Her head was so screwed up she couldn't tell if it was evidence for or against her. There was a whole blue sea out there, ready and waiting for it. Mummy always said that evidence was key. Real evidence. Not memories, opinions, probabilities. They could help but what clinched the deal was hard fact, evidence.

She filled the mop bucket and mopped it all away. The blood tracks. Hairs. Blood on the glass. On the chair. As she mopped and wiped, she plotted. She plotted and mopped and the glide of the water, the slide of the tiles as she did this dance, helped to calm her. She loved to dance. A gloss over it all, the shine of the water on the tile, the glint of light itself, like a dance. Dance and dance for now. She mopped and danced to a hum that . . . then she stopped. As if in 'hark', she held her head to the side and listened to the memory trace of the simple tune she'd just made up. The simplicity of the tune gave off an eerie sense of someone else at work. Something else, someone else taking over her body. After noticing this, the dancing didn't work so well. She couldn't dance so she worked it, the mop drawing streaks straight, diagonal, back and forth, she worked it, worked it. She decided to mop the whole room over. She emptied the bucket down the toilet and refilled it. Found the disinfectant and used it all up. She worked and plotted, washed and scrubbed. Rearranged the room entirely. She found her hairbrush on a chair, underwear, lipstick on the draining board, bits and bobs of her she found about the place and packed them all away in her suitcase.

When Jonathan returned, there'd be no trace of her. But how to go? She went to the balcony, bent over it and spotted the jeep. She found his keys and searched the bunch for car keys.

What if Jonathan knew about the money? What if he was in on all this? Did he know about the trick? Had he planned it with Jason? Why did Jason have the keys to the cupboard in his flat? She went to the bedroom. Looked again for his money belt. His papers. Anything. Found the letters from England and, shaking the papers, she read and re-read. The word prison made her stop instantly. He'd locked her in. Imprisoned her. Her adrenalin gone now, she was breaking down. She had to get away. And be quick about it. She dressed in her lemon picnic skirt.

But what about the suitcase? She'd never manage it on her own. She could barely lift her legs to walk. She rested a while on the balcony. Watched the rows of dead bodies baking away, not a care in the world, on holiday. Who would *they* believe, Jonathan or her? She'd be fine if she kept her cool.

Most people got caught by talking. She tried to remember some of her mother's cases. A few – more than a few – claimed they'd been framed. Or as her mother would say it, always laughing, so sick of hearing the same old tune, 'We was stitched up gav'ner, 'onest we was.' Oh mum. Oh mum.

The sea could convince her that all was well. It rested back and forth in its usual quiet state of lullaby. The people on the beach seemed lazier than usual today. There were no games. No children. She went downstairs to check the keys on the jeep. Got it going. Sat there, staring out of the window. Turned the engine off. Sat there. No energy to climb the stairs again. Wishing she'd brought everything down with her. Wishing she could just drive and be gone. The idea gave her the energy she needed. But when she reached the flat, she fell straight into bed. Slept a fitful sleep. Only half an hour but it did the trick. Back to the balcony. Binoculars. Scan. Nothing. She picked up the suitcase, her bag and the plastic bag of evidence, and then, like an old woman forced to leave her apartment, she staggered slowly but surely down the stairs.

A young man came to her aid. Lifted the suitcase into the back of the jeep for her. She got in the front, started at the sea for a while and still couldn't decide what to do. What to do about the video. It could get her off. Nail her in. Keep it just in case? Was the man that sold phones a policeman or a villain? She couldn't decide. They were all villains.

She looked for the key to the glove compartment. Guessed it first time. Opened it up, got ready to stuff the bag in and saw a gun. A gun. It was time to go home. She drove straight for Malaga. Death Highway.

It was Sunday but still. Putting himself right on offer, he drove round to his flat. The jeep had gone. He mounted the pavement, got out and looked up at the balcony. Hoping he might see her on it, bending over it. Wondering what he'd do if she did. Wanted to hear her shouting it, 'Romeo, Romeo.'

If he went upstairs and unlocked the padlock, she'd hear him. He'd not be able to stop himself going into her. He couldn't risk hanging about but couldn't risk seeing her for just seconds. She'd be so mad at being locked up, she just wasn't worth the risk. Go now.

Chapter Fourteen

He spotted her long before he knew it *was* her. Her yellow skirt. Not the jeep, tipping downwards, off the side of the road. Her skirt flapping. He'd caught her. Flying away from him. But she hadn't flown off that balcony without some help. He pulled up, got out the car and walked up behind her. She turned, saw him, turned back, carried on being sick. He wanted to tell her he was sorry but went for the more casual approach. A lighthearted approach to begin with.

'That's a water trough yer throwin' up in. 'S'meant to be for drinkin'. 'Ow about using them bushes over there.'

'Fuck off.'

'Bit strong innit?'

'Why did you lock me in?'

'How did yer get out?'

She threw up again. Then walked over to the bushes and crouched down. Her yellow skirt was stained wet brown, round the back. She'd shit herself, it looked like.

'Are you alright?'

'What does it look like?'

He turned to look at the jeep. 'Is that Jason's jeep?'

'No. There's more than one jeep in Marbella' . . . a retch to vomit . . . 'in case you hadn't noticed.'

'Are you alright to drive? Where yer goin'?' They were about 10K from Malaga. There was no need to ask.

'Home.'

'Shall I drive? I'll leave this car here. It's not mine anyway.'

'I can see that.'

'Is that your suitcase in the jeep?'

'Just shut up, Jonathan. Shut up.'

He was embarrassed to see her like that. 'Shall I get some clobber out yer case for yer. So yer can get changed. That skirt's gonna pong us right out.'

She turned and looked in such a way he moved back from her. The anger was huge and deep and all about her. Her toes were black. Her shirt wet under the arms. Her face ugly. She'd lost it. 'Don't you dare go near that suitcase.' She sounded like a car skidding, screeching. He did the arms-in-the-air stuff and backed off again. Then more quietly she said, 'Bring me my bag please.' And then after a pause, 'And the suitcase.'

'Anythin' you say.'

He'd gone off her total now. He didn't like girls freaking out. She looked ugly, greedy. Witchy. He didn't know what was worse. Women who tried to hide their real nature or women who showed it, whatever shade of evil it revealed itself to be. That most went in for hiding behind make-up and fancy hairstyles was probably an indication of how much rot had set in. But Wheezy hadn't been like that. She'd forgone the high heels, make-up and husband-hunting, and for what? To earn the money men earned, work the work men worked. For freedom. And just look at her. College girl. A girl with a start, with footsteps to walk in. A girl with a chance too lazy to take it. If *she* got pregnant, she'd abort. When Shirl got pregnant there was no question yet Shirl had the least to give. Wheezy had it all and gave nothing. Wheezy was a girl more willing to drop her knickers than wash dishes and wait on tables. A girl now after his sympathy and his guilt. A girl after his protection now she was out of the game, sick, dirty, ugly. A greedy girl. A fast girl. A dizzy conceited calculating bitch. A girl who should know better, who asks for it, who deserves it. A girl he no longer gave a shit about, he realised. At least Shirl turned whore for the love of her babby. This one had turned whore for money. She wasn't even a sicko junkie. What, so far, had she bought with her winnings? A ticket home to security? No. High heels and make up? No. To hide behind the illusion of taste and decency, she'd draped herself in designer finery and, quick as a bitch, splayed her legs for yet more money. Money money money. She'd turned whore for a purseful of bitch money. He didn't care what had happened to her. He was a lot more worried about Shirl and his mum and with his home-head on, he couldn't fit much else into his thoughts, certainly not some ex-girlfriend turned tart turning nasty on him.

He lifted her case out of the jeep. It felt full but empty. Light but serious. He picked up her bag and took them over to her. Then went back to his car. The traffic on the road, lively. Zipping along in both directions. Just two hundred yards away, a big billboard for Coca-Cola. Just stuck there, in the middle of dry brown earth, scratchings of grass on the side of the road. The can of Cola was frosted cold and sitting on a woman's naked stomach, a stomach dripping with sweat. If only. Further up, on the roadside, he made out a little fruit store, a family sat round it. Waiting for customers.

The car door-handle was metal and grill hot. He reached in through the back window to get his jacket and saw Sammy's tools in the swag bag. Did *he* get her out? Did he do something to her? He looked over but couldn't see her now. Did he get hold of her? He looked at his timeshare presentation pack and thought twice about taking it. Remembered he'd not had the pleasure of seeing Chas's video yet and decided it'd be a nice souvenir. He'd nothing else to go home with. Not her for definite. She was in a right state. He got into the jeep and decided to park it more safely, neatly. Didn't want some great lorry coming along, sidewiping it. Top jeep.

He still couldn't see her. Getting changed probably. The keys were in the ignition. She was more bothered about her suitcase than him nicking the jeep. Mitsubishi. Spots. Electrics. Quads. Auto-rewind. Radio tracker. He looked at the dash to figure out the controls then realised that a car had stopped, across the road, heading in the opposite direction. Long and black. Chauffeur-driven. A Roller. The chauffeur yelled across in Spanish. Asking him something. 'No comprende.' Then the back-seat window went down. Who was in the back? Cilla – Swillit Back. ''Ere love, yer couldn't tell us how far away the next petrol station is, could yer?'

'About another five kilometres. Eh, my mum really loves you.' He jumped out of the jeep, dodged the traffic and ran across the road.

Asked for her autograph. Went back across the road and got his presentation pack. Then dodged more traffic to get back to her. Got his free pen out and gave it to her. She wrote right underneath *Your Dream Come True*, 'To Hilda, with a lorra lorra love.' Then they were gone, into the dust. Leaving him standing there, gormless, dust in his mouth. He spat. Felt like a cowboy then, sauntering across to the jeep, gun down his trousers, sun on his neck. No traffic right then.

He got back in the driving seat. Still no sign of Louise. Perhaps he should see she was alright. Give it five more minutes, he thought. Didn't need another whip of that tongue in a hurry. He started the engine and parked up, square, half on half off the road, hazards on. Then tried the glove compartment. It was locked. He fiddled a key into it. Opened it. Saw the gun. Fuck it. Another gun. Saw the plastic bag. Saw a notepad. He flicked through it. Autographs of the Liverpool Team. To Jason, Kick It, Best Wishes Paul Walsh. Marbella. If he ripped off the top bit, it'd be worth having. He flicked through some more. The very first one was from Ian Rush. To Jason Clough. Any relation . . .? He took the pad and put it in his presentation pack. Then went back to the plastic bag. Opened it up. Saw the clothes. The clothes she'd had on when he left her that morning. Why in Jason's glove compartment? And then the video. Looked for her again. Thought sex. A video of Louise with her kit off would be a far more entertaining memento than one of Billy Butlin. So he swapped it. Hers had no label on but his did. His *Your Dream Come True*. It came off without a tear, a snag. Stuck it on her video and closed his pack up. Threw it in the back of the jeep and sat there then, wondering. About the gun. The shit on her skirt. Shirl. Thought of those snuff movies again. Couldn't get his head round Louise any more. 'A serious loon,' he said out loud.

Still, home soon. Back to normality. Forget all this. He was looking forward to the drive. Wished it was longer. Must make absolutely sure not to hit anything, he thought.

She was in a right state when he found her. Lying across her suitcase, crying her eyes out. Said she couldn't wear the shorts.

Couldn't get them on. Put her skirt back on. Wouldn't get anything else out of her suitcase. That got him thinking then, just what was in that suitcase.

'Don't talk to me. Don't touch me. Don't come near me, OK? Leave me and go back to the car. I'll be there in a minute. Just don't talk to me.'

He didn't want to. He didn't want to know anything about her any more. He could see the damage. He could tell there'd been trouble. And what could he do? Go back and sort them out or go home and forget all about it, her, the whole thing. She'd get over it. She had college lined up, a long row of mates lined up, an inheritance lined up, a life waiting to be lived. She'd bounce back, no problem. She had every reason to.

Sweat ran down his cheeks tempting tears. Goading him to not give up on her so easily. He wiped his face with his shirt and looked at the jeep shiny red in the road. Now he was wishing he'd run faster last night, when he'd seen her strapped in that man's jeep. He might have got to her, before it drove away. She'd be alright now if he had. If he hadn't run in to get his new phone off the bar. If he had lent her the money like she'd asked him to. Ifs and buts, but it was as much her fault as his. He wasn't her caretaker. He wasn't some Sir Galahad programmed to look after women in distress. They could look after themselves quite clearly. Jesus, they were running the fucking country. Badly, but running it all the same. She could have gone home any time she liked. She knew men weren't to be trusted. There's trust and there's trust. Johnno could be trusted not to inflict damage on purpose but could, not thinking, cause as much havoc as the next man. So therefore, not to be trusted. Bad men can be trusted to be bad. A bad man is open and straightforward and carries all the badges of danger up high, there for all to see. She should have read the signs. She should have known. She hadn't been that sheltered. She wasn't that dumb. She wasn't dumb at all and maybe that was the problem. Women educated with the mouth of reason but devoid of the sense they were born with. Clearly, they wanted men to walk all over them. To fill that void.

He'd watched the girls at his school do just that. They'd changed overnight, from being happy-go-lucky skippers and netball players into miserable panting females after the slightest glance from him, a touch, a smile. As if the personality they'd grown up with was no good any more. As if they *had* to become someone else. To be that someone else, they painted their faces and dressed up to the nines and stood on street corners in gangs, in readiness for a life on the game it would seem. They were all on the game in one form or another. His sister, his mother, every single girlfriend who'd sat and drank his money and ate his curries and waited on him hand and foot. They had all the power in the world, the power to breed and read and run the fucking country, but no idea how to use it wisely.

He knew she'd been raped. She had the same look about her as Mandy Rogers did at school. That vacancy. He didn't want to know it but he knew it. Could tell when something was missing from a girl. He'd had enough experience of them now. In fact, as if on the hunt for their own missing souls, for the missing parts of their very own body, they were the ones who fell into bed the quickest. They were the ones who felt nothing when they got there, who could be fucked again and again and it would never mean anything, until . . . until they confronted the fact of their emptiness. Till they stopped screwing and started to think. To screw such women was, in a way, to take on the mantle of the original thief. Was to take again. Was to be the very man who damaged her in the first place. Now, seeing Louise, in blazing heat on a clear sunny day, now he understood what that chill was. Why his stomach jumped when a girl went dead in his bed. Why he didn't really enjoy them. The chill on the face of a girl who's been done – that was the face Louise was wearing now. As if turned inside out. His days of bedding the dead were over. He couldn't settle for anything less than what Louise had given him, just yesterday. He was greatful for that. She'd managed to give him a taste of what he'd been looking for and he'd never forget her for that. He'd never settle for less. He wouldn't settle until there was some knowledge of the mind and soul for only then would he come to that true knowledge, the knowledge of the body. With her, he'd had all three. From Louise now, there would be nothing. She would need help to come alive again. She would need time.

He'd get her to the airport and then have nothing more to do with her. She was sick but he couldn't get involved. Not now. She was on her own and he was going home. She came clambering out from behind the rock and over towards the jeep. His instinct made him want to run and hold her, help her up the bank, but that chill on her face said stay away. He handed her his jacket to wear. It covered the stains on her skirt but only just.

He drove humming quietly to himself. She dozed off and then woke up, all in a panic.

'I wanna go to the sea,' she said.

'We're goin' home now, Wheezy.'

'I need to get to the sea. Just for a minute. Just drive down that road there.'

'No. We're going to the airport. Come on, go back to sleep. You were doin' just fine then.'

'Stop the car.' He stopped the car. She was back all lively again. Handing out her orders.

'What?' he said. 'You wanna drive now do yer? I'll tell ya what. You go to the sea. I'll hitch.' It was a threat he expected her to cave in on but she didn't.

'Give me the keys then,' she said.

'They're all yours.' He gave them to her and made to get out of the vehicle. He heard her fiddling with the keys while he leant in, to get his presentation pack out. When he looked up she was pointing the gun at him.

'Now get in and drive. Follow that sign there, "Playa". See it?'

This was turning out to be one hell of a day. At home, they'd accuse him of making it all up, to make his travels sound a bit more interesting. After five minutes' driving she said, 'Stop here.'

She put the gun and the keys in her plastic bag and got out.

'Can you get the suitcase out for me please?' Like he was her cab driver now.

'Sure can do.'

He got out, went to the back of the jeep and yanked it out. Put it by her feet. She put it on its wheels and, with her plastic bag in her other hand, off she went, down the path to the beach. He had the feeling she wouldn't come back. Remembered then the video. Had very dark thoughts about the contents of that video now. Very dark thoughts he shoved away, wiped away from the sweat of his brow. Felt ghastly. Sick. To the stomach. In a way, he hoped she didn't come back. He could quite happily never see her again.

He was sat outside a café, all broken-down, dark wood and greasy windows. Flowers growing between the gaps of the wooden steps leading up to the verandah. Just locals sat there, under the shade, a well-worn candy stripe plastic umbrella. The old men had been eyeing her up as she walked down to the beach, slapping the tables, talking, smiling leers at her. Weren't bothered that he could see them. On a board outside, pictures of meals you could have, yellowed by the sun. Just one look at the old lady clearing up plates told you all you needed to know. Her apron was filthy.

He went in and bought himself a Coke. Then went back for another. He sat and waited in the jeep for her. Felt the back of his money belt. Yep. The gun was still safe. Hurting a little now. He decided to turn the jeep round ready to go and away from the onlookers. Then he put the gun in the glove compartment and locked it. And then he threw away the key. That was the end of that. And then, from nowhere, a little Spanish girl appeared, long hair with pearls in her ears. She climbed up the side of the jeep and smiled at him. He tickled her nose, offered her his Coke and she ran off then, screaming. Two of the men on the balcony stood up. That was the closest he'd come to an unmarried Spanish girl since he'd been here.

She'd left her bag behind. He had a look in it. Crumpled-up shorts, make up, tissues, mirror, her passport. Louise Clements. He flicked through it. Hong Kong. St Vincent. Austria. He opened her make-up bag. Found contraceptive pills. Checked the days. She'd missed one. Yesterday.

She came back with just the suitcase. Nothing else. The plastic bag gone. The gun gone. 'Well thank Christ for that,' he said out loud.

She got back into the jeep and they were off again. All she said was, 'I'm sorry about that.' He offered her the Coke. She drank it all in one.

'How d'yer know I'd still be here?'

'I'm sorry. OK? About the gun. I'm sorry. Can you stop the car. I want to be sick.'

When she got back in the car. 'Louise, I was gonna come back for yer but . . . well I 'ad the police after me. I 'ad to leave town.'

'That's just what I needed to hear, Jonathan. Please, just get me to the airport.' She was crying now. Not noisily. Just tears falling.

'You alright?'

'Just get me to the fucking airport, Jonathan.'

They drove the rest of the way in silence. Nearly.

'Guess who I saw back there on the road?'

'Who?' She was still on the verge.

'Cilla Black. I got her autograph.'

The next flights to England with any seats free were to Manchester and Bristol. Bristol not till seven the following morning. Manchester at midnight. Jonathan said, 'Looks like this is where we part company.' He was feeling quite jolly now. Glad to be rid of her. 'You'll have to stand by for London,' he said.

'I'll go with you,' she said.

'Eh?'

'I've got friends in Manchester. I'll stay there.'

'But you live in London.'

'I can't sit in this place on my own. Do you have a problem with that, Jonathan?'

He did yes. He wanted to leave her, not take her with him.

He bought one of those tiny travelling chess sets to pass the time and take his mind off her. They sat in the main public lounge, waiting to check in. He'd paid for her ticket too. Still squawking skint yet she'd been out working all night. She still hadn't told him how she'd got out of the apartment. From the look of her, he could believe she'd jumped the balcony, done the sheet trick, bawled her way out. There was a whole seat between them. The tiny chess box sat in the middle of it, like an umpire. He insisted on playing white. She didn't care, she said. She always had in the past. She was always white. When they screwed the pieces into the holes, her hand touched his. She'd sat back suddenly, as though he'd hurt her. She was grimacing, as if in pain.

'You alright, Louise? D'yer want some pain-killers or somat?'

'No.' She kept her head down and played. Never looked up once. It was like she was afraid of something. Afraid to look.

'I'd quite like a banana,' she said.

'Well go and get one then.'

After every move, he looked around, the amount of armed security making him feel nervous, not safe. He sighed heavily, like a really challenged opponent would sigh. He noticed her concentration was firm, even when it wasn't her go. She was into it. Playing to win. Wouldn't take her eyes off the board.

He was planning on taking her queen with his knight but she rooked him, and then mated him. No checks. Straight to mate. It seemed to give her some confidence. The confidence to sleep, legs up on her suitcase.

It was gone ten when he woke her. 'Come on. Check-in time.' She picked up her bag and made to move away. 'Don't forget yer case.' She put it on its wheels and followed him over to the desks. He was strutting now. Happy. He figured, the more smiley he was, the less suspicious he'd look. The less attention he'd attract. He hated airports.

He was thinking, thinking hard. Working a lot harder than when he'd been playing chess.

'Louise, how did yer get out the apartment?'

'I called the police,' she said.

'Did yer tell 'em about me? That I locked yer in.'

'No.'

'Good.'

'I said it was a mix-up. It turned out they had my suitcase. I recognised one of them. He gave me the lost property number to ring and then gave me a lift to go and collect it. Jonathan, I'm sorry about the gun and everything.'

'It was Jason's gun, wasn't it? Jason's jeep.'

'Yeah.'

'How come?'

'I stole it. I just wanted to go home, Jonathan.'

'What was in that placky bag you had to get rid of so desperately?'

'Clothes. Sick and poo all over my clothes.'

'What else?'

'Nothing else.'

'I just want to go home, Jonathan.' On the verge again.

He took her hand for the first time that day. 'We'll get you home, don't worry.'

She pulled away from him violently. Then silence. Then, 'Where was Jason when you took his jeep?'

Nothing.

Then silence. Then, 'Listen, Louise . . . about . . . well I . . .'

'Jonathan, I'm exhausted. No more quizzing please.'

'I was gonna ask yer back to our house for the night. Meet me mam 'n' that. You always said . . .'

'I'd rather not.'

'Is this your suitcase, madam?'

She didn't answer. Jonathan nudged her.

'Yes.'

'Did you pack it all yourself?'

Jonathan nudged her again.

'Yes.'

'And it's going to Manchester, yes?'

'Yes, Manchester.'

'No luggage for you sir?'

'No. Only this,' he said, waving his carrier bag of duty-free in the air.

They walked through to the departure lounge but not together.

Jonathan walking fast. Sulking. He'd done his best. He'd not try again.

On the plane they were sat towards the back. Just in smoking. Jonathan was sat in the middle, Louise on the outside, a man who looked like he was half dead next to the window. Jonathan pretended sleep. Louise likewise. The automatic silence prior to take off promised a quiet flight home. As the plane left the ground, Louise expelled a great sigh of relief. And from the front of the plane a loud surge of yob song. The dying man by the window reached for his vomit bag.

She undid her seatbelt and stared straight ahead. She never slept a wink. He kept his eye on her all the way. She never ate the meal. Didn't drink. Didn't talk. Just stared straight ahead. Tears lashing down her face. Silent. She didn't wipe them away. Just let them stream down. Like a washing off. A washing away. Spain gone now. The chill still there. The chill like a frozen mask that even those tears wouldn't melt.

He leant away from her. The yobs had settled on a tune they quite liked and they sang it, *all the way, all the way, all the way* home. Just over half way, she went to the toilet. Was in there a while. Was in there till just before the plane landed. The stewardess got her out.

'The door was stuck,' she said, when she sat down for the landing.

'You gettin' a cab when we get in?'

'Yes.'

'What with? Yer skint, remember.'

'Would you?'

'Do I 'ave any choice in the matter?'

'I've got the money, I just don't think I can . . .'

'Spend it. Is that what yer gonna say? Yer can't bring yerself to spend any of it. Fuckin' 'ell. I musta bin off my head 'aving owt to do with you.'

The conveyor belt took an age to start. Round and round. Round and round. Took her a while to spot it. She pointed at it. Like a child, pointing it out to mother. She looked so obvious. So mad. Her hair

246

was all over the place. His jacket on her looking not like the million dollars it had looked that morning. The conveyor belt was on a go-slow, it took so long to come round.

And then customs. The list of what and what not to declare was neither here nor there. He had nothing. Full stop nothing. She was looking guilty as sin now, trying to tidy her hair. It looked alright. She'd wet it in the loos, flattened it down a bit. They were boyfriend and girlfriend, obviously. When they got round the corner, the customs staff were waiting for them, with big wide smiles and open arms.

'Put yer case on there love and open it up please?' The customs man leant over to help her lift it up. Maybe to make sure Jonathan didn't run off with it. 'Ave a nice time did yer, miss? Yer've a fair tan. Nearly catchin' 'im up look.' Jonathan put his hands in his pocket and walked on, past all the desks. Absolutely nothing to declare. 'Now then, let's see what we've got in 'ere, shall we?' Jonathan turned to see them open the case and, before he was through, a woman customs officer was in front of him, almost on top of him. He lifted his hands in the air and stood back. His presentation pack fell to the floor. The woman picked it up and read it. '*Your Dream Come True*', 'To Hilda, with a lorra lorra love'.

Who's Hilda?' she asked him.

'Me mum,' he said and just then, saw her in his head, as if he was there, home already. He'd missed her so much. She was there in his head, for the first time in ages. Lying in her bed, dead to the world, eyes firmly fixed on the telly. And as he pondered the thought and followed the customs woman back to her counter, he saw that chill on his mother's face. He saw the glaze. He remembered her two faces quite clearly now. The woman who'd played with his Dinky cars up and down the stairs. And the woman who she'd turned into. He could remember the day that he lost her. His birthday. He walked in a daze now, tired. It was late. He walked back towards Wheezy and then saw it on her. That look. That chill. And then he heard that screech from his past drill right through his brain to the mouth of the woman standing in front of him now. Wheezy was screeching at him. Screaming. Moving backwards and away from him. Everyone was staring at her.

'It's his,' she screamed, bending over, ranting and raving, ugly as hell, holding bundles in her arms, clutching and rocking them like a baby. And then whoosh. She raised her arms above her head and threw the money everywhere. Piles of it. And then she screamed again.

'It's all his.'

A NOTE ON THE AUTHOR

Born in London, Joanna Traynor grew up in
the north of England and now lives in Plymouth.
BITCH MONEY is her third novel. Her novels are
SISTER JOSEPHINE, winner of the 1996 Saga Prize,
and DIVINE, both published by Bloomsbury.

A NOTE ON THE TYPE

The text of this book is set in Linotype Sabon, named after the type founder, Jacques Sabon. It was designed by Jan Tschichold and jointly developed by Linotype, Monotype and Stempel, in response to a need for a typeface to be available in identical form for mechanical hot metal composition and hand composition using foundry type.

Tschichold based his design for Sabon roman on a fount engraved by Garamond, and Sabon italic on a fount by Granjon. It was first used in 1966 and has proved an enduring modern classic.